THE TAMING OF ALEXA

Alexa lifted her chin defiantly. "You're wasting your breath giving me orders, for I have no intention of obeying them . . . I am not in the habit of obedience."

"Nor in the habit of being punished for disobedience, I dare say," Rowan thundered. He had been holding his own temper on a tight rein but it was beginning to fray at last. "Defy me, Alexa, and I shall be forced to show you how easy it will be to bring you to heel," he grated. "You may be a headstrong little madam with no consideration for others or thought for your own future, but I am the head of the family and as such it is my duty—"

"You're not my father, my brother or . . . or my husband . . ." Alexa flared.

"Indeed not! And God help the man who takes you to wife!"

D0885614

Other Leisure books by Sue Deobold:

SAVAGE SPLENDOR

THE MILITANT HEART

SUE DEOBOLD

Book Margins, Inc.

A BMI Edition

Published by special arrangement with Dorchester Publishing Co., Inc.

If you purchased this book without a cover you should be aware that this book is stolen property. It was reported as "unsold and destroyed" to the publisher and neither the author nor the publisher has received any payment for this "stripped book."

Copyright© 1989 by Sue Deobold

All rights reserved. No part of this book may be reproduced or transmitted in any form or by any electronic or mechanical means, including photocopying, recording or by any information storage and retrieval system, without the written permission of the Publisher, except where permitted by law.

Printed in the United States of America.

Chapter 1

The shiny new Rolls rounded the corner of Downing Street and came to a screeching halt. Its sole passenger, a top-hatted, frock-coated gentleman, lurched forward, the sheaf of official documents he had been perusing slithering off his knees and scattering around his feet.

"What the devil, Chalmers!" Rowan Traherne exclaimed, ducking down to retrieve the documents. It was fortunate that he did so, for at that moment a stone hurtled through the air and cracked the windscreen.

Chalmers was not so fortunate as his employer. The chauffeur received a nasty cut from a shard of shattered glass. Dabbing his bloodied face with his handkerchief, he gasped, "Sorry, sir. It's another one of those demonstrations . . . those cursed suffragettes!"

It was obvious that Chalmers's assessment of the situation was correct, Rowan Traherne thought glumly, eyeing the milling mob of women blocking the street and unfurling banners proclaiming "Votes for Women!" One banner, a particularly large one, caught Rowan's jaundiced eye. It depicted a symbolic woman with a broken chain in her hands and bore the inscription "From Prison to Citizenship!"

He frowned. Since June of 1913, when suffragette Emily Wilding Davison had thrown herself under the hooves of galloping horses at the Derby, the women's movement had grown ever more vociferous and militant. As if German militarism, with all Europe precariously poised on the brink of war, were not enough for the Government to contend with, thought Rowan with a sigh. But then, the man—or rather, woman—in the street was not privy to official secrets, as he was, and remained blissfully unaware that the delicate balance of international diplomacy was teetering towards a breakdown.

Reminded of the importance of the documents he was carrying, Rowan stuffed them hurriedly back into his briefcase and, after assuring himself that his chauffeur's injuries were superficial, sallied forth on foot, intent on battling his way through the milling mob to Number Ten Downing Street where his Foreign Office superior, Sir Edward Grey, and Prime Minister Asquith were awaiting him.

Rowan's broad shoulders and habitual air of command ensured an easier passage than he had anticipated as embattled women and beleaguered bobbies alike fell back before his determined assault. The surging crowd made way before him and he gained the steps of Number Ten just as a slender girl in a grey skirt and a white shirtwaist with a sash of purple, green and white, the colors of the Movement, slipped through the police cordon.

Rowan frowned. There was something vaguely familiar about that slim, hatless figure with the tangled bramble bush of undisciplined curls cascading down her back. The hair was an unusual shade of reddish brown—almost the color of autumn leaves shot through with golden lights.

Rowan's frown deepened. He knew of only one person with hair that particular hue—Alexa. Then, as the girl glanced around furtively before drawing a length of chain from her skirt pocket, he caught a glimpse of her face and realized with a sense of shock that—good Lord, it *was* Alexa!

Alexandra Traherne's whisky-colored eyes sparkled with excitement. She felt a heady sense of triumph. Several young women had been equipped with lengths of chain and instructed to break through the police cordon and shackle themselves to the railing of Ten Downing Street as a symbolic protest of the political bondage of womanhood, but none

had succeeded except herself. She owed her
success to a sudden strategic maneuver—
that of jabbing a much-tried police constable
in the rear with her hatpin. In the ensuing
melee she had, of course, lost her headgear,
but the loss of her second-best chapeau
troubled her not a whit. She was willing and
eager to sacrifice more than a hat for the
Cause.

She glanced around furtively. She would
have to work fast. Already a Black Maria had
drawn up to the curb and police were busily
engaged in bundling yelling, protesting
women into the conveyance bound for Holloway, via a police magistrate's court.

Prison! A sobering thought. And her ultimate destination, she supposed, once a
locksmith had been summoned to release
her from her self-imposed shackles into a
more onerous captivity. As a relatively new
recruit she had not yet suffered any of the
dire penalties so many brave women had
already undergone, not once but many
times—incarceration, hunger strikes, force
feeding by means of a tube through the
nostrils and a steel gag. She shuddered at the
thought. Yet she was sure that her spirit
would be equal to the occasion, when the
time came. With a toss of her head she
whipped the chain from her pocket and
began to wind it through the railings.

She was on the verge of snapping shut the
clasp when a hand like a steal vise gripped
her wrist. "I wouldn't do that if I were you,"

a crisp voice warned her in forbidding tones.

Alexa looked up apprehensively, expecting to see a police constable at her elbow—perhaps even the one who had suffered the business end of her hatpin! Instead, she found herself looking into the glacial grey eyes of her cousin, Rowan Traherne.

"Row-Rowan . . . !" she stammered. "Wh-what are you doing here?"

"I might ask the same of you," he grated harshly. "In fact, I will!" His rather heavy chiseled lips were set in a straight stern line. "I find it hard to believe you've joined forces with this fanatical bunch of harpies, Alexa. I credited you with more sense than that!"

Usually Alexa had plenty of spirit but she quailed before his wrath. Rowan Traherne in a rage was a formidable figure, seeming to tower over her. As a former Guards Officer he had to be at least six feet tall, she knew, and in Rowan's case it was six solid feet of intimidating bone and muscle. He was, moreover, one of the "black Trahernes" and his square-shaped handsome face was as dark as any gypsy's. His midnight black hair was worn slightly longer than was the fashion and waved about the nape of his neck. He was, Alexa had to admit, stunningly handsome, but "handsome is as handsome does," as her old nurse used to say!

If Rowan thought that his undeniable physical superiority, his sneering tone, the barely concealed contempt in his voice, and his insolent air of authority that seemed to demand instant and unquestioning obedience were going to intimidate *her*, well, he couldn't be more wrong! Alexa decided. No doubt he had been used to ordering his subalterns about but he had no authority over her. He was, after all, only a very distant cousin, not her guardian, and anyway, she was of age now and could do as she pleased.

"As it happens, I *am* a suffragette and proud of it!" she retorted loftily. "The time has come for women to ... to cast off their fetters ... to be more than a man's plaything ... to take charge of their own lives and destinies!"

Rowan's jaw dropped. "My God, you *have* swallowed the suffragette line!" he jeered. "Have you lost all sense of self-respect ... of decorum and propriety, Alexandra?" His eyes roamed over the demonstration in disgust. Women, most of them well-dressed, grappled with police in a flurry of white petticoats and blue tunics. "The behavior of these women is a public scandal!"

"The scandal lies in the way they are treated; in the shameful abuse that is meted out to them!" she retorted.

Rowan's hand itched to smack some sense into her. He restrained himself with difficulty, though his eyes narrowed threateningly and a muscle twitched at the corner of his jaw. He was tempted to give her the dressing down she so richly deserved, but this was neither the time nor the place. He was already late for his appointment, and one did not keep the Prime Minister waiting with impunity! What was more, the police were succeeding in quelling the demonstrators and it would not be long before official attention was directed towards himself and Alexa.

Making up his mind with his customary despatch, he rapidly divested Alexa of her suffragette sash, snatched the chain from her fingers, and deposited both in the shrubbery.

"Wh-what are you doing?" she gasped.

"Trying to keep you from reaping the results of your folly!" he snarled. His fingers bit painfully into her arm as he watched a police constable detach himself from the crowd and approach them in a purposeful manner, the buttons of his tunic flashing in the spring sunshine.

"No histrionics, Alexa!" Rowan muttered in an undertone. "And remember, if you don't play along with me, it will be the worse for you."

Before the man had a chance to open his mouth, Rowan said loudly, "Well done, Constable! You and your squad did a fine job of rounding up these rioters. You're to be commended!"

"Er . . . thank you, sir. These suffragettes . . . this lot deliberately caused a riot here in Downing Street and would have stormed Number Ten if my men hadn't prevented it." He shook his helmeted head. "We've got most of them rounded up now, sir, but . . ." he looked searchingly at

Alexa as he spoke.

"The young lady is with me, Constable. She had nothing to do with this disgusting exhibition." Not abandoning his grip on Alexa's arm, Rowan fished an identifying card from his wallet. "I can vouch for her."

The constable scowled at the card Rowan presented to him, glancing from it to Alexa's flushed face, tangled tresses, and disheveled appearance. "Well, sir, if you vouch for her," he said doubtfully.

"I do," Rowan said firmly. The pressure of his fingers biting into her arm warned Alexa to hold her tongue. "We got caught up in the demonstration and fought our way to the steps when the lady—my cousin—was overcome with giddiness. I judged it best to remain here until the mob was dispersed. And now, if you'll kindly step aside, Constable, I'll conduct my cousin back to our motor car. I'm sure she'd like to sit down. Wouldn't you, my dear?"

Feeling the warning fingers nipping at her arm, Alexa murmured an almost inaudible assent. What an inglorious ending to her first assignment! If only Rowan hadn't interfered, she thought resentfully, she might have distinguished herself in some way— perhaps by heckling a cabinet minister on his way into or out of Ten Downing Street!

She could see that the constable was unconvinced. There was more to this than met the eye, his experience told him, but the gentleman's credentials were impeccable and he wore an inbred air of authority with an unconscious ease that commanded respect. With a deferential salute, the policeman stepped out of their way.

Alexa was half-tempted to denounce Rowan's statement as the tissue of lies that it was, but he hustled her away before she could collect her wits or screw up her courage. Consoling herself with the notion that she could do more for the Cause on the outside of Holloway rather than within it, she made up her mind that she would make her way to suffragette headquarters at the first opportunity and request a new assignment.

But this was going to be easier said than done. Bundling her unceremoniously into the Rolls, Rowan ordered Chalmers to drive her to his Cadogan Square residence and extracted a promise from her to remain there until he arrived home. Seeing her mutinous expression, he said sternly, "I want your word of honor, Alexa."

"Oh, very well. You have it," she said ungraciously. It crossed her mind that she was as much a prisoner as if she had been herded into the police van with her fellow protestors, the difference being that the Rolls was a much more luxurious conveyance.

She leaned her head back against the seat with a heavy sigh, enjoying the unaccustomed luxury in spite of herself. Both she and Rowan had been born, so to speak, with silver spoons in their mouths, but hers had quickly tarnished, she thought ruefully. Her father and his had been cousins, but while Rowan's papa had a most ungentlemanly flair for making money, hers had had an aristocratic penchant for losing it at the gaming tables, gambling away first his own not inconsiderable fortune and then her mother's portion. And when Reginald Traherne had run through his wife's money he had abandoned her, running off to France with a light-o-love, whom he had abandoned in turn for a Parisian demimondaine. Papa's defection had taught her at an early age that men were simply not to be trusted.

But even after Papa left them, life had still been good, Alexa reflected. True, Mama had had to practice stringent economies, letting most of the staff go, swathing much of the furniture in dust sheets, and closing up one wing of the sprawling Elizabethan manor house. But this had not mattered greatly to Alexa.

What *had* mattered to her was the absence of Papa—so handsome, gay, charming, and carelessly indulgent, as long as indulgence of her childish whims did not greatly inconvenience himself, she'd realized only later, with bitterness. She'd missed him terribly at first, when her world—except for the servants—had shrunk to a world of women— Mama, Nanny, and Miss Pringle, her governess, an extraordinarily well educated vicar's daughter who held advanced views on the role of women, views she had passed on to her charge.

From time to time, Rowan and Lucinda had come to stay—Lucinda as a playmate for Alexa and Rowan because he was the heir.

She hadn't realized that, either—not then. As a child she had idolized him, this handsome, dashing cousin in the Guards' uniform who occasionally came for tea with her and Mama and who seemed to take a proprietary interest in them, which pleased and flattered Alexa.

But his proprietarial interest was in the estate. And when Alexa realized that, she hated him for it.

It was only after Papa died in Paris that Mama and Mr. Smithers, the estate agent, explained to her that the estate was entailed and would pass to the nearest male heir— her cousin Rowan. Simply because he was a man and she was ONLY A GIRL!

"It isn't fair!" she'd cried to Mama.

"But, darling," Mama said gently, "there's no way we could afford to keep up Nun's Farthing, even if it weren't for the entail. There's no money—not even enough for you to make your debut . . . to be properly introduced into society." Mama seemed even more distressed on that score than she did about the prospect of leaving Nun's Farthing, Alexa realized.

"In the course of time you'll marry and go to a home of your own," Mama said comfortably. "And in the meantime, Rowan has kindly asked us to stay on here. So you see, nothing has changed."

"Everything has changed!" cried Alexa. Her pride was too great to allow her to stay on in her beloved home on sufferance—a poor relation dependent on Rowan's generosity. So when he resigned his commission and came down to take possession of his inheritance, she had persuaded her mother to take up residence in an inexpensive and unfashionable quarter of London where they could live quietly on the pittance that was left of her mother's fortune and where Alexa, at eighteen, could train for some kind of work that would enable her to earn her own living. Never, she vowed, would she be dependent on the whims of some man—no, never ever again!

With such an attitude it was not surprising that she was attracted to the contagious enthusiasm of the suffragettes. It didn't take long to convince her that the way to better the lot of all women (including her own) was to obtain the vote. But in deference to her gentle mother's opinions she had not actively sought martyrdom or, as yet, done much more than pass out a few leaflets for the Cause. Mama was still firmly convinced, despite her own less than idyllic experience, that the only suitable career for a woman was marriage and that a girl who made a public exhibition of herself was hardly likely to find a husband.

No, Mama didn't understand, Alexa thought moodily, and perhaps it was just as well that she would have the opportunity to pin up her hair and make herself presentable before going home to face her mother.

Rowan's housekeeper, Mrs. Brownell, a buxom motherly woman, tut-tutted over Alexa's bedraggled appearance and led her upstairs to wash her face and hands and brush out her hair. With her tangled curls turned into a neat bun and a rip in her skirt pinned up, Alexa felt much refreshed and ready to face an irate Rowan whenever he should return home.

She settled down to wait for him in the library. To take her mind off the forthcoming interview (sure to be an unpleasant one) she was leafing through his fine collection of first editions when she heard someone at the door.

Alexa put down the book with a sigh and braced herself for the fray, but it was only a girl with a round, pretty face, dancing black curls, and a beaming smile. "Alexa!" she exclaimed, "Browney said you were here. How lovely it is to see you again!" Lucinda Traherne embraced her cousin affectionately. "Why haven't you come sooner?" This in a tone of reproach.

"I didn't know you were in town," Alexa explained, rather taken aback by the change in her cousin, whom she hadn't seen for some time and whom she remembered as a rather pudgy schoolgirl with spots. But Lucinda had slimmed down somewhat and the spots had disappeared. Goodness, she

must be seventeen or eighteen now, Alexa
calculated, for she was fifteen years younger
than Rowan.

"I've come up for fittings," Lucinda said
gaily. "Such a bore . . . but I'm to 'come out'
this season, so . . ." She led her cousin to a
large comfortable sofa by the fire and sat
down, patting the sofa cushions invitingly.
"Sit down and tell me about yourself. Shall I
ring for tea?"

"Er . . . no, thank you. I can't stay long. I'm
waiting for your brother and I don't expect
he'll be long." A shadow crossed Alexa's face
as she spoke, and Lucinda was quick to pick
up on it.

"Is anything wrong, Alexa?" she asked
anxiously. "You haven't quarreled with
Rowan, have you?"

"Umm—not exactly," Lucinda was too
sharp by far, Alexa decided ruefully. And
then she found heself pouring the whole
story into Lucinda's inquisitive ears—her
involvement with the suffragettes, the
incident in Downing Street, culminating in
Rowan's parting shot as he slammed the car
door shut, effectually imprisoning her in the
Rolls, that he would "deal with her later."

Lucinda's grey eyes opened wide. "In that
case you simply must have some tea to
fortify you," she declared, ringing the bell
pull energetically. "I always thought Rowan
was the dearest, most wonderful brother a
girl could have," she ssaid thoughtfully, "but
he's unalterably opposed to women's suf-

frage. He simply won't listen to reason and refuses to wake up and face the fact that a new day is dawning—that we women won't allow ourselves to be downtrodden any longer."

Alexa blinked. She had scarcely expected to find an ally in Rowan's own household! "Are you a suffragette sympathizer?" she asked with rising excitement. It was too much to hope for.

"Yes!" Lucinda said stoutly. "And, oh, Alexa, I do admire your spirit ... your willingness to sacrifice for the Cause. I wish I had your courage."

Alexa forebore to mention that she hadn't actually made any sacrifices yet (except for her second-best hat) and basked in the younger girl's admiration.

Over tea, cakes, and hot buttered scones, she regaled Lucinda with more of her suffragette experiences and was not above a little judicious name-dropping.

Lucinda sighed with envy. "To think that you've actually met and marched shoulder to shoulder with Mrs. Pankhurst and her daughters!" Clearly Lucinda was impressed.

But the younger girl shook her head regretfully. "Rowan would be furious. I daren't even bring suffragette literature into the house."

"Pooh! He doesn't own you!" Alexa declared spiritedly.

"N-no," Lucinda agreed doubtfully. "But ever since Papa and Mama went down on the

Titanic Rowan has been more like a father than a brother to me and he has the greatest aversion to—" she quoted her brother with a grimace, "unwomanly women." She sighed. "He insists that no sister of his is going to get mixed up with the suffragettes."

Alexa sniffed. "Well, you're associating with one now!" she pointed out. She frowned thoughtfully. Rowan *would* be furious, she knew, if she led Lucinda astray. But then she was already in his black books, wasn't she; she might as well be hung for a sheep as a lamb. To recruit the sister of an under-secretary for Foreign Affairs would be a definite feather in her cap. And if Lucinda was old enough to make her debut in Society she was surely old enough to make up her own mind about such things. Rowan couldn't keep her wrapped up in cotton-wool forever!

So she said hesitantly, "Suppose you come along with me to Clement's Inn tomorrow. I'll introduce you to Mrs. Pankhurst. Neither of her daughters will be there, I'm afraid. Sylvia works in the East End and Christabel had to leave the country to avoid arrest. She sets W.S.P.U. policy, you know, and is too valuable to the Cause to languish in Hollo-way," Alexa said knowledgeably. "But some of the other leaders are sure to be at head-quarters and you could meet them. Annie Kenney, Grace Row, or Mary Richardson."

"Isn't she the one the newspapers call Polly Dick? The one who slashed the

Velásquez *Venus* in the National Gallery?"

"The very same." Alexa confirmed.

On Lucinda's pretty face, prudence warred with temptation. She took a deep breath. "I'll come with you," she promised. "But ..." Her brow wrinkled. "How shall we manage it? I have to take a maid along whenever I go out. I'm never allowed to go anywhere alone."

"How perfectly medieval!" Alexa was indignant. Really, she thought, Rowan belonged to the Dark Ages rather than the dawn of the twentieth century. She was thankful that she wasn't his dependent and under his thumb as Lucinda so obviously was. A deep feeling of protectiveness towards the younger girl welled up in her. "Never mind," she said kindly, patting Lucinda's hand. "We'll think of something."

The two girls had their heads together plotting their strategy when Rowan strolled in some ten minutes later, so absorbed that they didn't even hear him until he spoke. "Ah, keeping our guest entertained, Lucinda?" he said jovially, going over to the cake stand and helping himself to a generous slice.

The girls sprang apart guiltily. Lucinda flushed and busied herself in pouring a cup of tea for her brother while trying at the same time to avoid his eyes.

Now what have those two been up to? Rowan wondered as he took the fragile piece of china from Lucinda's hand. It trembled

ever so slightly and the cup rattled against
the saucer and a little of the fragrant brew
was spilled during the transfer.

Rowan's eyes narrowed speculatively.
Lucinda looked as though she were suffering
from a case of bad conscience, and Alexa—he
transferred his speculative gaze to the older
girl—looked as smug as the cat that's been in
the cream jar. Hmmm—this wanted looking
into.

Feeling his hard stare focus upon her,
Alexa blushed, and Rowan with a start of
surprise acknowledged something he had
overlooked in the confusion of their earlier
meeting—that his little cousin had
blossomed into a rare beauty. How had his
rackety cousin Reggie and Reggie's mousy
wife, Mary, produced such a vivid creature?
he wondered. Alexa's coloring had always
been striking, of course—the wealth of
tawny-bronze hair and the strange whisky-
colored eyes. But he had not realized till now
how dainty and perfectly proportioned she
was. The bone structure of her face was
delicately aristocratic with high cheekbones
and a long sweet curve to the jaw. He
followed the fragile line of her throat to
where it disappeared into the collar of her
white silk blouse.

No, this one wouldn't fare well in Holloway, he thought with a frown. Though he
was indifferent to suffragette aims and outraged by methods he could not possibly con-
done, he'd been shocked more than once by

the sight of some of the poor devils who emerged gaunt and hollow-eyed from a stretch in Holloway. Some, like Lady Constance Lytton, had had their health permanently undermined by the strain and degradation they had endured.

He couldn't let that happen to Alexa, he decided abruptly. Not just because she was, if only distantly, family but because she was too fine-drawn and fragile to be exposed to such experiences and emerge from them unscathed and unscarred. Somehow, he decided, he would have to save Alexa from herself.

Alexa found herself wilting under Rowan's steady contemplative gaze. Unaware of his thoughts, she supposed that he was mentally rehearsing the tongue-lashing that was in store for her. Suddenly she felt as if she were in the schoolroom again and Miss Pringle was about to rap her over the knuckles for a trifling misdemeanor. It was all she could do not to fidget and she wished wholeheartedly that he would do it and get it over with.

As if he could read her mind, Rowan drained his cup of tea and rose to his feet. "If you'll excuse us, Lucinda, your cousin and I have certain matters to discuss in my study."

Lucinda shot a commiserating glance at Alexa and said encouragingly, "Till tomorrow then, Alexa."

"Tomorrow?" Rowan, who was leading a reluctant Alexa towards the door of his study, stopped short and glanced back at his sister quizzically.

"Yes . . . er . . . ah . . . Alexa and I have arranged to have tea at Gunter's," Lucinda mumbled unhappily, aware that she had let the cat out of the bag. "You've been promising to take me there for a treat for so long, Rowan, but ever since I've come up to town you've been too busy." Lucinda, who was not used to deception but was learning fast, pouted prettily.

"Hmm . . . come to think of it I have been remiss," he admitted readily enough. "Suppose I join you tomorrow and treat you both. Better late than never, so they say!"

Lucinda couldn't quite conceal the look of dismay that spread across her face, but Alexa said quickly, "That would be delightful, Rowan. Quite a family party. But Lucinda and I had planned to do some shopping first. I . . . er . . . I lost my hat during the fracas today and I need to replace it. Lucinda tells me that Mademoiselle Madeleine in Bond Street has a delightful selection of new hats, all in the latest mode," she improvised swiftly, quite sure that Rowan would be averse to cooling his heels in a millinery shop while she and his sister dawdled over their choices.

She was right. "In that case, perhaps I should arrange to meet you at Gunter's later on—say four-thirty," he suggested. It was a good sign, he thought, that Alexa was still feminine enough to care about the latest

fashions and in relief he began teasing the
girls. "Between you and Lucy, you'd buy out
the shop, if I were along to foot the bill."

But once the study door closed behind
them, Rowan's good humor faded. This was
a serious business he was engaged upon—
that of. bringing Alexa to her senses. Unfortunately, he took the tack of speaking to
her as if she were a little sister, in a rather
heavy-handed fashion, and his difficulties increased as he realized with amazement that
the feelings engendered in him by this
defiant red-haired chit of a girl were not at
all brotherly.

It went from bad to worse as the interview
proceeded until finally Alexa's temper
snapped. "Don't patronize me, Rowan!" she
said irritably. "I'm not a child still in the
schoolroom and I do not view participation
in the suffragette movement as a childish
prank. I'm quite well aware of the possible
consequences of my actions!" She set her
stubborn chin and insisted, "I am quite
willing to suffer for the Cause."

Rowan sighed. "Are you also willing to see
others suffer, Alexa? Your mother, for instance. Have you any notion of the shame
and anguish she will endure if her only child
is thrown into prison?"

Alexa bit her lip. It had been out of consideration for her mother's feelings that she
had not joined the Women's Social and
Political Union long ago. Rowan had probed
and found her weak spot with devilish skill.

"Sometimes a Cause must transcend one's personal feelings," she began loftily.

Rowan's fist slammed down on the desk between them with such force that some small articles rattled off onto the polished hardwood floor. "Damn the Cause!" he snarled. "You are a Traherne, Alexa, and I expect you to start behaving like one. It is a proud old name and I do not intend to stand by and see it—and you—dragged through the dirt. I will not have you become the butt of music-hall jests, nor will I allow you to bring disgrace upon our name. Is that perfectly clear?"

"I don't see how it is possible for me to bring any more disgrace on our name than Papa did!" she retorted.

Rowan was startled. "That is an entirely different thing," he said. "A man may gamble at cards, even lose at cards, and still be a gentleman."

"Even *cheat* at cards?" Alexa said softly.

Rowan was shocked into truthfulness. "How did you know? Surely your mother—"

"Not from Mama," Alexa said swiftly. "It was the servants—"

"You shouldn't listen to servants' gossip and tittle-tattle, Alexa," Rowan said severely. "And you most certainly should not repeat it to anyone."

"As you've taken pains to remind me, it's all in the family," Alexa retorted. "And I still maintain that no one could possibly disgrace the family any more than Papa already has.

With his gambling debts and his cheating at cards and . . . and his women! Don't you see, Rowan," she pleaded desperately, "I'm not defying the conventions to satisfy a whim or for self-indulgent reasons but for . . . for a principle—to advance the rights of women. There's a new age dawning and it will be the age of the free woman and . . . and I intend to do my part in bringing it about." She paused for breath, her bosom heaving, then hurled her defiance at him. "I assure you that I *will* carry on with my suffragette activities, with your approval or without it!"

"And I say you will not."

Alexa sprang to her feet, her hands clenched in anger. "Don't you give me orders, Rowan! You may stand in loco parentis to Lucinda but you have no authority over *me*!"

"Have I not?" His voice was deceptively soft and silky. "We shall see."

Alexa lifted her chin defiantly. "You're wasting your breath giving me orders, for I have no intention of obeying them. I am not in the habit of obedience."

"Nor in the habit of being punished for disobedience, I dare say," Rowan thundered. He had been holding his own temper on a tight rein but it was beginning to fray at last. "Defy me, Alexa, and I shall be forced to show you how easy it will be to bring you to heel," he grated. "You may be a headstrong little madam with no consideration for others or thought for your own future, but I

am head of the family and as such it is my
duty—"

"You're not my father, my brother or . . .
or my husband . . ." Alexa flared.

"Indeed not! And God help the man who
takes you to wife!" The exclamation burst
forth involuntarily. Suddenly he got up from
behind the heavy oak desk and came around
it, moving towards her until there was
scarcely a hairsbreadth between them. His
face was suffused with anger and, despite
herself, Alexa gave way, dropping her eyes
and taking a step backward. To her distress,
angry, frustrated tears sprang to her eyes.

"I . . . I hate you, Rowan!" she declared in
a trembling whisper. "I hate all men. You're
just like all the rest—expecting that a
woman should have no other purpose in life
than to please and humor and cosset a man!"
She took another step backward and then
another until she was fumbling at the door
handle. "All . . . all you care about is some
antiquated notions of honor and propriety.
Well, I don't give a fig for either. And . . . and
I hate all men! Selfish egotistical brutes!"
she cried hysterically. Fumbling the door
open, she turned and ran, slamming it behind her as doors were seldom slammed in
Cadogan Square.

Chapter
2

It came to him in a flash. How to save Alexa from herself. It was so incredibly simple he wondered why he hadn't thought of it earlier. He would marry her off!

The idea came to him over brandy and cigars. He had dined at his club and, after a day that had proved trying, to say the least, he was feeling relaxed and expansive after a good dinner in these exclusively masculine precincts.

When Alexa had slammed out of his study, he had followed close behind. But she ran through the vast entrance hall as if the devil himself were at her heels until she came to the front door, which a startled footman opened for her. Rowan was just in time to see her run down the steps of Number Twenty-two Cadogan Square and out into the street. Fortunately, he had earlier on had the foresight to have the Rolls brought around so that Chalmers might drive her home after their interview, and now, as Rowan watched, he saw the quick-witted chauffeur usher the distraught girl into the vehicle.

Relieved that she wouldn't be wandering through the streets of the city in her emotional state, Rowan watched the motorcar pull away from the curb and then returned to his study. He had a report to prepare on Balkan affairs that couldn't be postponed. For the moment, at least, the problem Alexa posed would have to be shelved.

And now he had the answer to the riddle. Although he was usually an abstemious man, Rowan refilled his glass from the decanter on the sideboard and cradled the glass in his hands, swirling it gently and sniffing the aroma. Before he took a sip, he lifted the glass and made a toast—To Marriage!

She should have been married off long ago, of course. Properly speaking, it was the duty of her mama to see her daughter creditably settled in life with a husband and a home of her own. Obviously Cousin Mary had been negligent and it behooved him, Rowan, to take a hand and rectify matters. The girl shouldn't be left hanging on the shelf any longer. Why, it was no wonder she'd gotten herself mixed up with the suffragette crowd. She should have been properly launched into society at eighteen, with a court presentation and a "coming-out" ball. Lovely as she was, she would have been snapped up in her first season, penniless or not.

Rowan studied the glowing tip of his cigar. Well, it wasn't too late now. She wasn't more than twenty-one or twenty-two. And a husband was just what she needed—a mature man, strong-minded enough to curb her willful ways—a man of means who had no need to hold out for a rich wife. He began assessing possibilities among his friends and acquaintances. There was Owen Forbes-Hamilton, for instance, a captain in the Scots Guards, whose family seat comprised a draughty and crumbling castle in Wester Ross. It was just the place for Alexa. She could utilize that crusading zeal of hers to good account in bettering conditions for crofters on the estate—far, far from London and the suffragettes. Or, take Derek Cathcart—a second son, but there was money in the family for his mother had been an American heiress. The Cathcarts were notoriously prolific as well. Once married to Derek, Alexa would soon find herself busy setting up a nursery and adding a new pledge of her affections to the family every ten months.

Rowan grinned wickedly—and then a sudden scowl replaced the signs of mirth. Somehow he didn't fancy seeing her surrounded by small replicas of Derek Cathcart; the mental image he had formed—of her with a baby in her arms and Cathcart toddlers clinging to her skirts—didn't please him as much as he thought it would.

Well, dammit, it wasn't as though he would be insisting that she marry the first man who offered for her! She would have a wide choice; he would see to that. Half the eligible men in London would be at her feet when she turned those extraordinary eyes upon them. All he had to do was give her the opportunity of a London season and let nature take its course.

Accordingly, the next day, while the two girls were on their innocent shopping expedition (or so he supposed) he sallied forth to consult with Alexa's mama. The sooner his plan was put into operation, the better for all concerned.

Lady Mary Traherne received him in the stuffy and extraordinarily hideous drawing room of a small and inconvenient house in an unfashionable district of London. The best that could be said of it, he supposed, was that the rent must be cheap, and he felt rather guilty that he had not prevailed upon his Cousin Mary to stay comfortably in her own home at Nun's Farthing. At the time, he had assumed that too many unhappy memories haunted her there, but since meeting Alexa he decided that she—not her mother—had insisted on their removal to London. Obviously she was the stronger character of the two.

Once the polite preliminaries were out of the way, Rowan broached the subject of Alexa's involvement with the suffragattes as gently as he could. He did not want to unduly shock her mama, who was thin and pale and apparently far from well. But he felt it was incumbent on him to make painfully clear how dire the consequences might be if Alexa continued on her present course.

Lady Mary blanched when she heard how close her daughter had come to arrest and imprisonment. "I'm at my wit's end, Rowan," she said, with a quaver in her voice. "Alexa simply won't listen to me any more. Ever since she became self-supporting, she's insisted on going her own way and—"

"Self-supporting?" Rowan's black brows rose incredulously.

"Oh, she doesn't go *out* to work, of course. That I could not allow," Lady Mary re-assured him. She gestured towards a crowded corner where a large black machine sat incongruously on a table that was surely an antique. "It's one of those typewriting machines," she said unnecessarily. "Alexa taught herself to use it . . . she types manu-scripts for novelists and also literature for the W.S.P.U., the Women's Social and Political Union. Though in that case there is no remuneration, of course."

In spite of himself, Rowan was impressed. It was practically unheard-of for a young woman of Alexa's social station to exercise such initiative. Most would prefer to exist in genteel poverty, on the scraps doled out by beneficent relatives. Alexa had plenty of spirit, he mused. He would have to give her credit for that, at least.

He moved to the table and, with a murmured "May I?" and without waiting for his hostess's nod of permission, took up the top sheet of a pile of transcript. It was, he saw at a glance, neatly and professionally typed, but the subject matter brought a frown to his face. A sample of Alexa's volunteer work, it was a suffragette tract that described, in lurid detail, the process of force feeding. His eyes skimmed down the page. "One end of the nasal tube is put up the right and left nostril on alternate days ... great pain is experienced during the process ... the drums of the ears seem to be bursting and there is a horrible pain in the throat and breast ..."

With a grimace, Rowan discarded the sheet of paper. "Have you read this, Cousin Mary?" he asked.

She shook her head. "I fear I have not the courage," she said. "It is so appalling for me to think of Alexa undergoing such brutal treatment ... yet I know if she continues her present course ..." Her voice broke and she dabbed at her eyes with a lace-trimmed handkerchief.

Rowan frowned. "I wish she would at least limit her suffragette activities to typing and handing out tracts and pamphlets instead of taking part in riots and demonstrations."

"And so should I!" Lady Mary looked at him hopefully. "Do you have any suggestions, Rowan?"

"As it happens, I do," he said briskly. "It occurs to me that if Alexa were to have a London season—a formal coming-out—she would have little time left to devote to the Movement. Indeed, she might well lose interest in it altogether."

Lady Mary sighed. "I fear you misjudge the strength of Alexa's devotion to the Cause, Rowan."

"Nonsense!" Rowan broke in roughly. "I'm convinced that, given the chance to meet eligible young men during the London season, she'll forget all this suffragette foolishness. What the girl needs," he said authoritatively, "is a home and a husband—a strong, determined man who is capable of making her toe the mark."

"It may be that you're right," Lady Mary mused. "Alexa *was* very disappointed when she couldn't make her debut at the proper time."

"Exactly," Rowan said triumphantly. "She's turned to the suffragettes out of natural frustration at being denied the pleasures of other young girls of her social standing. The parties, the balls—"

"And you think if Alexa were similarly occupied . . ." Lady Mary, who knew her daughter rather better than did Rowan, was still dubious.

"I'm sure of it," he said firmly.

If Rowan could have seen his sister and his cousin at that particular moment, he would not have been so cocksure.

Alexa didn't like telling lies, even when circumstances forced her to do so. She and Lucinda had gone to Mademoiselle Madeleine's millinery shop exactly as she had told Rowan they would. Once there, Alexa chose a new hat—a beige sailor with dark brown velvet ribbons—with a speed and dispatch that astonished Lucinda. Chivvied by an impatient Alexa, the younger girl, unable to make a choice between two more elaborate concoctions, decided to purchase both and then sent her attendant maid off in the motorcar, laden with hatboxes. On their own at last, the two girls set off towards suffragette headquarters at Number Four Clement's Inn.

It was a veritable beehive of activity. Mrs. Pankhurst herself, thin and worn from her latest incarceration, was in the roof garden at the top of the huge rambling old building, making plans, it was rumored, to lead a deputation to Buckingham Palace to present a petition to the king. But she took time out to greet Alexa kindly and to be introduced to Lucinda, saying, "So you've brought us a new recruit, Alexa." She clasped the younger girl's hands with warm friendliness, murmuring, "How pretty you are, my dear. You remind me of my daughter, Christabel."

Alexa smiled on seeing that her cousin was suitably impressed by the renowned suffragette leader. When she led the girl off on a tour of inspection, Lucinda whispered to her, "Why, Mrs. Pankhurst isn't at all as I pictured her, Alexa. She must have been quite beautiful when she was young. I'd heard she was a harpy—a regular virago. Rowan has often said as much."

Alexa sniffed. "Rowan is not an oracle," she said tartly. She was delighted that her young cousin was quite in awe of Mrs. Pankhurst but she was beginning to wonder what Rowan's reaction would be to his sister's sudden conversion to the Cause. She hoped that Lucinda would have enough sense to keep a still tongue in her head when they all met later at Gunter's for tea. After her own explosive interview with Rowan last evening, she feared that the atmosphere would be fraught with tension enough, without an overenthusiastic Lucinda letting the cat out of the bag. She had just opened her mouth to warn Lucinda when a shrill whistle rent the air.

"It's a raid!" someone cried. "In retaliation for our demonstration yesterday. We must get Mrs. Pankhurst away!" For Emmeline Pankhurst, as Alexa knew, was out of prison on a ticket of leave. Under the much-hated Cat and Mouse Act of Parliament, suffragettes on hunger strike were sometimes released on sick leave without remission of sentence. If found at headquarters and certified in good health, Mrs. Pankhurst would be returned to prison to complete her sentence.

More whistles blew, but most of the suffra-

gettes remained at their posts, hastily
destroying compromising documents while
others went off to escort Mrs. Pankhurst to a
place of safety through a secret exit. Lucinda
clutched Alexa's arm excitedly as a squad of
detectives entered and began ransacking the
building, looking for evidence of conspiracy,
Alexa presumed. They turned out desks and
filing cabinets while an officious inspector
lined up the women against a wall. He then
went slowly down the queue, looking closely
into each face. Lucinda shook with fright,
but Alexa, who felt quite calm, endeavored to
comfort her. She was whispering reassur-
ances to her young cousin when, to her
surprise, the inspector stopped in front of
Lucinda and said in a gratified tone,
"Aha—so we've nabbed you at last, Miss
Christabel Pankhurst!"

Lucinda's pretty mouth fell open. "Oh, but
I'm not—!" she squeaked.

Alexa kicked her sharply on the ankle,
realizing instantly what had happened. Dark-
haired, round-faced Lucinda did bear a
resemblance to Christabel. If the police had
been keeping Clement's Inn under sur-
veillance, as they must have done, they
would have been elated when a young
woman answering to Christabel's general
description went openly into the building.

"No sign of Emmeline Pankhurst?" the
inspector asked one of his subordinates who
had been searching the premises.

"No, sir."

The inspector looked momentarily disappointed but said resignedly, "Oh, well, we may have lost the old vixen but we have the vixen's cub. Take her out to the van, Jenkins. I'll finish up here."

Lucinda clung, half-fainting, to Alexa, her eyes wide with fright. "Come along now, miss," Jenkins said gruffly. "You know the routine as well as I do. It's down to the magistrate's court at Bow Street and then off to Holloway. It must be like a home away from home for such as you."

Alex put a protective arm around the younger girl. "I'm going with her," she announced defiantly.

The police sergeant looked dubious. "We don't have a warrant for you, miss."

"Well, then, I'll give you a reason to take me into custody," she said swiftly and, suiting her action to her words, kicked him sharply in the shins.

The Black Maria looked like a hearse with elephantiasis whose dark maw gaped open to engulf the suffragettes. Lucinda quailed before it, and even Alexa, who had never before been taken into custody, felt that entering it was a sort of living death.

Lucinda spoke plaintively. "Why . . . why wouldn't you let me tell them I'm not Christabel Pankhurst? And . . . and what will they do to me when they find out, Alexa?"

"Wipe the egg off their faces and release you," Alexa assured her anxious cousin promptly. "What else can they do? It wasn't

your fault. You weren't impersonating
Christabel. You just happened to be there
and you do look a bit like her. They wouldn't
have believed you anyway, even if you had
told them the truth." Alexa tossed back the
heavy mane of hair that, as usual, had
slipped through its pins and cascaded
untidily over her shoulders. "Don't you see,
Lucinda," she went on impatiently, "their
mistake turned out to be a marvelous diver-
sionary tactic. It gave Mrs. Pankhurst an
opportunity to get away. That odious police
inspector was so cock-a-hoop over capturing
the notorious Christabel Pankhurst that he
didn't bother to conduct a thorough search
for her mother. And they simply mustn't get
Mrs. Pankhurst in their clutches just yet,"
Alexa said earnestly. "She is planning a very
important demonstration next month and
she simply must be there to lead it in person.
You're performing a very important service
for the Cause."

Even in the dimness of the van Alexa could
see that Lucinda looked unconvinced. "I
don't know what Rowan will say," she sighed
worriedly.

It was an aspect of the situation that had
not occurred to Alexa. There was no way to
keep it from him; he would have to know.
Alexa's heart sank. He was going to be
furious with her. Not only had she, within
twenty-four hours of his prohibition against
her suffragette activities, managed to get
herself arrested, but she had embroiled his

young sister with the suffragettes as well. He would never forgive, nor forget this escapade.

Of course it wasn't all her fault, she told herself bracingly. How could she have foreseen that an overeager police inspector would mistake Lucinda for Christabel Pankhurst? She couldn't. But it would never have happened if Lucinda hadn't gone with her to suffragette headquarters, and for that, she Alexa, was responsible. She shivered, picturing the rage on Rowan's dark face when he found out about it.

Rowan was already furious. He had waited for the girls to keep their appointment, first with indulgent masculine complacency (trust a woman on a shopping spree to forget all about time), then with increasing irritation. As the minutes ticked away, irritation gave way to outright anger. Lucinda would never have kept him waiting; it must be Alexa who was the culprit. No doubt she was aping the unpunctual habits of her namesake, the widowed Queen Alexandra.

His fingers were rapping an impatient tattoo on the tabletop when a waiter brought him a note on a silver salver. He could hardly believe the message it contained. With a muttered oath, he crumpled the note and sprang to his feet.

> "March on, march on
> Face to the Dawn
> The Dawn of Liberty"

A number of suffragettes had been crowded into the Black Maria with the two young cousins and kept their spirits high by striking up the Women's Marseillaise. Even Lucinda, who didn't know the words, hummed the tune until she too could sing out, "March on, march on . . ." But when the police van jolted to a stop outside Bow Street Station and everyone was herded into a smelly dark cell to wait for court to convene, Lucinda's pretty face crumpled. Alexa helped her find a seat on one of the hard benches that lined the walls and did her best to comfort her.

The younger girl clutched at her, whimpering. "Oh, Alexa, I'm . . . I'm afraid I'm not the stuff of which heroines are made. I . . . I want to go home!"

"And so you shall," Alexa comforted her. "Nobody but a . . . a noodlehead could mistake you for Christabel Pankhurst." She was confident that her cousin would be released, for the judge would have had the real Christabel up before him on numerous occasions and would realize as soon as Lucinda entered the dock that a mistake had been made. But what about herself? She would be charged with assaulting a policeman and/or hindering him in the performance of his duties. To her dismay, Alexa found that her courage and bravado were seeping away. She didn't want to go to prison; she wanted to go home quite as much as Lucinda. But she squared her shoulders, she wasn't going to snivel!

Alexa's prediction proved correct. Lucinda's case was called first and the justice, Mr. Curtis-Bennett, needed only a cursory glance at the shrinking, half-fainting girl to throw the case out of court.

Because Alexa was next in line, her case was called next.

"Alexandra Traherne, you stand accused of assaulting a police officer. How do you plead?" a bored voice intoned.

Alexa licked her lips. "Guilty, Your Honor," she admitted in a small subdued voice.

"Thirty shillings or fourteen days," that same bored voice pronounced.

Alexa stiffened her spine and took a deep breath. This was the moment she had been waiting for—the moment when she would stand proudly in the dock and announce that she would go to prison because she was fighting for her rights and the rights of all women!

But the words stuck in her throat. "I will . . . I will . . ." she stammered.

"Your Honor, I will pay the lady's fine and I further ask that she be remanded into my custody!" The voice rang out in the stuffy courtroom.

Alexa swung around in disbelief. It couldn't be . . . but it was . . . Rowan was standing beside the dock, his face black with fury.

Before she quite grasped what was happening, Rowan had paid the fine, Mr. Curtis-Bennett was calling for the next case, and Rowan, one hand grasping her arm and the other Lucinda's, was propelling them speedily out of the courtroom.

Dinner was a silent affair. Rowan was tight-lipped with fury, Lucinda sniveled into her soup, and Alexa could only toy with the food on her plate. Finally Rowan, whose eagle eyes noticed everything, said nastily, "Going on a hunger strike, Alexa?"

She shook her head. "I simply don't have any appetite," she said listlessly. She hadn't wanted to stay for dinner, hadn't wanted to come back to Cadogan Square at all, but when, in the Rolls, she had expressed a wish to be dropped off at her own home, Rowan had fixed her with a riveting stare and grated, "Not one word, Alexa. Not one word!" Utterly routed for once in her life, she had subsided, shriveling into her seat.

He had listened to Lucinda, though. The younger girl was shaking with relief, but she insisted on babbling explanations. With breathless gasps and broken sobs, she described how she had been mistaken for Christabel Pankhurst and how terrible the experience had been. Rowan listened intently, occasionally giving her shoulder a comforting pat.

"I . . . I don't know what I would have done if it weren't for Alexa. She was wonderful, Rowan!" Lucinda wiped her eyes with a handkerchief borrowed from her brother. "They didn't want to let her go with me, you know. And . . . and that's when she kicked that horrid policeman in the shins. So he would take her into custody too."

"Indeed." Rowan's sole comment was totally noncommittal but Alexa, sneaking a peep at him through the veiling of her thick curling lashes, saw, or thought she saw, the corners of his mouth twitch. She was tempted to ask him then, since it seemed explanations were in order, how it was that he had popped up at the opportune moment, but when she opened her mouth to put the question to him he affixed her with a look that would have curdled milk and she subsided into herself again.

When they arrived at the Cadogan Square house, he sent Alexa upstairs to borrow a dinner frock from his sister while he telephoned a message to Alexa's mother, to inform her of her daughter's whereabouts.

"Perhaps I should speak to her," Alexa said quickly.

"That won't be necessary," Rowan said dismissively. "Run along now and change for dinner."

Just as if she were an errant child being sent off to the nursery, Alexa thought indignantly. She would have liked to be privy to his conversation with her mother but apparently she was going to be denied even that small privilege.

So now she sat uncomfortable in an ill-

fitting frock of Lucinda's. A maid had hastily
taken a tuck in it, but Alexa was sure she
looked a fright, which only served to increase her discomfiture. She shifted uneasily in her chair, feeling as if seated at that
banquet in ancient Greece at which Damo-
cles was forced to sit under a sword sus-
pended by a single hair to demonstrate the
precariousness of fate. The advantages of a
classical education, Alexa thought, a trifle
hysterically. Thanks to Miss Pringle's tute-
lage, she could find a classical allusion to fit
any situation in which she found herself.

The well-trained maids moved soft-footedly around the table, removing in turn
almost-untouched soup plates, a joint of beef
that had scarcely been sampled, the sweet,
the savory—for it seemed that nobody had
any appetite.

At last the interminable meal was over.
Lucinda rose, eager to leave her brother to
his port and cigar which Alexa devoutly
hoped would temper his disposition.
Judging by his facial expression, it could
best be described as savage.

But on this particular evening Rowan was
not disposed to linger. He followed the girls
to the drawing room where he took up a
stance before the marble fireplace, in which
a small fire crackled cheerfully. It was the
only sound in the room.

Alexa exchanged a nervous conspiratorial
glance with Lucinda.

The silence stretched out—a heavy,

ominous, tension-fraught silence. If it went on any longer Alexa was sure she would scream.

She cleared her throat and said with forced brightness, "Th-thank you for the lovely dinner, Rowan. It was delicious! But . . . but I really should be going home now. Lucinda is quite worn out and Mama will be anxious—"

The expression on Rowan's dark face was inscrutable. "Sit down, Alexa."

"But I—"

"Sit down!" His tone brooked no argument. Alexa sank down on the sofa beside a wan and worried-looking Lucinda.

"You won't be going home. Not tonight. Not at all," Rowan said flatly.

Alexa couldn't believe her ears. "Not going home! But I—"

"Your mama agrees with me that Mrs. Brownell's chaperonage will be sufficient for this one night. In the morning you—all of us, in fact—will be going down to Nun's Farthing. Your mother will meet us at the station with her baggage and yours. She is packing up tonight."

"Nun's Farthing!" Alexa and Lucinda spoke at the same time, Alexa in bewilderment, Lucinda in dismay.

"Oh, Rowan," Lucinda wailed. "Do you mean to cancel my debut? Is that to be my punishment?"

"Not at all," Rowan reassured his little sister quickly. "Your punishment—if you choose to consider it as such—is that you will have to share your coming-out ball, your court presentation, and sundry other amusements with Alexa."

The two girls exchanged bewildered glances. Lucinda was the first to recover from the shock of this surprise announcement. Overjoyed that she was not to be deprived of her debut, she jumped up and hugged her brother.

"Oh, Rowan, you're the most wonderful brother a girl could have!" she exclaimed. "What fun it will be for us to come out together! We'll take the town by storm!" she prophesied happily.

Alexa sat still in a stunned silence. "I don't understand . . ." she said faintly.

"What is there to understand?" Rowan said coolly, disentangling himself from his sister's excited clutches. "The necessary arrangements have been made with your mama for you to be launched into Society at the same time as Lucinda. Since your mother is in delicate health, my aunt, Lady Salter, will present you both and act as your joint chaperone. Nothing could be more suitable."

"And . . . and Mama has agreed to this?" Alexa asked in disbelief. Her mind in a whirl, she grasped at a straw. "Why, the expense alone would be—"

"Your mama has come into a small legacy which will cover all the expenses," Rowan said mendaciously, for he himself intended to supplement Lady Mary's slender purse.

"In any case, she will be giving up her London establishment and returning to Nun's Farthing to act as my hostess, so she'll be spared the expense of renting and keeping up a London house."

"But . . . but I don't want to go back to Nun's Farthing!" Alexa cried. "And I don't want a London Season!"

"What you want has very little to do with it," Rowan said in measured tones. "Like it or not, Alexa, you are going to be launched into Society. And, like it or not you are going down to Nun's Farthing in the morning. You have no choice in the matter. Do I make myself clear?"

Alexa tried to brazen it out, though in spite of herself her chin trembled. "You . . . you have no right!" she cried, catching her lower lip between her teeth.

"Now that's where you're wrong," Rowan interrupted her. "I have every right." He sighed. "Must I remined you, Alexa, of a little matter you appear to have forgotten?"

"F-forgotten?" she stammered.

"That Mr. Justice Curtis-Bennett himself remanded you into my keeping!"

Chapter
3

There were those who would say she had gotten off lightly, Alexa supposed. Lucinda, for one. Her brief flirtation with women's suffrage was thoroughly squelched, and Lucinda was glad, pitifully glad, Alexa thought scornfully, that she was not to be deprived of her debut.

No, Lucinda was no ally. Neither was Alexa's mother, whose capitulation to Rowan's arrogant masterfulness was instantaneous and complete. In fact, by the time the train pulled into the little station of Chumleigh Halt, the nearest rail point to Nun's Farthing, it was plain that Mama was absolutely besotted by Rowan, fondly regarding him as the son she had never had.

So Alexa took her grumbles to Nanny, who had been pensioned off and who lived in a small thatched cottage on the estate. But Nanny was, if possible, even worse than Mama

—full of lavish praise for "Master Rowan," waxing enthusiastic over the improvements he had made on the estate, his kindness to old retainers such as herself, his popularity with staff and estate tenants alike. Moreover, Nanny had already heard that Alexa was to make her debut at long last, and she couldn't be more delighted at the prospect. In Nanny's experience, debuts inevitably led to weddings, and weddings just as inevitably led to babies. Nanny hastened to reassure Alexa that she was ready and able to come out of retirement and take charge of her nurseling's firstborn. Her dear mama had been so obliging as to produce Alexa just nine months after her wedding day, and it was to be hoped, hinted Nanny, that Alexa herself would be just as prompt (though more prolific).

Alexa gnashed her teeth with rage. She felt trapped. Nanny saw her as a brood mare, Mamma as a marriageable daughter whom (now that the opportunity was available) she was eager to get off her hands, and Rowan . . . ? Rowan saw her, she was sure, as a Potential Disgrace to the Family Name.

Her eyes narrowed thoughtfully. So *that* was his game. Of course, *that* was why he was so anxious for her to have her long-deferred debut! It was his intention to put her on the marriage market and sell her off to the highest bidder! Her imagination suddenly caught fire. Since she was penniless, she thought feverishly, she would probably be married off to some horrible fat old man of property who could afford a pretty, well-born, young wife. And she would . . . she would have to *sleep* with this creature. Since Alexa, in common with other well-bred young women of her time, had only the haziest idea what went on in the marriage bed, her mind boggled at the thought. But at the very least, he, this mythical husband, would be the sort who would lock her in her room on a bread and water diet if she so much as smuggled a suffragette tract into the house. Rowan would see to that.

She shuddered. She couldn't let it happen to her. Not without a fight! With fire in her eye she went in search of Rowan.

She found him in the estate office, conferring with the agent he had installed when he took up his Foreign Office career. For the estate, once it had been restored to its former productivity and was running smoothly, had not been enough to absorb Rowan's restless energies. Alexa privately thought that since he had been lucky enough to inherit, he ought to have remained on the estate and managed it himself, but that was neither here nor there.

"I have to talk to you, Rowan," she said without preamble.

He stood up, looking surprised at her rudeness. He seemed, Alexa couldn't help thinking, even more impressively masculine in his well-cut country tweeds than in the starched and snowy shirt and dinner jacket he had worn the previous evening.

"As you wish," he said coolly. "But first let me introduce you to Alec Macpherson, my agent. Alec, my cousin Alexa."

Alexa inclined her head, and sandy-haired Alec Macpherson, who seemed extremely bashful, muttered something in broad Scots and edged towards the door.

"No, don't go, Alec," Rowan said decisively. "Alexa and I will take a turn in the garden and I'll get back to you later." He opened the door and ushered Alexa out.

Like the rest of the estate, the rose garden had undergone a startling transformation. In the old days, the gardening staff had consisted of one arthritic old man and a young boy. Old Turner had preferred food for the stomach rather than food for the soul and though justly proud of his prize cabbages and brussels sprouts had shamefully neglected the flower beds.

But Rowan had not, she noticed grudgingly. The old bushes had been pruned back and lovingly trained over rustic pergolas, and new tea roses in shades of cream, peach and smoky apricot had been planted in beds intersected by charming footpaths laid down in sandy-golden brick. But she wasn't going to let herself be impressed by the transformation he had wrought, she told herself sternly. Her mother, who loved flowers, could have done the same if she'd had the means. It was wonderful what miracles money could accomplish, she thought bitterly.

As they strolled along the brick paths, she found herself wondering for whom Rowan had planted the rose garden and why he had not yet found a mistress for Nun's Farthing. His wealth and social position automatically rendered him a highly eligible parti in the eyes of socially ambitious mamas, while his rugged good looks must have set the susceptible hearts of debutantes aflutter season after season. She herself was not, of course, susceptible! Oh, she knew what men were—none better. Gay deceivers, like Papa. Or pompous, overweening brutes, like—like Rowan himself! Oppressors of her sex. Yes indeed, it was men like Rowan—arrogant, self-assured men—who were keeping women in subjugation. Well, she wasn't going to be subjugated—not she!

Having worked herself up to a pitch of indignation she went on the attack. "It won't work, Rowan," she said abruptly.

He had paused to pluck a bud from a Gloire de Dijon rose with the intention of presenting it to her but thought better of it and tucked it into his buttonhole instead. Judging by the mutinous expression on her face, the friendly gesture wouldn't be appreciated. He sighed. "All right, Alexa. Out with it. Just what is it that isn't going to work?"

"Your nefarious scheme."

"My what?" Rowan's jaw dropped.

"You heard me. Your evil scheme."

"And just what does that consist of?" he asked.

She told him. In detail. Not forgetting the fat old man.

He threw back his head and laughed. He *laughed!* at her, she thought indignantly. Notwithstanding her irritation, she was poignantly reminded of another, earlier Traherne—the seventeenth-century Traherne whose portrait graced the Long Gallery. Dark of skin and black of hair as Rowan himself, that earlier Traherne who had fought for his king at Edgehill and Naseby had been painted in a similar pose, his portrait captioned *The Laughing Cavalier.*

Why she should suddenly have been reminded of that portrait, Alexa couldn't have said. The two men bore a family resemblance—at least they were both black Trahernes—but there was nothing at all cavalierlike about Rowan—was there? No indeed. He was a stuffy, conservative, hidebound, arrogant bully! With a misplaced sense of humor!

"I don't see what there is to laugh about," she said with asperity.

Rowan's ringing laughter died away to chortles. "A fat old man, forsooth! Believe me, Alexa, you have no need to fear an overweight, elderly husband." Merriment danced in his eyes. "You'd be the death of him! And then where would we be? Alexa Traherne as a Merry Widow!" He almost went off again but sobered suddenly, troubled by the very real concern reflected in her eyes. "No one is going to coerce you into a marriage of convenience, my dear," he reassured her gently.

"No?" Alexa was unimpressed by his assurance.

"No," he said firmly. "Naturally the ultimate object of a young woman's debut is matrimony..." Seeing the flicker of fear reappear in her eyes he added hastily, "but both you and Lucinda will be introduced to a variety of young men so that you will have a wide choice. In fact, I'm planning a house party this weekend so that you will get to meet a few young people in an informal way."

"Then you have no objection to my making a love match?"

Rowan hesitated, knowing full well how few marriages in their social circle were made for love. "If you meet a suitable young man for whom you have a decided partiality, you will have my blessing," he said cautiously.

"I have your word on that?"

"You have my word."

"You've been out in the world a number of years, Rowan, and yet you haven't found anyone for whom you have a decided partiality," she observed slyly. She had got him to make a concession—that she would not be forced into a marriage of convenience—but what she was angling for was a declaration that she need not marry at all, if she didn't choose to. A husband, even a complaisant one, would cramp her style, she considered. If only she had the money that Mama was putting into her social debut, she thought resentfully, she could study for a profession instead. Take up law, like Christabel Pankhurst who already had her LL.D from Manchester University. At present women were barred from actually practicing law, but all that would change when women got the vote. Of that she was sure.

Rowan was startled by her thrust. No, by God, he thought, he hadn't yet found a woman for whom he was willing to give up his freedom. He had a comfortable arrangement with Lady Wyndham, who had already given her husband an heir and a spare and who, by the prevailing social code, was free to amuse herself as she chose as long as she exercised discretion. But Lady Wyndham was beginning to pall. Compared to Alexa, he reflected, his voluptuous mistress would look as blowzy as an overblown rose beside a bud, its petals just beginning to unfurl.

"It's different for a man," he assured her. "A woman *must* marry. What else is there for her?"

"For me, there is the Cause," she said incautiously.

"The Cause!" A frown creased Rowan's dark brow. "The Cause won't father your children or warm your bed of nights!"

She blushed, unaccustomed to such frank language even from Rowan. "There's no need to be crude," she said tartly, turning away from him a little shocked.

He grabbed her shoulders and forced her
to face him, giving her a little shake. "Listen
to me, Alexa . . . is this Cause or any cause
worth giving up your life for? Do you really
want to waste your life between committee
rooms and Holloway?" And it *would* be a
waste, he was sure of that. She had too much
to give—too much warmth and love—too
much fire and spirit. Deep within her he
could sense a deep well of as yet untapped
passion. If only she could be persuaded to
give the devotion to a man that was wasted
on an ideal, he mused. It struck him forcibly
that what she needed was to be soundly
kissed—awakened to the realities of life. But
he was not the man for the job, he decided
regretfully. She was his cousin, after all. And
she was too young for him. Experienced,
worldly wise women had always been more
to his taste. He tore his gaze away from the
fire smoldering in those lovely eyes, from the
softly inviting lips that cried out to be
kissed, and summoned all his patience. "My
dear girl, the millennium won't come when
women get the vote, you know."

"Perhaps not, but we'll be just a little bit
closer to it," she insisted.

Rowan sighed and tried another tack.
"Alexa, a woman needs a man to take care of
her and—"

She gazed up at him defiantly. "*I* can take
care of myself!" she asserted, trying to
squirm out of his grasp.

His grip on her shoulders tightened. "As you did yesterday?" he taunted her.

She flushed. "There was no need for you to come rushing to my rescue."

"No need?" Rowan ejaculated.

"How did you know where we were, anyway?" she asked. It had been puzzling her ever since—Rowan's opportune appearance at Bow Street Station. *She* certainly hadn't sent for him and she knew quite well that Lucinda had not had the opportunity. He had appeared out of nowhere, like a devil in a puff of smoke.

"Oh, that," he said carelessly. "I told Chalmers to follow after you in the Rolls. He trailed after you to Number Four Clement's Inn. When the police bundled you and Lucinda into the Black Maria he hot-footed off to send me a message."

Alexa's whisky-colored eyes darkened with fury. "You . . . you sent a servant to *spy* on me!" she gasped.

"Don't twist my words, Alexa!" he said angrily. "Chalmers was there for your own protection—yours and Lucinda's. She doesn't know her way around as you do—or, as you think you do! And as for you, my hoity-toity little madam, you can be damn glad that he was there or you'd have spent the night cooling your heels in Holloway!"

Rowan had to shout the last words after her, for with a cry she had wrenched herself from his grip and was gone.

Rowan went up to London the next day. Which was a good thing, Alexa thought privately, for his temper was savage and everyone from her mother down to the lowliest housemaid was glad to see the back of him.

"If only you'd be a little more civil to Rowan, dear," her mother expostulated with her. "After all, if it weren't for him you wouldn't be able to come-out this season."

"Why? He isn't subsidizing it, is he?" asked Alexa suspiciously.

"No, dear, of course not," her mother faltered a little over the white lie. "You know I had expectations from Uncle Paul." It was true her brother had left her a small bequest which she had put aside for a rainy day, Lady Mary mused. But dear Rowan was so generous about supplementing it, taking her aside before he left and insisting that Alexa must have the very best. "I won't have her dressing like Lucinda's poor relation," he'd said bluntly. "Whenever you run short, charge it to my accounts."

Lady Mary bit her lip. "No, dear, Rowan isn't subsidizing your debut," she repeated as if repetition would make it true. "I only meant . . . well, he *has* made arrangements for you to be launched by dear Lady Salter."

Indeed he had, Alexa thought indignantly. Rowan's aunt, summoned by him, had arrived promptly on the next train, come down to assess her prospects. She had looked her over, Alexa thought stormily, like

a filly at a horse auction. It was a wonder she
hadn't been ordered to show her teeth.

"Your gel's a beauty, Mary," Lady Salter
had boomed. "She'll go off in her first
season, mark my words. Bound to outshine
Lucinda, who's pretty enough but common-
place." Alexa was glad Lucy was not present
to hear herself thus casually dismissed. "But
Lord," Lady Salter continued, "I never saw
such a sulky debutante. What ails the gel?"
Just as if she weren't there at all! Alexa
raged.

To which her mother had no answer, for
she couldn't understand her daughter's state
of mind and said so frankly.

"Darling, I don't understand you," she said
again, plaintively. "Any other girl would leap
at the chance to come-out in Society . . .
to . . ." her mother flushed a little, "to make
a good match."

"To make a Society marriage, that's what
you mean, isn't it, Mama? Well, I want more
than that. I won't be satisfied with the empty
civilized relationships that characterize
such a marriage. I want to marry for love! If
I marry at all."

"If you marry at all!" her mother gasped.
And at the very hint that Alexa might not do
any such thing, she began fanning herself
vigorously and sent her daughter running
for hartshorn and water.

Alexa's only escape from the ever-present
discussion of fashions, furbelows, feathers
and fittings which the two older women and

Lucinda enjoyed was a refuge she had often sought in former years—the stables. Mounted on her little black mare, Gypsy, Alexa could savor at least the illusion of freedom in a gallop across the downs.

But by Friday afternoon, she needed more than a gallop to soothe her ruffled temper. The house was in an uproar—the servants in a dither; Mama, unaccustomed to entertaining after years of solitude, having palpitations; Lucinda in a pet because her maid had forgotten to pack the gown she wanted for dinner that evening. Alexa herself had quarreled with Lady Salter, who declared that she was a headstrong chit who needed her ears boxed, merely because Alexa had thrown out the corsets the older woman insisted were de rigueur.

The conventions of society were straitjacket enough without being tight-laced into such instruments of torture, Alexa decided rebelliously. She was one of the "New Women," wasn't she? At least she thought of herself as such. She might as well start as she meant to go on. No more corsets for her. And . . . a slow smile curved her lips . . . no more sidesaddles either.

With a sparkle in her eyes she dived into her dresser drawer and rummaged until she found her breeches. She'd bought them with the first money she'd earned but had never dared to wear them. They'd have brought on Mama's palpitations for sure.

She got out of the house undetected. Mama

was resting in her room, Lucinda pouting in
hers, Lady Salter was out—gone to the devil,
Alexa hoped—and the servants were busy at
their various chores.

Old Saunders, the head groom, who had
been at Nun's Farthing ever since she could
remember, never batted an eye. "I won't be
needing the sidesaddle today, Saunders,"
she said blithely. "Will you change it for me,
please?" Saunders, knowing her habits, had
had Gypsy saddled and waiting for her in the
courtyard.

While waiting for the saddle to be
changed, Alexa went down the row of stalls.
A glossy head, black, brown or bay, poked
out over the half-door of each loose box for
the pat and sugar lump that Alexa dis-
tributed impartially.

This was one innovation of Rowan's that
Alexa approved wholeheartedly. In the old
days, Mama's first act of economization was
to sell off the horses, except for the carriage
horses and Gypsy, and Alexa had wept her
eyes out as each one of them was led away.
But Rowan had filled the stables with
hunters and hacks, and, much as she hated to
admit it, he was an excellent judge of horse-
flesh. She bestowed a special pat on Rowan's
silky-coated black stallion, Shaitan, eyeing
him with longing. She would give her eye-
teeth to ride him just once and had already
teased Saunders for permission to try him
out, but the old man who never refused her
anything had looked at her in alarm. "It

would be as much as my job is worth, Miss Alexa," he protested. "And me due to retire with a pension and a cottage on the grounds, come Michaelmas."

"You don't need a cottage, Saunders," she chaffed the old man gently. "You live, eat and breathe for horses, you know you do!"

"Now, miss. You know I daren't let you up on the Black. The master's very generous, that he is, but it don't do to cross him!"

So, bestowing a final pat on the stallion's gleaming hide and whispering, "One day I'll ride you, you beauty. One day after Michaelmas," she turned away. She didn't want to get Saunders in trouble or cause him to lose his promised pension and she knew Rowan's temper. When roused, he could be a devil!

She had forgotten her bowler so she borrowed a cap from Saunders and crammed it down on her head so that it almost concealed the burnished curls that were already threatening to spill from the heavy knot she had twisted them into. It would be as well to look as much like a boy as possible, she considered, just in case anyone spotted her. Flaunting the conventions was all very well, but there was no use in deliberately courting disaster by making herself even more conspicuous and the talk of the countryside.

It seemed distinctly odd at first to be straddling her horse like a man instead of curling her knee around the high horn of a ladies' saddle. But before long she grew accustomed to it and found that she quite liked it. In fact it was quite a relief to be free of dragging, hampering, cumbersome skirts. The hobble skirt that was in vogue had always been a particular destation of hers, in that it restricted a normal stride. No wonder men like Rowan could bestride the earth like the Lords of Creation, she reflected. Their clothing permitted them a heady freedom of movement that women were denied.

Her gallop across the downs succeeded in restoring Alexa's spirits, and with the wind ruffling her hair and blowing the scent of the sea into her nostrils she turned homeward in a much better frame of mind than when she had first set out. Better, that was, until she spied Rowan, mounted on Shaitan, emerging from the Home Farm woods and heading her way.

Oh, Lord, she thought ruefully, it's a good job I didn't manage to coax poor old Sanders to mount *me* on Shaitan. He'd have been turned off without a reference, for sure!

And then she remembered her breeches, looking down at herself in horror. While she wasn't precisely sure what Rowan thought of women wearing pants (the subject had never arisen) she had a shrewd suspicion that he would be outraged and that that outrage would be expressed loudly and forthrightly. Oh, bother! What was he doing home so early anyway? she wondered with vexation. He wasn't expected until teatime and it couldn't be anywhere near that yet. Or was it? Had she lost track of time?

But that didn't matter now. What
mattered was evading Rowan, if at all
possible. She brightened. Perhaps he hadn't
even seen her—he was still a goodish
distance away—and seeing her at that range
he might well take her for a stable lad out
exercising one of the horses and pay her no
mind.

Faint hope! Within minutes he had spied
her and was calling peremptorily, "Hi, you!
Lad! Wait up!"

At that point there were a couple of
options open to Alexa. She could have obe-
diently waited up and meekly taken a
tongue-lashing. Or she could have cut across
into the Home Farm woods and hoped that
Rowan wouldn't bother to retrace his steps
and follow her.

But she did neither of these things.
Instead, she altered her course slightly,
flicked Gypsy with her crop, and set off
across the Home Farm pasture, scattering
startled sheep ahead of her as she went. Why
she chose this course she didn't know herself, for, as good a horsewoman as she was,
she ought to have known perfectly well that
her little mare was no match for Rowan's
stallion whose long strides ate up the
ground.

She ought also to have remembered the
five-barred gate that divided the Home Farm
pasture from the park proper. Gypsy could
have jumped the low hedges that kept the

sheep from straying, but the gate was coming up directly ahead of her.

Glancing back over her shoulder, Alexa could see that Rowan was gaining on her fast. Indeed, she could hear the thudding of his horse's hooves in pursuit. Common sense told her that she should draw rein and let Rowan catch up to her, but a little demon that lived inside her urged her to show off her horsemanship first. So she set Gypsy at the gate that loomed ahead.

But Gypsy was already winded, and Alexa's momentary hesitation put her off her stride. Her foreleg bumped the top rail and she went down, pitching Alexa over her head.

It was Rowan who, making the jump she should have made, cleared the bars with ease on Shaitan. When he landed, Gypsy was limping away and Alexa, who had been thrown clear, was lying off to the side, the burnished curls spilling out from under her cap betraying her identity.

Rowan cursed. Until he espied the betraying brazen curls, he had taken her for a groom riding out with a message to the Home Farm, though he'd thought it odd that a groom or stable lad would be mounted on Gypsy when there were so many hacks needing exercise. He'd been amazed that when hailed the "lad" had turned tail and run from him.

Alexa! He might have known! He cursed again and knelt down beside her, feeling for a pulse. It was beating rapidly.

At the touch of his fingers on her wrist her eyes flickered open. She moaned and tried to sit up.

"Lie still. I've got to make sure nothing is broken," he commanded her. Her thickly fringed dark lashes fluttered up at him and he wondered if she knew just how provocative the sweep of those dark lashes was to watch.

"Are you in pain?" he asked anxiously, his hands gently probing.

"No . . . no . . . I don't think so," she gasped, surprised at the genuine note of concern in his voice. "Where's Gypsy?" She tried to struggle to her feet. "I've got to see to Gypsy," she insisted.

Rowan spared a glance for the mare who was quietly cropping grass a short distance away. "She appears to be all right. No thanks to you," he added, for now that he was sure that Alexa was all right his irritation was beginning to surface.

She struggled to her feet. "I have to see . . ." Her voice trailed off and she clutched at Rowan as the world began to whirl around her.

He sighed. "Your concern for your mount is commendable but it comes a little late in the day," he said dryly. He eased her back down onto the greensward. "Stay where you are, I'll check her over." He got up and went to where the mare was grazing, running experienced hands down her legs. "Her right foreleg seems hot and tender to the touch," he reported. "But at worst she's only strained a tendon."

Alexa got up to see for herself. Rowan groaned. "Alexa, for once in your life can't you do what you're told! Sit down!" he boomed in a parade-ground voice.

Since her legs were buckling under her, Alexa obeyed him rather more abruptly than she meant to.

"Not going to pass out on me, are you?" he said bracingly, a strong arm going around her in support.

"Of course not! I've never fainted in my life," she said indignantly, though she felt uncommonly like doing that very thing. It would be a relief, she thought, to slip away into the beckoning darkness, spots of which were whirling before her eyes.

"Hold on. I'll get the flask I carry for emergency purposes. You could do with a drop of something . . ."

But Alexa clutched at his hacking jacket. He was the one focal point in a dizzy spiralling world. "Don't . . . don't leave me," she begged. Her stubborn pride made her add, "I'll be all right in a minute. Truly I will. Just don't leave me."

"Very well. But get your head right down between your knees," Rowan advised. He waited patiently for the dizzy spell to pass off and when he saw that she was looking more herself, he detached her slim white fingers from his lapels and went off to get his flask of restorative brandy.

The stimulant brought her back to life, sputtering and choking and causing color to flutter in her pale cheeks. Taking out his handkerchief to mop up the drops of brandy that dribbled down her chin, he said whimsically, "You know, Alexa, I can foresee a time when my life might become intolerably dull without you around to rescue from a predicament, say, once every forty-eight hours."

Was it the brandy that loosened her tongue? She decided afterwards that it must have done, for to her horror she heard herself answering back pertly, "Dull? I don't wonder that your life is dull. How can it be otherwise when you're so . . . so stuffy and stodgy and pompous and hidebound and . . . and . . ."

Her voice trailed off. She caught herself up short, aghast at her own temerity.

Rowan drew back, affronted. "Stuffy, am I?" he said wrathfully. "Pompous, am I? Stodgy? Hidebound?"

Alexa trembled. Retribution, she knew, was sure to come but she couldn't guess the form it was to take.

Chapter 4

Retribution took a most unexpected form. Alexa had issued a challenge which, she knew with a sinking heart, a man of Rowan's caliber could not let pass.

He brought his face down very close to hers as he snarled a repetition of those careless words she devoutly wished she had left unsaid. "Hidebound!" he repeated in a strangled tone. "Pompous!" His darkly menacing face loomed closer and closer, so close she could see the pores of his skin, the hard planes of his face, the burning resentment in his eyes. "Stuffy!"

Alexa's heart began to pound and her mouth went dry with fright. She tried to moisten her parched lips with her little pink tongue, parting them slightly to run her tongue over them.

Suddenly Rowan knew that he must take

his revenge on those soft half-parted lips, and his handsome head descended to claim them.

They were all that they had promised, sweet and warm and eminently kissable, tasting faintly of fine French brandy. They were lips such as he had never sampled before—the unwittingly provocative lips of an innocent girl, as unlike as possible to the lights o' love with whom he usually conducted discreet liaisons.

Yes, kissing Alexa was an unexpectedly pleasant experience, Rowan realized with something akin to amazement. It was definitely an experience worthy of being prolonged! He had intended the kiss to be punishing and punitive, but the velvet softness of her virgin lips stirred something deep within him, something that made him want to prolong the experience and extract from it the maximum pleasure.

Alexa's knowledge of kisses was far less comprehensive than Rowan's. In fact, she hadn't any prior experience to go by at all, no basis of comparison other than episodes from the romantic novels she had typed for lady authoresses. At the time she had thought them ridiculous, discounting the descriptions as so much drivel. The caress of a man's lips along one's mouth couldn't possibly set one aflame! she had thought critically. One couldn't possibly feel as if one's bones were melting, one's heart about to leap out of one's chest! But now that it was actually happening to her, she mentally apologized to Miss Ethel M. Dell and Miss Elinor Glyn, even as her lips clung to his and the world spun. dizzily around her. She hadn't known that the touch of a man's lips could send shock waves through her entire body, astounding her by the unexpected strength of her response to them.

But was it only the novelty of the thing? she wondered in utmost confusion. Possibly one man's kiss was very much like another, always providing, of course, that that man was sufficiently attractive. But surely there were few men as attractive as Rowan Traherne, she thought confusedly.

As he smothered her mouth with demanding mastery, all thought ceased and she gave herself up utterly to enjoyment of the exquisite sensations he evoked within her. Twining her arms about his neck, she pressed her body against his in innocent abandon and yielded her mouth to his.

The ba-a-a-ing and bleating of a Home Farm sheep which had strayed from its pasture to poke its black face through the gate and gaze at them with a mildly inquisitorial air brought them back to reality. With a heavy sigh Rowan withdrew from her and got to his feet. "You *are* a minx, Alexa," he said huskily. "I must get you back to your mama."

He extended a helping hand and drew her to her feet. "Come on," he said gruffly, not meeting her eyes. "We'll have to double up on Shaitan and lead your mare."

The remark was unnecessary. Alexa knew perfectly well that Gypsy wasn't fit to bear a rider's weight, but the last thing in the world she wanted to do was ride double with Rowan. As it was, she was beset with a number of conflicting emotions that she didn't in the least understand.

But there was no help for it. She watched quietly as Rowan mounted the restive stallion, checked his prancing with a firm hand on the reins, and reached down to help her up, kicking a foot loose from the stirrup as he did so. She inserted her own booted foot into the stirrup, and with one effortless fluid movement he swung her up and settled her comfortably against him.

Instinctively she relaxed against that hard muscular body, liking the feel of it pressed against her own, liking the way its movement blended with that of the horse, for Rowan was a born horseman, riding as if he were part of the animal.

He was surprised at how neatly Alexa fitted against him as he cradled her slim body in his arms. Despite her slenderness and seeming fragility, her body was soft and gently rounded in all the right places. She would have no need of padding inserted in the bodice of her gowns or rows of ruffles sewn across the front, he reflected. How could he have mistaken her for a boy, even in shirt and breeches? he wondered. It crossed his mind that he really ought to give her a dressing-down for donning such a getup and riding astride but, somehow, this didn't seem to be the right time or place. Later, perhaps, he thought hazily, his protective arm tightening around her, just under the curve of her breasts.

Yes, he mused, it was high time Alexa found a husband—or, one was found for her! She was a bud just ripe for plucking. But *not* by him, he assured himself hastily. Lord, no! That kiss should never have happened and he must make sure that it was never repeated.

He couldn't understand it himself. He had never before been attracted to the ingenue type; his taste ran to more mature women of the world, to sophisticated Society ladies.

His cousin Alexa might be a bewitching combination of innocence and allure but she was also, he reminded himself, a meddling, willful little hoyden who positively relished making a noise about her "rights" and her second-class citizenship. He very much suspected that if she hadn't latched on to the popular cause of women's suffrage some other crusade would engage her attention, for she was, he felt sure, just the type to rush in where angels fear to tread.

Now that he was past thirty it was high time he began to give serious consideration to marriage and the necessity of getting himself an heir, but his bride, when he took one, would be the very antithesis of Alexa. A well-bred, demure, unassertive young woman. He needed a wife who would be a good Society hostess; someone who could advance his career. She must be biddable and placid in temperament. Capable of managing his household with the minimum of fuss and the maximum of efficiency. It struck him suddenly that such a creature might be insufferably dull. Rather cowlike in fact.

He frowned, brushing back a lock of Alexa's hair that had blown into his face. It was soft and clean and sweet-smelling and its tawny-bronze beauty suddenly irritated him unbearably. It had, as usual, come loose from its pins and hung down her back in a riotous mass of curls.

"Do you always go around looking as raggle-taggle as a gypsy?" he asked irritably.

Alexa craned her neck around to look back over her shoulder in bewilderment. She had been riding along in a dreamy haze lulled by the motion of the horse beneath her and the comfort of Rowan's strong arms about her. This sudden and unprovoked attack left her momentarily stunned. "Wh-what?" she stammered.

"Your hair. It's blowing back in my face. I can hardly see where I'm going!" he complained.

Alexa stiffened, swiveling her head front and forwards, staring out between Shaitan's black ears, affronted. Dragging the heavy offending mass of curls over her shoulders and tucking it around each ear, she said, with a bite in her tone, "*Nobody* can be expected to look bandbox neat after a gallop on the downs. Especially when they've just taken a tumble!" she retorted. Stung by his criticism, she added sarcastically, "I'm *deeply* sorry if my appearance offends you!"

Her impudent tone had the effect of putting his back up. He said explosively, "You're damned right it offends me! And your flyaway hair is the least of it. What the devil do you mean riding about the countryside dressed like a boy?"

Alexa grated her teeth. She might have known he would get around to that little item sooner or later!

"How I choose to dress in the privacy of my own home is my own affair!" she retorted. Carrying the battle into the enemy's camp, she added slyly, "You did invite Mama and me to consider Nun's Farthing as our own home, did you not, Rowan?"

This was unarguable. Rowan's lips set firmly in a thin hard line. "I did indeed," he admitted. "But at the time I did not expect you to contravene the rules of good behavior, of decorum and propriety, by flaunting yourself in breeches!" Not that those breeches weren't vastly becoming, he thought to himself. He had already noted that the boyish garb suited Alexa's slim figure to perfection.

"Flaunting myself!" she gasped in outrage.

"Exactly. I won't stand for your making a spectacle of yourself. Most especially when the house is full of guests. Do you understand me, Alexa?" he said sternly.

"Perfectly!" she said icily, sitting stiff as a statue in the circle of his arms. The embrace that only a few minutes ago had seemed so comforting was now well-nigh unendurable and Alexa breathed a small sigh of relief as they drew near the stables. As soon as Rowan drew rein, she slithered down from her mount unaided and with no word of thanks for the timely rescue Rowan had performed flounced off towards the house. She didn't care if she was being churlish. She couldn't trust herself to speak another word to him just at present.

So he didn't care for her appearance, did he? she thought as she ran up the stairs. Well, he hadn't seen anything yet!

Rowan had not come down by train. Chalmers had driven him down to Nun's Farthing in the Rolls, which was thus available to convey houseguests from the little station of Chumleigh Halt to Nun's Farthing. The early contingent was due to arrive at teatime; the later contingent was coming down on the 7:15 in time for dinner.

Rowan had gone over the guest list very carefully with Lady Mary. In addition to his good friends Derek Cathcart and Owen Forbes-Hamilton, either of whom, in his estimation, would make an excellent parti for Alexa, he had invited a sprinkling of younger men who might take either her fancy or Lucinda's. Derek's younger brother, Dabney Cathcart, was one of those he considered eminently suitable for little Lucy.

He had toyed with the idea of inviting
Winston and Clementine Churchill.
Winston's political views coincided with his
own and he would welcome the opportunity
of quietly sounding out the First Lord of the
Admiralty on the current naval armaments
race with Germany. But he abandoned the
notion with regret. He simply didn't trust
Alexa not to create a scene. Winston's
opposition to women's suffrage was well-
known, dating perhaps from the day he had
been publicly attacked by a suffragette
wielding a dog whip.

No, Rowan decided, this house party must
be kept strictly apolitical. The prospect of
fiery-spirited Alexa airing her suffragette
views to a pugnacious Winston was enough
to make a strong man (and Rowan was a very
strong man) blanch!

Naturally a few ladies had been invited,
mostly girlish friends of Lucinda's and their
attendant mamas, in order to keep the
numbers even.

Rowan frowned. One guest he had been
unable to exclude was his current mistress,
Lady Wyndham. She was just back from the
south of France where she had been summoned to her ailing elderly husband's bed-
side, and her return could not have been
more untimely as far as Rowan was concerned.

She had been away for several weeks and
he had hoped that time and distance might

naturally have extricated him from a relationship that was beginning to pall. Frances had become cloyingly possessive of late, even going so far as to hint that if poor dear Hubert was carried off in one of the dropsical attacks to which he was subject, she would not be averse to discarding her title in favor of becoming plain Mrs. Rowan Traherne!

Much to Rowan's relief, poor dear Hubert had miraculously rallied once again. When it became apparent that he was on the mend he had unselfishly sent his wife home to enjoy the London Season, for the social whirl was the breath of life to her.

But Rowan was uneasily aware that next time he might not be so fortunate. Lord Wyndham might not rally from a similar attack. Rowan was unlikely to be reprieved a second time, and if he did not want to make the late Lady Wyndham Mrs. Rowan Traherne, it behooved him to break all connection with her as soon as might be.

Rowan was (justifiably, he thought) annoyed. This was *not* the way the game of love was played out in Society. He should not be expected to marry his inamorata if she suddenly became free of her matrimonial bonds. The devil take Frances! he thought irritably. *He* would not! She was a shallow, self-centered (though incredibly beautiful) woman with a long string of amours behind her, and he would be damned if he would take her as his wife! Why, he would as soon marry—he cast around in his mind for another such ludicrously unsuitable candidate—as soon marry . . . Alexa!

But freeing himself from the silken toils of Lady Wyndham was proving more difficult than Rowan had supposed. Absence had not weakened the bonds between them—in fact, in the case of Frances it had had the effect of making the heart grow fonder. Rowan was not unskilled in breaking off liaisons of this nature when it suited him, but Frances was an extraordinarily difficult case. She clung like a limpet, insisting, for example, on an invitation to the house party. In vain he had protested that it was merely a "children's affair," a means of gently introducing his little sister and his young cousin to Society on an informal basis so that they would have an opportunity to acquire a little social polish, a little savoir-faire, before making their official debuts.

"Lord, yes, there's absolutely nothing so agonizingly gauche as a schoolroom miss," said Lady Wyndham in a languid tone. "I feel for you, Rowan, with two such chits to get off your hands in one season. How is it that this cousin of yours has never been presented? She is some years older than Lucinda, is she not?"

"By some three or four years," Rowan said. "Her mama suffers from poor health" seemed sufficient explanation and one which he offered rather tersely. He found himself curiously reluctant to discuss his cousin with Lady Wyndham. In some inexplicable way it seemed somehow a betrayal of Alexa.

"So you see, Frances," he marshaled his arguments and concluded, "no one of any consequence is being invited to this house party. I assure you, you would find it an intolerable bore."

Lady Wyndham opened her blue eyes very wide, abandoning her languid pose. "However can you say that, my darling?" she said reproachfully. "*You* will be among those present." She pouted prettily. "Surely we will be able to snatch a few precious stolen moments to ourselves." She hesitated delicately. "And . . . and there are always the nights. Never tell me you have forgotten the house parties at Blenheim and Chatham and Belvoir that we attended together," she reminded him. "Since you will be host at Nun's Farthing, surely nothing will be simpler to arrange than the placement of the rooms." She tinkled a light laugh. "Possibly you could even arrange for us to have adjoining rooms."

Rowan, who was taking tea with her at the time, hid a slight moue of distaste with his linen napkin. He had not forgotten (though suddenly he wished he could) those house parties at which tactful hostesses, knowing of their liaison, had arranged for them to have rooms conveniently close to one another's.

Good Lord, he thought impatiently, did Frances really expect him to creep around

the corridors of Nun's Farthing to have a
secret assignation with her under the very
eyes of his aunt, his cousin Lady Mary, and
his innocent little sister? Evidently she did.

And Alexa! He could visualize the scorn in
her clear candid eyes for such tawdry hole-
in-the-corner behavior and felt suddenly
overcome with disgust for Lady Wyndham,
for the social structure that permitted, nay,
encouraged such behavior, and last but not
least, for himself.

Little wonder Alexa was so determined to
make a love match, he mused. Not for her
was the round of musical beds that Society
ladies indulged in—not for her the shoddy
affairs, the playing at love. For her the world
would be well lost for love.

He pulled his scattered thoughts together
to deal with Lady Wyndham who was eyeing
him curiously. "I fear what you are sug-
gesting is impossible, Frances," he said
stiffly. "My aunt, Lady Salter, is, as you
know, a stickler for the proprieties. And with
young girls in the house . . ." his voice trailed
off.

Nevertheless, Frances was impossible to
dissuade altogether and Rowan, knowing of
the lengths to which she would go to get her
own way (it was one of the reasons he had
"gone off" her), wearily issued her an
invitation to the house party. He could not
afford a scandal at this stage of his political career and with two young girls to
marry off. Even a breath of scandal would

irretrievably damage their chances for a
good match. He must handle Frances with
the utmost caution, he realized uneasily, for
he knew that she was perfectly capable of
cutting off her nose to spite her face. Society
would accept almost any peccadillo one
cared to mention, except the cardinal
sin—being found out.

Lady Wyndham arrived at teatime but
Alexa did not go down for tea. She was
feeling a trifle seedy and begged to be
excused, using her tumble as reason to rest
in her room. In truth, it was not so much the
fall from her horse that had unsettled her as
the emotional upheaval she had experienced
today. The Kiss—and its aftermath.

She felt bewildered, for she had never
thought that a seemingly simple thing like a
kiss could be such an earth-shattering
experience. She didn't even understand how
it had come about or *why*. One moment
Rowan had been looming over her and the
next his mouth had fastened on hers and it
was as if she had received some kind of
cosmic shock, forever separating what had
gone on before from what came after.
Nothing, she was sure, would ever be the
same again. She felt dazed, confused, be-
fuddled. The more so as, only a short time
later, he had begun browbeating and
berating her again. What did it all signify?

A kiss was supposed to be a sign of affection, wasn't it? But Rowan didn't have

any affection for her, did he? Not a jot, as far
as she could see. Oh, when she was a child
and he had come to visit at Nun's Farthing,
he had shown her a condescending kindly affection, much the same kind of tepid tolerant
affection he had for Lucinda.

And she? In those days she had adored him
wholeheartedly. But that was long ago.
Before Papa had deserted her—them, she
corrected herself hastily. Before Rowan had
driven her out of her home! She tried to
work up some indignation about that but
failed miserably. A blind man could see that
the estate had benefited under Rowan's
astute management. And he *had* invited her
and Mama to stay on here when he came into
his inheritance; it had been her own stubborn pride that had refused to allow her or
Mama to remain under his roof as poor
relations. And Rowan could not be blamed
for their poverty; it had not been him but
Papa who had squandered the family
fortunes. Nor could he be blamed for the entail; the estate had been entailed to the
nearest male heir for generations.

No, she decided, if Rowan had ever had
any real affection for her it had dissipated
long ago. These days irritation with her
seemed to be his predominant emotion!
Irritation, on the whole, was putting it
mildly, she thought ruefully. Antagonism,
outright anger, and rage were more like it!
But, to be fair, she had done her very best to
provoke him, had she not? He had tried to

get her out of the scrapes she had gotten her-self into and she had shrilled defiance at him.

But she hadn't done anything to provoke his latest explosion of rage, she thought with resentment. It had come as a bolt out of the blue, totally unwarranted and unexpected, and unprovoked.

As much so as The Kiss. If affection had not prompted The Kiss, what had? she wondered. Passion? She shivered. Could there be passion without affection, without love? She didn't know. She knew nothing at all of passion between a man and a woman and she wasn't altogether sure she wanted to learn! She'd sensed vaguely, at the time, that Rowan's kiss was meant to be punitive, and then . . . then something had happened be-tween them, between one breath and the next, and it had changed into something quite different . . . so different that . . .

Oh, she might as well give it up. She didn't know how he felt about her and she didn't know how she felt about him any more and all this going round and round in circles was giving her a headache.

She tried lying down for a while to ease her throbbing head but she couldn't rest. Giving it up as a bad job, she got up again and prowled restlessly around her room. A little fresh air might help her head, she decided listlessly, and she went to the window to open it wider.

Her bedroom overlooked the rose garden,

and before she turned away from the
window she spotted Rowan down below. He
was strolling through the rose garden with a
woman on his arm. A tall, statuesque woman
with a magnificent head of golden hair elegantly arranged in elaborate coils and puffs.

The woman, whoever she was, was
strikingly beautiful, Alexa noted a bit enviously. She was groomed and gowned and
coifed with exquisite care. You couldn't
imagine her in a state of disarray, Alexa
thought gloomily, or with even a single hair
out of place.

The two of them appeared to have a good
deal to say to each other, she noticed, not
wishing to spy on them but lingering by the
window for another look. That is, the woman
was talking and Rowan was listening atten-
tively. He appeared to be devoting his full
attention to her—and a great deal of
admiration as well, or so it seemed to Alexa.

Impatiently she drew the curtains together
with a snapping sound. She would have a lie-
down. There was plenty of time before
dinner and her headache might be the better
for a little nap.

But she didn't get it. Mama came in shortly
afterwards to ask if she was feeling better
now and would she be able to come down to
dinner, because if not, there would be
thirteen at table and that was so dreadfully
unlucky. Alexa promised to come down and
Mama fluttered away, her maternal feelings
ruffled because her difficult daughter had

rejected, all in one breath, her offerings of
headache tablets, hartshorn and water, and
cold compresses over the eyes. "I only want
to *sleep*," pleaded Alexa.

Lady Salter came in to say that in *her*
young day girls weren't mollycoddled and to
ask after the horse.

Lucinda came in, ostensibly with an
offering of ginger biscuits because Alexa
might be feeling peckish after missing her
tea, but really to regale her cousin with an
account of teatime in the drawing room.

Alexa sighed and sat up in bed, seeing
clearly that she was going to have to forgo
the nap. Besides, she was curious about the
members of the house party. Especially the
beautiful blond woman she had seen with
Rowan in the garden.

But Lucinda was, not unnaturally, more
interested in the male houseguests. Captain
Forbes-Hamilton was one of those coming
down on the late train, but the Cathcart
brothers had already arrived and Lucinda
was in raptures trying to decide which was
the more handsome of the pair. Derek was
dark, like Rowan, Lucinda reported, while
Dabney, the younger, had "a thick lion's
mane of burnished golden hair." Alexa
blinked at this extravagant description. They
both had an easy charm and rather free and
easy manners, said Lucinda, probably because their mama was an American. There
was an elder brother, too, the viscount, but
he had been married last year, sighed

Lucinda with visible regret.

When her young cousin's transports had run their course, Alexa ventured to enquire as to the identity of the beautiful woman she had seen with Rowan. "Beautiful . . . fair-haired . . . statuesque . . ." she described her to Lucinda.

"Oh, that must be Lady Wyndham," the younger girl said carelessly, helping herself to a ginger biscuit.

"One of the mamas?" guessed Alexa. Somehow she didn't think so. The woman hadn't looked or acted like anybody's mother with Rowan. She had looked, Alexa thought, like a beautiful lioness. Sleek but definitely predatory.

Lucinda broke into a peal of laughter and promptly choked on a cookie crumb. "Goodness, no!" she gasped when she had recovered. "Whatever gave you that idea?" Assuming a worldly-wise air, she said importantly, "Lady Wyndham is Rowan's mistress."

ROWAN'S MISTRESS! For the second time that day the world whirled dizzily around Alexa. She had not been so stunned when she had toppled from her horse and the ground had risen up to knock the wind out of her. Rowan's mistress! And yet . . . yet why should she be surprised? she thought feverishly. All men had mistresses. Especially handsome, wealthy men-about-town like Rowan. Papa, even, had had mistresses—several of them—and no one had thought the worse of him until he made a scandal by running off with one of them. The important thing was not to get talked about—not to create a scandal—and she was sure Rowan would never allow such a thing to happen.

"How . . . how do you know?" Alexa asked faintly.

"About Lady Wyndham?" Lucinda looked a bit disconcerted. She didn't want to admit that she had overheard a bit of servant's tittle-tattle not meant for her ears—a conversation between Rowan's chauffeur Chalmers and her own lady's maid. So she said airily, "Oh, Alexa, everyone knows. They just don't talk about it or . . . or acknowledge it." Rather proud of exhibiting her worldly knowledge to her older cousin, she said, "If they did talk about it, if it became a scandal, neither she nor Rowan would be received in Society. But she and Rowan are always very discreet."

"Yes, of course," said Alexa quickly.

Lucinda's curiosity was piqued. "Whyever are you so upset about it?"

"Upset? Who's upset?" Alexa essayed a tiny but hollow-sounding laugh. "I . . . I was just curious, that's all."

Lucinda looked doubtful. "You're looking rather pale all of a sudden.

Alexa mumbled something about her aching head.

Tenderhearted Lucinda looked suitably repentant. "Oh, poor you! I'd forgotten all about your taking a toss. You probably ache all over. Shall I ask Violet to run you a bath so you can have a nice leisurely soak before dinner?" she asked, burning to be useful. Violet was the lady's maid whose services the two girls shared.

"That would be lovely," said Alexa faintly. The bathroom was likely to be the only place she would have peace and privacy, she decided, and she was thankful that the installation of several such amenities was an innovation that Rowan had insisted upon.

A short while later, the tubful of hot steamy water soothed her physical aches and pains though, of course, it did nothing for her sore and aching heart. Though why the discovery that Rowan had a mistress should distress her she could not have said. It meant nothing at all to her . . . absolutely nothing! It was, after all, the way of the world, she told herself resolutely. She understood perfectly that a single man of Rowan's station in life was allowed the privilege of a mistress—of course she did!

A beautiful and voluptuous mistress, she thought morosely as she stepped nude from the high claw-legged bathtub. Wrapping herself in a soft and fluffy bath towel from the heated rail, she toweled herself dry, wishing she were a little more generously endowed. She had never given much thought to her figure, but now, all of a sudden, she found herself utterly dissatisfied with it. Oh, she

was far from flat-chested; she had a trim
little figure that (could she but realize it)
suited her tiny, small-boned frame to perfection. But suddenly, passionately, she
wished that she were taller, more imposing,
more ample of breast and hip and thigh . . .
like . . . like Lady Wyndham. Rowan's mistress, she thought miserably, had a lush
opulence worthy of Juno herself. While she,
she thought discontentedly, was a skinny,
scrawny little half-pint.

But . . . wasn't that lush, voluptuous style
of beauty just a little passé? The boyish silhouette was IN, and the hourglass figure, for
years a standard of feminine pulchritude,
was OUT. As were corsets and tight-lacing,
Lady Salter's strictures notwithstanding.
Suffragrette or not, Alexa was sufficiently
conscious of fashion to know *that*!

The boyish silhouette . . . hmmm. Alexa
tossed her red head. Maybe she couldn't
compete with Lady Wyndham's style of
beauty but she could make the most of what
she had. She could set her own style! And
Rowan's acid comments earlier about her
flyaway hair gave her a little idea. Flinging
the towel carelessly aside, she snatched her
dressing gown from its hook on the door
and, belting it around her slim waist,
hurried back to her room.

A few minutes later, a little housemaid,
coming into the room with an armload of
linen, uttered a gasp of shock and dropped

the stack of sheets and pillowslips. "Miss, oh, miss," she choked out. "What have you done?"

Chapter 5

The curly crop was really very becoming, Alexa decided, staring in a rather woebegone fashion at her reflection in the dressing-table mirror. And her head felt amazingly light and cool now that it was relieved of all that excess weight. So why, she wondered rather desperately, did she feel like crying? She wasn't afraid of Mama's reaction, was she? She caught her full underlip between her little white teeth. Or . . . or of Rowan's?

Well, what was done was done. Her tangled bramble bush of undisciplined curls was gone forever. In its place remained a shining sleek cap of curls that fitted her small neat head, suited her delicate features better than that heavy mass of hair, and curved round her high cheekbones in a balanced sweep on each side, enhancing the depth and wide spacing of her whisky-colored eyes.

She looked rather like a young page boy out of the court of Camelot, she decided, moving her head experimentally so that the wings of hair that framed her face swung and bobbed against her rose-petal cheeks. She liked it; she quite liked it, she told herself firmly, and she was not going to cry. Especially not in front of Hetty whom she had sent scurrying for a broom and dustpan to sweep up the mess. She frowned, watching the maid sweep the long locks of hair into a dustpan.

Hetty straightened from her task. "Will that be all, miss?"

"Yes, thank you." Alexa helped herself to two long red curls, one to give to Mama and one for Nanny to save forever after. Slipping the two locks of hair into separate envelopes and labeling them, she felt as if she were signing her own personal declaration of independence. Few women at this time went about with bobbed hair—not even the Pankhursts, although a handful of suffragettes sported what had come to be called "Eton Crops."

The little maid was halfway out of the room when Alexa remembered that she would need help dressing in order to be ready when the dinner bell rang. The dressing bell had already gone off, and Rowan did not tolerate tardiness at table.

There was no use in exacerbating him any further, she decided. "Oh, Hetty, would you send Violet to me, please, as soon as she's finished helping Miss Lucinda dress," she called.

"Yes, miss." Hetty bobbed a curtsy and hastily went out of the room, hoping she would not be accused of complicity in the deed. What Master Rowan would say to the new hairstyle she dared not think!

Neither did Alexa. As so often happened, she was beginning to regret her impulsive spur-of-the-moment action. Thoughtfully she worried at her underlip with her tiny white teeth. Perhaps she should not go down to dinner after all. Perhaps she should plead illness or fatigue and ask for a tray to be sent up. But no, that was a coward's way out. And she, Alexa Traherne, was no coward! She would not cower in her room like a frightened child!

Violet, forewarned by Hetty, made no comment on her young mistress's altered appearance but quietly buttoned her into the simple white frock considered suitable for a jeune fille, a young girl not yet out.

When Violet was done, Alexa looked at her image in the mirror disparagingly. The frock was definitely insipid, more suitable for a schoolroom miss than a young woman of one-and-twenty. But it, and similarly styled frocks, were all she had and it would have to do.

It didn't suit her "New Woman" haircut

either, she thought discontentedly.
Longingly, she remembered some of the new
styles she had seen in London shop windows,
styles inspired by the Oriental look of
Diaghilev's Russian ballet which had taken
the town by storm the previous year. Frocks
in vivid colors (like the turquoise tea gown
she had seen Lady Wyndham wearing earlier
in the day), frocks with gold and silver embroidery and jeweled shoulder straps. Skirts
which revealed the ankles or, even more
daringly, the calves!

But such styles were not for unmarried
girls—not even girls who were officially
"out." Such styles were reserved for married
women, for daring young matrons whose
complaisant husbands did not mind their
being considered "fast." Possibly, Alexa
reflected, the married state would not be so
bad after all, if one's husband were sufficiently complaisant and—the thought
skittered across her mind—if he could kiss
like Rowan!

The thought brought a blush to her pale
cheeks, tingeing them with becoming color,
just as the dinner bell rang. Alexa straightened her shoulders, took a deep breath and,
consoling herself with the thought that both
Mama and Rowan were too well-bred to
make a scene in front of guests, went downstairs to face the music.

The company was gathered in the drawing
room, the ladies partaking of sherry and the
gentlemen whisky-and-soda. The subdued

hum of polite conversation ceased abruptly when Alexa, the door opened for her by an impassive footman, stepped into the room. Heads turned, eyes swiveled, and, for a moment, a shocked silence prevailed.

Lucinda's clear voice cut through the silence like a knife through butter. "Ooh, Alexa, you've bobbed your hair!" she squealed.

Rowan uttered a strangled curse more fitted for the barracks than the drawing room.

Mama gave a soft sigh and sank gracefully down on the Aubusson carpet in a ladylike swoon. As a device to divert attention from her wayward daughter, it succeeded wonderfully well. Everyone crowded around proffering advice and suggestions for reviving her. Lady Salter seized the bell pull and rang it masterfully, demanding smelling salts and sal volatile from the maidservant who answered the summons.

Alexa, by no means a hard-hearted girl, was not unduly perturbed. She knew from experience that it was simply Mama's way of coping with a sticky situation. Just so had she reacted on a number of stressful occasions in the past, as when Alexa first announced her intention of joining the W.S.P.U.

The more exciteable Lucinda grabbed a bowl of hyacinths from an end table and raised it with the obvious intention of dashing the flower water in Lady Mary's face, but Alexa caught her arm and restrained her.

Rowan, with truly admirable presence of mind, rang for Peacham, the butler, and directed him to inform Cook that dinner must be put back a quarter of an hour. Alexa could not but admire his sangfroid. He then knelt down by the prostrate Lady Mary and began chafing her wrists gently. She moaned softly and her eyes fluttered open when Rowan applied the restorative smelling salts handed him by a wide-eyed maidservant.

The others had withdrawn to a corner of the room at Alexa's soft-voiced plea to "give poor Mama more air." She had joined them and thus could not hear the brief low-voiced conversation Rowan conducted with Mama, after which, murmuring his excuses to the assembled company, he swept her into his arms and carried her upstairs.

So they were thirteen at dinner after all, for Lady Mary dined off a tray in her room. The contretempts had put a damper on dinner, but the guests with well-bred aplomb did their best to ignore the incident, studiously avoiding mention of either hair-styles (length of) or fainting fits (causes of). The talk was all of the entertainments planned for the forthcoming Season—whose daughter/sister/cousin was going to make her debut—the chances of Durbar II winning the Derby—which of the contestants was most likely to win the Men's and Ladies Singles at Wimbledon—and the anticipated delights of the Henley Royal Regatta.

Alexa, seated between Owen Forbes-Hamilton and Derek Cathcart, did her best to keep the conversational ball rolling as she had been trained to do, even as she snatched glances at Rowan's totally unreadable face. Only once did that imperturbable face change fleetingly—into an expression that in his army days had reduced incompetent sub-alterns to gibbering terror.

Alexa sighed and applied herself to her lemon soufflé. She knew she was in for it.

She heaved a sigh of relief when Lady Salter, who had taken Mama's place as hostess, led the ladies into the drawing room, leaving the gentlemen to their port and cigars. Carrying on diner conversation with Owen Forbes-Hamilton had been an up-hill battle, for the Scotsman had exuded polite but nevertheless icy disapproval from every pore. Derek Cathcart, on the other hand, gave the appearance of being secretly amused, which suited Alexa no better.

In the drawing room, Lady Wyndham displayed that same condescending amusement, as at the antics of a wayward child, and it set Alexa's teeth on edge. She had no intention of being patronized by Rowan's mistress! As soon as she decently could, she made her escape, excusing herself on the grounds of wanting to see how "poor dear Mama" was getting on.

Poor Mama appeared to be getting on very well indeed. She was sitting up in bed, propped on pillows, with a dinner tray across her knees and looking very pretty in a frilly bedjacket of blue silk. Hers was a delicately feminine room, decorated in the style of la Belle Epoque with deep pile carpets, embossed wallpaper also in pale blue, gilt-framed mirrors and paintings and photographs (mostly of Alexa) and fragile rococo furniture. Alexa never felt quite comfortable in the fussily feminine room.

But never less so then now.

"Oh, Alexa, how *could* you?" Mama exclaimed in soft-voiced reproach as soon as her daughter had entered. "Your beautiful hair! Your crowning glory!" Mama put down her spoon and pushed the tray away feebly. "I haven't been able to eat a bite of this. Take the tray away, do!" she said fretfully.

Alexa reached for the tray and set it out of harm's reach, noting silently as she did so that, except for the custard which Mama had been eating when she came in, all the plates were well cleaned.

"I'm so very sorry, Mama," she said dutifully. "Er . . . how are you feeling now?"

"How do you expect me to feel?" her mother countered. "Utterly . . . utterly shamed . . . *humiliated*!" She pulled a lace-trimmed hanky from the pocket of her bed-jacket with the obvious intention of settling in for a good cry. "How I shall ever be able to face our guests tomorrow, I cannot think! Oh, Alexa, how *could* you?" She shook out the hanky and wept into it. "Oh, sharper than a serpent's tooth," she wailed, "is a thankless child."

Alexa drew up one of the fragile-looking rococo chairs and, patting Mama's hand, settled down to endure a litany of soft-voiced reproaches and lamentations guaranteed to melt the heart of a stone.

Surprisingly, it was Rowan who rescued her from them some little while later. His sharp eyes had noted Alexa's absence from the drawing room as soon as the gentlemen had joined the ladies and he had immediately gone in search of her.

Mama was right, Alexa thought guiltily. She *had* been thoughtless . . . and selfish . . . and, as usual, far too impulsive. Just at the moment she couldn't think what had come over her. Why had it seemed so important to her to bob her hair at that particular juncture, knowing full well what distress it would cause her family, and, as Mama so rightly pointed out, with a houseful of guests? It . . . it was because she had wanted to show Rowan . . . show Rowan *what*? she wondered confusedly.

"I'm very sorry, Mama," she repeated in a small voice. "I . . . I just didn't think—"

"You *never* think, Alexa," said Mama in the same fretful voice. She took a deep breath preparatory to starting in all over again. "Oh, the disgrace . . ." she began, but a knock sounded on the door and Rowan poked his head in.

"Ah, so there you are, Alexa," he said, advancing into the room at Lady Mary's invitation. "How are you, Cousin Mary?" he asked thoughtfully.

Lady Mary beamed. Dear Rowan—always so concerned for the welfare of others. So kind and considerate—always.

"Better, thank you," she said. "No thanks to this naughty, naughty child." She caught at Alexa's hand. "But she's very sorry for all the trouble she's caused." Her mother squeezed Alexa's hand. "And she's ready to apologize. Aren't you, Alexa?"

Apologize for *what*? Alexa thought, rather dazed. For cutting her own hair? Or for creating a scene? But surely it was Mama who had created the scene, she thought in confusion, not herself. Though she supposed she was, by extension, to blame for it all. It was her rash act that had brought on Mama's fainting fit. She had been the catalyst . . . and if an apology would smooth things over . . .

"I am very sorry, Cousin Rowan," she said meekly. "Truly I am."

Rowan looked at her with narrowed, suspicious eyes. A meek and mild Alexa was a new thing in his experience. But apparently her mother's strictures still carried some weight, he decided. For once in her life, the chit looked suitably chastened. There were deep violet shadows under her eyes, her full red lips trembled ever so slightly under his steady gaze, accentuating her vulnerability as did the slight hollows in her too-pale cheeks. Her cheeks were brushed by feathery fronds of tawny-bronze hair which was what this brouhaha was all about.

It was, he decided swiftly, a tempest in a teapot. The new hairstyle, if a little outré, was quite becoming, accentuating as it did her fragile, fine-boned beauty, not detracting from it. The times, Rowan reminded himself, were changing and one had to adapt oneself to them. Obviously, Alexa was born to be a trend-setter. She was no sheeplike follower of the old ways! There was much to be said for tradition, of course, but one *could* become too set in one's ways . . . stultified. Not, he thought ruefully, that there was much danger of becoming stultified with Alexa around, defying the conventions with every breath she drew!

Oh, well, it was not as if she had jeopardized his plans for her future, he reminded himself. The chit had a style, a special flair all her own that caught and held the imagination. He was not slow to see that she had charmed his houseguests. Notably Derek Cathcart. Rowan had not missed the warm light of admiration, intermingled with amusement, in his friend's eyes when he turned his gaze on his dinner partner. No doubt Derek found her a refreshing novelty—as would others, Rowan was sure, when she was officially "out." And that was all to the good. It was, he reminded himself, all part of his plan for her!

"Very well, Alexa," he said agreeably. "I accept your apology." A small smile hovered round his lips. "Yours was not an offense that can well be repeated!"

"Indeed not, Rowan," Alexa's Mama interposed swiftly. "The child simply acted on impulse, prompted by . . . prompted by . . ."

Lady Mary faltered to a halt, quite unable to account for the inexplicable impulse that had overtaken her willful daughter. "As you say," she substituted feebly, "it is not an offense that can well be repeated."

"And now Alexa must remember our guests and come downstairs before she is missed," Rowan said smoothly. "That is, if you can spare her, Cousin Mary."

"Oh, by all means." Lady Mary waved her daughter away. "Run along, dear child, and make my excuses to our guests."

"As you wish, Mama." Alexa bent dutifully to brush her lips across her mother's faded cheek. "I'll see you in the morning," she promised, before allowing Rowan to escort her from the room.

They went along the winding corridor, Alexa's hand firmly tucked in the crook of Rowan's arm, as if, she thought resentfully, he had some idea that she might escape. Oh, well, in view of his suppressed anger at dinner and the enormity of her offense, she had to admit that she had gotten off lightly once gain. When he'd popped his head in at Mama's door, she fully expected him to read her the riot act and she was rather surprised that he did not. Mama's presence had restrained him, she gathered, feeling sure that she had her mother to thank for jollying him along to the point where he was willing to accept her apology without a severely worded rebuke. Yes, she mused, she was lucky to get off so lightly and she resolved to do nothing more to rouse his demonic temper. From now on she would be as meek and biddable as the sternest taskmaster could wish—at least for the duration of the weekend!

She chuckled inwardly, remembering suddenly the rather childish remark that the late Queen Victoria was said to have made upon her accession: "I will be good." Well, she, Alexa, would be "good," she promised herself. Butter would not melt in her mouth. She would be a veritable angel. Rowan would have no further cause to complain of her behavior and . . .

"What are you smiling about, Alexa?" His voice broke into her thoughts.

"Smiling? Was I smiling?" she prevaricated, casting about in her mind for a suitable reason for levity.

They had cut across the Long Gallery and paused in its shadows to look down into the Great Hall where young couples were dancing to music provided by Lucinda's victrola. The house was ablaze with lights and gay with laughter and chatter. Alexa thought she hadn't seen the old house so lit up, so bright and gay, since her earliest childhood. Her lips curved upwards again, this time in a smile of happy reminiscence. "Do . . . do you remember the last party we had here before . . . before Papa went away?" she asked, giving him a sidelong glance. "It was very grand."

"Oh, yes, I remember it well," he said

easily. "I also remember looking up here into the gallery and seeing you skulking about like a little ghost in a long white flannel nightie." The rather hard lines of his face softened, undergoing an almost magical transformation, taking on the tender expression he reserved for children and other small helpless things. Taking on, Alexa thought, the look it had worn then, when he was a young subaltern, not long out of Sandhurst.

"I was waiting for Papa," she mused. "He'd promised to bring me comfits from the kitchen—little iced cakes and meringues and a strawberry tart. I waited and waited for him to come," she went on rather sadly, "but he'd forgotten all about me. So I crept out of my cot, while Nanny was snoring in the night nursery, and came along here, hoping to catch his eye." She smiled again. "Only I caught yours instead."

Rowan's rather hard grey eyes softened in remembrance, becoming warm with humor and compassion. "I came up to see what you were doing out of bed," he remembered. "You looked so woebegone that I found myself going back downstairs and sneaking treats for you off the supper buffet . . . we had a little feast up here all by ourselves."

"You *do* remember!" Alexa's whisky-colored eyes sparkled. "Lemonade and fairy cakes and meringues. You even gave me a small sip of your champagne." She laughed. "And the bubbles went up my nose!"

"Good Lord, did I?" Rowan looked startled. "I must have thought it would put you to sleep."

She laughed again. "It didn't though. I was more awake than ever. And then we danced." She sighed, remembering the tall youth accommodating his steps to the little girl in the long white nightdress who was happy to pretend that she was a grown-up lady and her cousin was her Prince Charming, come to claim her.

"And then I carried you back to the nursery and tucked you up in bed and promised you that when you were a grown-up young lady we would dance together again." The music downstairs had temporarily ceased while somebody changed the record and wound up the victrola, and when it began again, the strains drifted up to them.

Rowan, who had been leaning negligently on the gallery rail smoking a cigarette, straightened up suddenly and, in a gesture which surprised her, bowed low over her hand. A whimsical smile played about his full lips as he said, as he had some fifteen years before, "May I have the honor of this dance?"

Alexa shook her red head, a teasing smile hovering about her own lips. "But *this* dance isn't a waltz," she reminded him, as that first dance had been. "It's a tango."

Rowan arched a quizzical black brow at her, pretending to take offense at her words.

"Do you really think I'm so stuffy and stodgy that I don't know all the latest dances imported from America?" He linked arms with her and escorted her down to the dance floor. "As a garrison officer based in London I had to learn them all. The tango, the two-step, the maxixe, even the Castle Walk. An inept dancer would have been a disgrace to the regiment," he said with a grin. "And it's a social skill even more indispensable to a diplomat." Expertly he guided her onto the floor and swung her into position.

As they dipped and swayed to the strains of Lucinda's ragtime music, Alexa decided that Rowan was definitely not as stuffy and staid as she had supposed. By no means!

It was only much later, when the party broke up for the evening, that she remembered something she had forgotten earlier. On that long-ago occasion about which they had been reminiscing Rowan had kissed her goodnight. Apparently, she mused, he did not remember that. She rather wished he had.

Chapter 6

The remainder of the weekend passed in a flurry of activity. There were boating and tennis and croquet and lavish teas taken al fresco on the lawn and more dancing in the evenings.

It all would have been quite enjoyable, Rowan reflected, but for two things—the flirtation that developed between Derek Cathcart and Alexa, and the presence of Lady Frances Wyndham.

He could have danced with Alexa all night, he mused. She was an exquisite dancer—graceful, light on her feet, weightless as a feather in his arms, following his lead instinctively.

But of course he could not monopolize her. He had his duties to perform as host. And she was in much demand. Before that first evening was over, Rowan could see that

Derek Cathcart was badly smitten with her. Even the somewhat dour Owen Forbes-Hamilton had been won over, while young Jeremy Fortescue, a fresh-faced youth of good prospects, had observed ingenuously, "I say, sir, have you any more pretty cousins hidden away?" Fortescue was employed as a very junior secretary at the Foreign Office, and Rowan supposed that his own capacity as a senior service official entitled him to respect, but nevertheless that "sir" grated on his ears, making him feel every one of his thirty-three years. It jarred him to realize that Alexa and Jeremy Fortescue were exactly the same age and that Alexa was only a few years older than Lucinda, to whom he was accustomed to act in loco parentis.

So he handed Alexa over to Jeremy Fortescue and watched from the sidelines as the young people disported themselves. Lucinda had her share of admirers as well and was obviously enjoying herself. From the looks of things, neither of the girls would be wallflowers, Rowan decided. No doubt they would both have their dance cards filled at every ball they attended during the Season, and obviously neither one was going to be troubled by shyness or gaucherie. He ought, he supposed, to be gratified, for it was, after all, the object of the house party to introduce the girls to a few select friends "en famille." From that point of view, everything was going swimmingly and, dammit, he was gratified by it—wasn't he?

Lady Wyndham was sitting out and looking discontented about it, and Rowan, a man who knew his duty and did it, sighed and asked her for a dance.

As the weekend progressed, the young people naturally began pairing off at their various activities. Alexa most often was with Derek Cathcart and Lucinda with his brother, while Jeremy Fortescue transferred his attentions to a fellow guest, a pretty but painfully shy debutante friend of Lucinda's. Which naturally left Rowan paired off with Lady Wyndham, a state of affairs he found highly unsatisfactory, though Frances quite obviously did not.

Alexa, observing Rowan's preoccupation with Lady Wyndham, found herself compelled—for what reason she could not have said—to flirt with the handsome and carefree Derek Cathcart. The flirtation, she made sure, was conducted with the utmost propriety and decorum, and Rowan, observing it with an experienced eye, knew that he had no reasonable grounds for complaint. He did not even know *why* he would want to object—the flirtation was all part of his strategy for taking Alexa's mind off the suffragette Cause, was it not? It was his own master plan, and once again he told himself he ought to be gratified it was working out so well.

But somehow he found it harder and harder to convince himself that he was gratified, especially when Cathcart put his arm round Alexa's waist at the tennis court, ostensibly to show her how to improve her backhand. Rowan's jaw set when he saw Alexa, quite relaxed in Cathcart's embrace, laughing up at him and brushing back the wings of tawny-bronze hair that bobbed against her cheeks and blew across his bent head. Rowan remembered with a pang how soft and sweet-smelling that hair could be.

The two chaperones, Alexa's mama and Lady Salter, had turned a blind eye to this byplay, and Rowan supposed that he had no cause for complaint. But he intervened anyway, telling Cathcart quite shortly that he was a duffer at tennis and had no business giving lessons—a claim that was soon disproved when his friend good-naturedly challenged him to a match and trounced him soundly, two games out of three. With Alexa standing by and cheering Derek on!

The two opponents were actually well-matched in skill, but Cathcart, a couple of inches shorter than Rowan, was leaner and more agile, covering the court just that little bit more quickly. Rowan, taller, more muscular and heavier-boned, became winded sooner, and Cathcart added insult to injury by advising him to "give up your after-dinner cigars, old man."

Rowan had not lacked his own cheering section, comprised of his sister and Lady Wyndham, who, like everyone else, was dressed in tennis white though she declined to play. Frances, he recalled, had never en-

joyed exertion (unless it was in bed). Too
afraid of getting her face smudged or a hair
out of place, Rowan thought sourly, comparing her with Alexa who threw herself into the
game as she did everything else, wholeheartedly, and was consequently looking disheveled, though quite attractively so, Rowan
couldn't help thinking.

Yes, taken all in all, he was glad to see the
weekend draw to a close—or he would have
been if Lady Wyndham had not taken it into
her head to motor back to London with him
instead of going back by train with the rest
of the guests.

The devil take Frances, he thought uncharitably. He had been no more than civil to
her all weekend. He had given her numerous
hints that their affair was over, and she had
chosen to ignore every one of them. He had
strenuously avoided all opportunities for a
tête-à-tête with her and had rigorously kept
to his own room at night.

As soon as he had deposited her at her
town house he would not, he decided, see her
again. He would avoid any and all invitations
from her; he would leave her telephone
messages unanswered. Sooner or later she
would, he hoped, take the hint without his
having to spell it out for her. A true lady
would understand the situation—that their
affair had run its course—but he was beginning to wonder if Lady Frances, despite
her title, had any of the hallmarks of the true
lady at all. Judging by the disgustingly

blatant overtures she had made this weekend, he decided that she had all the hallmarks of a whore!

Her conversation during the ride to town
was comprised of sly innuendoes and quite
vicious gossip, and the sickeningly sweet
scent she wore would permeate the uphol-
stery of the Rolls for days afterward, Rowan
knew. He wondered what he had ever seen in
her. A beautiful beddable body, he supposed.
Certainly she had no other qualities to
attract a man and hold his heart ensnared.
No qualities of mind or heart or spirit, such
as Alexa, say, possessed in abundance. But
then his affair with Lady Wyndham had
never been truly an affair of the heart, but
merely—he barked a bitter laugh at himself
—an affair of the glands.

Alexa had watched them depart on
Monday afternoon with a slight frown creas-
ing her pretty forehead. She wondered if
what Lucinda had claimed was true—that her
brother and Lady Wyndham were lovers.
Wasn't it possible that Lucinda had been
mistaken? Certainly the two of them had
paired off for drives and rides and talks, for
dancing and croquet. But, on the other hand,
she had not seen him display any very lover-
like devotion to his lady. In fact, Alexa had
noticed that on more than one occasion he
had been quite brusque with her—at times,
barely civil. But perhaps such an attitude
had been feigned in order to throw dust in
everyone's eyes—to divert suspicion in an

attempt to avoid a scandal. That was how the
game of love was played in Society, was it
not? And Rowan *must* enjoy her companionship—otherwise he would not have invited
her to the house party at all—much less
motor up to London with him, thought Alexa,
her shoulders slumping. She was not to
know that it had been quite the other way
round—that it was bold Lady Wyndham who
had invited herself on both occasions.

Ah, well, Rowan's affaires du coeur were
no concern of hers, Alexa reminded herself.
A properly brought-up young woman of good
family was not even supposed to know that
such situations existed, much less speculate
about them. And it was nothing to her anyway. Why should she care? She *didn't* care,
she told herself strenuously, straightening
her shoulders and going back into the house.
But all the same, she could not help wishing,
a trifle wistfully, that Lucinda had been
mistaken. She had not liked Lady Wyndham,
summing her up quite accurately as a
shallow, self-centered Society beauty, spoilt
and selfish and living for admiration and
adulation. She hated to think of Rowan ensnared in such a woman's toils.

Quite soon she had other things to think
about.

After a day or two to allow Mama to rest
and recuperate from the fatigues of the
house party (for the duties of hostess at such
an affair were not to be taken lightly; she had
to supervise the cook, the butler and the

housekeeper, approve menus and wine lists, write out dinner cards in a fine hand, see to the flowers, and ensure that suitable entertainments were planned and that no guest suffered from boredom, exclusion or ennui) the two girls and their chaperones went up to London by train. They joined Rowan at the Cadogan Square house, where they were immediately plunged into a flurry of pre-presentation activities.

First and foremost were the fittings. Lucinda's wardrobe was already well-equipped for the Season, but Alexa had to start from scratch and there was very little time left, for Lady Salter had arranged for her to be presented in the same drawing room as Lucinda, at the end of May.

The girls had to learn, as an essential part of the deportment expected of debutantes, how to make a proper court curtsy while weighed down with a heavy brocade train and carrying a bouquet. Lucinda was a mass of nerves, sure that she would drop her bouquet, catch her feet in the lace and chiffon flounces of her skirt, and topple over at the feet of royalty; or lose the two white ostrich feathers—de rigueur for all debutantes—out of her headdress of tulle veiling; or otherwise disgrace herself forevermore. But Alexa, who considered the whole business an antiquated exercise in futility, remained cool as a cucumber throughout their practice session.

"You must have nerves of steel!" Lucinda

moaned enviously, practicing her curtsy
over and over and each time becoming
entangled in the heavy slippery lengths of
her train. She kicked at it petulantly. "I feel
as clumsy as a cow."

"It's because you *care* too much, Lucy,"
said Alexa kindly. She stooped and rearranged the heavy folds of the unruly pink
brocade. "There you are. Now try it again,
and this time don't wobble so."

"And don't you care?" asked Lucinda, a bit
resentfully. Her cousin's self-possession was
downright inhuman—and irritating.

"Not so very much," Alexa said honestly.
"There are other things I care about far
more. More important things . . ." she said
vaguely.

Lucinda's grey eyes opened wide. She
didn't see how anything could be more
important than making one's debut and said
so forthrightly.

Alexa eyed her cousin thoughtfully. She
realized that the younger girl was a bundle
of nerves because she was honestly convinced that if she made a fool of herself in
front of royalty the sun would never rise
again. Perhaps if she gave Lucinda something besides herself to think about, it
would put this whole ridiculous business of
the presentation into perspective for her.
Help to calm her nerves.

"Really, Lucy, you would know what is
going on in the world if you ever read the
newspapers," she remarked with asperity.

"Something besides the Society columns, that is." How could Lucinda be so empty-headed? "Don't you know that Mrs. Pankhurst has been arrested again? Haven't you heard about the horrible brawl that took place at the gates of Buckingham Palace? The papers are comparing it to Black Friday of 1910 when the police rode their horses through mobs of women like cossacks and bludgeoned them down with clubs!"

"The papers are probably exaggerating, Alexa." The younger girl attempted to soothe her cousin. Looking uncomfortable, she began to pick at a piece of lint from the carpet that was adhering to her train. "I thought you had put the Cause out of your mind. I'm sure Rowan thinks you have done."

"Does he indeed?" They had seen little of Rowan since coming up to town. He had taken refuge at his club, well away from the feminine flutterings of debut preparations, and had been heard to say that he "would be damned glad when it was all well over!"

Alexa looked pensive. She had not dared to set foot in suffragette headquarters since her return to London. Lady Salter was proving to be a much more rigorous chaperone than Mama had ever been. A veritable dragon, she refused to let either girl out of the house unaccompanied. And since the demonstration at the Palace, Alexa knew that she, in particular, was being watched even more carefully. It was practically like being under house arrest, she thought resentfully.

All that she could do was follow the doings of the suffragettes in the newspapers. Since the demonstration on May 21 when Mrs. Pankhurt had led a deputation in person to Buckingham Palace to present a suffragette petition to the king himself, the newspapers had had a field day. According to newspaper reports, the Government was making a last desperate attempt to crush the W.S.P.U., to remove all leaders and destroy their papers and records. Suffragette headquarters and even private homes were raided, efforts had been made to suppress their newsletter, *The Suffragette*, and wholesale arrests and subsequent hunger strikes were the rule of the day.

Alexa had followed the news avidly, wishing there were something she could do. She could hardly bear to sit down to dinner and eat her way through several courses for thinking of her friends and comrades incarcerated in Holloway, suffering the tortures of hunger and thirst and the nasal tube and the steel gag.

Something ought to be done! It wasn't fair! It wasn't even English, this despicable war on women! Oh, if only there were something—anything—that *she* could *do*!

She tapped a fingernail thoughtfully against her small white teeth. Mrs. Pankhurst had always asserted that it was a subject's right to go to the foot of the throne itself to seek redress of political grievances. There were, she claimed, any number of precedents for such actions. Yet when she and her associates had attempted to do so they had been turned away—brutally turned back. And then arrested and imprisoned, simply for exercising their rights.

It was *so* ironic that in just a few days she, Alexa, would be approaching the throne to make a curtsy to the king in observance of a silly social custom. She frowned. Mrs. Pankhurst and the other suffragettes were debarred from approaching the king, but *she*, for one brief moment, would have access to him. Hmm. It certainly gave one to think and Alexa thought furiously, the glimmering of an idea taking shape in her brain.

If only she could . . . well, why not . . . why couldn't she . . . ? A slow smile spread across her vivid little face and her eyes began to sparkle with mischief. She, and she alone had the opportunity—a heaven-sent opportunity—to do what no one else, not even Mrs. Pankhurst, could do for the Cause.

"Alexa?" Her cousin's voice broke into her reverie. "Alexa? Whatever are you thinking about? You look a million miles away."

"Hmm? Oh, nothing . . . nothing special." Alexa was evasive. The idea was too vague . . . too amorphous as yet . . . and perhaps too bizarre . . . to confide to anyone, least of all the excitable Lucinda. This would be no schoolgirl prank, performed with her usual impetuosity. It would require the most careful planning and coordination.

"Come on. Let's try it again, Lucy," she said encouragingly. "Maybe if I help you manage your train. Remember what Lady Salter told us—that there'll be footmen in the Throne Room to slide it along behind and keep it from getting twisted."

This time, Lucinda acquitted herself creditably with Alexa's help, but all the time the older girl was playing the footman's part, following behind her jittery cousin and managing the heavy folds of brocade, her brain was whirling at top speed, ticking off the essential steps in her plan.

First of all she would need to acquire a copy of the suffragette petition—preferably a condensed version, since she would have to conceal it on her person. The cumbersome train would be ideal for the purpose, she judged, since one end of it would be looped over her arm much of the time. It would require a certain amount of dexterity to manage train, petition, and floral bouquet, but she was sure she could do it.

She must also obtain the sanction of suffragette leadership. She was sure that approval of her scheme would be automatic, for the Movement as a whole was still aware of the value of publicity. This would be a welcome propaganda coup, especially at a time when the suffragette forces were in disarray. She would be performing an invaluable service for the Cause. Why, she might even go down in history—she, Alexa Traherne!

But she banished the thought as unworthy almost as soon as it crossed her mind. She would not do this for self-glorification; she would do it to further the Cause! She had been prevented from marching shoulder to shoulder with the demonstrators. Very well. But this was something she could do for her suffering "sisters" in Holloway. She decided that at the moment she presented the petition to the king she would make a verbal appeal to him—a petition of her own to stop force feeding. Yes, that would be an extra added touch!

She frowned. How to get in touch with the suffragette leadership in their present demoralized condition was a problem. Headquarters had been shifted to Lincoln's Inn, she knew, but according to the newspapers the building had been raided and the suffragettes dispersed or arrested. Well, a few telephone calls should suffice to give her the address of one or more of the leaders.

But *how* was she going to get out of the house alone and unchaperoned in order to meet with them? It seemed an insoluble problem. She chewed her lip thoughtfully. Well, she would find a way. She just had to!

Chapter
7

As it happened, what seemed the hardest problem was the easiest to solve. Derek Cathcart's mother had invited her to tea, and since the Cathcart town house was but a short distance away, even rigid Lady Salter agreed that chaperonage could be dispensed with.

Ever since they had come up to London, Derek Cathcart had run tame in the Cadogan Square house. Seeing the fast friendship developing between the two young people, Mama and Lady Salter had concluded that a better match for Alexa could not well be found. The young man was a highly eligible and quite unexceptionable parti—well-born (though a second son) and well-to-do, connected through his mother to the American plutocracy. She was an independent-minded American woman of advanced views and was thought to be a suffragette sympathizer.

Mama and Lady Salter agreed between themselves that no more suitable mother-in-law for tempestuous Alexa could be found.

So the well-meaning matchmakers relaxed their vigilance where Derek Cathcart was concerned and began gently nudging the two young people into (what the elders fondly hoped would be) each other's arms. Since Alexa was not yet "out," she could not go to evening entertainments, but Derek had been allowed the privilege of escorting her to matinees and to Gunter's for tea after the performance.

It did not take Alexa long to ferret out what her elders were up to, and she was amused by it. She had not the slightest intention of becoming romantically involved with Derek. She was not attracted to him in that way, but she did enjoy his companionship, and if it suited her guardians to play at matchmaking, she was not averse to humoring them, especially if she might thereby gain a little more freedom.

Rowan was seldom at home these days, but whenever he did appear he was annoyed to find himself tripping over his friend, who seemed to be always about the house. When he joined the family at tea one afternoon, he was amazed to find Cathcart in the drawing room in full-dress uniform of His Majesty's Life Guards. "Good God!" Rowan ejaculated, his strong jaw dropping. "Why the fancy dress at this time of day?"

His friend, resplendent in a scarlet

uniform with gold braid, merely grinned.
"Just dropped in for a cuppa, old man. I'm on
duty in half an hour. In fact," he said regretfully, "I should be on my way." Stooping, he
picked up his helmet with its nodding white
plumes and made his goodbyes to the ladies.
At a nod from her mama, Alexa walked him
to the door.

"What was all *that* about?" A bewildered
Rowan asked Lady Mary, sotto voce, as she
poured him a cup of the fragrant brew.

"Oh, I expect he just wanted to show himself in full fig to Alexa, dear," her mother
said placidly. "Young women are always so
impressed by uniforms." She sighed after
them and Rowan guessed that it was not only
the young who found a man in uniform
appealing!

"Dear Derek seems to be quite 'epris' of
Alexa," Lady Mary remarked approvingly.
"It would be *such* a good match, don't you
agree? And to think, if *anything should come
of it*, we will have you to thank for bringing
them together."

Rowan spilt his tea.

Nothing was easier, Alexa found, than to
enlist her smitten swain as unwitting co-con-
spirator. She did not, of course, tell him
exactly what their little side trip to a quiet
house in a London suburb was in aid of. Not
in detail, at least. And though Derek was
quite shrewd enough to guess that it had
something to do with Alexa's suffragette

sympathies, he was by now too besotted to care. He thought it a mere foible, found her enchanting and amusing, and in any case his sympathies lay with the suffragettes, in a mild sort of way. He thought that they had been hard done by, that women suffrage was bound to come sooner or later, so what was all the fuss and bother about? His own American-born mother, though not an active participant, had contributed heavily to the Cause.

He also thought that the Traherne family was handling Alexa all wrong. She was a spirited filly who needed careful handling. Controlled by a curb bit, she was sure to make a bolt. His mama had allowed his sisters more freedom than Alexa and Lucinda enjoyed and they had been the better for it, in his opinion, acquitting themselves creditably and, after a Season or two, marrying well.

They took tea with Derek's mother first, Alexa explaining beforehand that she would like to slip away early in order to run a little errand.

Derek's brow had quirked. "An errand? A suffragette errand, I suppose?" he had guessed, for he was sufficiently well acquainted with Alexa by now to know where her enthusiasms lay.

"Ye-e-es. As a matter of fact it is." Alexa held her breath lest Derek refuse to accompany her or fly into a rage as no doubt Rowan would have done.

But Derek merely laughed good-naturedly. "Not going to beard the prime minister in Ten Downing Street, are you?" he teased. "Or 'rush' the House of Commons all by yourself?" He sobered suddenly. "Or plant another bomb in Lloyd George's vacant house?"

"No—no. Nothing like that," Alexa assured him hastily. "It's merely to do with some—ah—some paperwork," she improvised. Which was not quite a lie, not quite the truth.

This satisfied Derek, who knew that Alexa had done volunteer typewriting for the W.S.P.U. and assumed that her current errand was something of the same. Considering the Union's present demoralization, he supposed it was understandable that she should want to do her bit for the poor beggars, he thought indulgently. He was therefore a little surprised when, after a prolonged wait in an antechamber, she came out of an inner room wearing a self-satisfied expression but empty-handed.

"No papers to type up?" he asked, a bit puzzled, as he fell into step beside her.

"Wh-what?" Alexa, who was delighted to have received official approval for her scheme and was engrossed in a daydream in which His Majesty kindly consented to read her petition and then acted upon it, overriding the harsh policies of his ministers. Thus, she thought, she was in the position of the innocent young maiden who tames the unicorn! She abandoned this delicious fantasy and came back to earth with a dull thud.

"What? Oh, no, no, nothing like that. Ah . . . what I mean is . . . the draft has to be revised. I . . . er . . . I arranged for them to deliver it to Madame Lucille's when I go in for my fittings," she explained, rather flustered.

"Very wise of you," Derek commented. "I expect you'll want to smuggle it into the house in a box of finery, what? Much better if old Rowan doesn't find out about it."

"Oh, very much better!" Alexa agreed with fervor. "You . . . you won't tell him about . . . about our little outing today, will you?" she asked anxiously.

"Not a word," Derek promised rashly, liking the idea of sharing a secret with Alexa. He smiled to himself, well pleased. He could foresee that Alexa, a bewitching little minx, would be the belle of her (and Lucinda's) coming-out and he would be in an excellent position to claim her for several dances and take her in to supper as well, by George!

From then on, for Alexa time seemed to take wings and fly. She was in a fever of anxiety that the abridged version of the petition would not be delivered in time. It simply *must* be ready when she went to Madame's for her final fittings, she thought anxiously.

Mama and Lady Salter, themselves busy with preparations for the grand coming-out

ball which would follow hard on the heels of
the presentation, noticed Alexa's agitation
but attributed it to pre-presentation jitters.
Lady Mary actually breathed a sigh of relief
that her difficult daughter had lost that
scornful blasé attitude so . . . so unnatural in
a debutante. She herself had been a bundle
of nerves at her own debut—and then, when
she had had to go back the following year
and be presented as a married woman it had
been even worse, she remembered, for Alexa
had already been on the way and she had
been plagued with the nausea and dizziness
of early pregnancy, as well as nervous
tension. She was thankful that it was Lady
Salter, not she, who was sponsoring the two
girls. She would not relish climbing the
grand staircase again (which would surely
bring on her palpitations) and waiting an
interminable time in the glittering but stuffy
anteroom which would be crowded with
debutantes and their sponsors.

Lady Salter, to whom she had confided her
maternal worries, was also gratified to see
her charge become jittery as the big day
drew nearer. It was, she considered, altogether appropriate for a debutante to be
nervous and on edge. Alexa's new attitude,
though hard to live with, was, pronounced
Lady Salter, "very proper."

Alexa herself found that her worries were
not over when, on the day of her final fitting,
she picked up the plain brown paper parcel
at Madame Lucille's. She managed to slip it

unobtrusively into her dress box while
Lucinda, who had accompanied her, was still
in the dressing rooms. But, on their return to
Cadogan Square, Lucinda, who was bubbling
over with excitement, had seized upon the
dress boxes and borne them off to her
brother's study, with Alexa trailing along
behind voicing protests. It was her misfortune that today, of all days, Rowan would
be home, she thought apprehensively,
watching as Lucinda, without even knocking,
burst unceremoniously into her brother's
sanctum.

Rowan, who was engaged in a detailed
analysis of the Balkan situation, was glad to
take a breather. The Balkans had been a hot-
spot for years, ever since Austria had
annexed Bosnia and Herzegovina in 1908, to
the annoyance of the pan-Slavs of Russia.
England, allied with Russia and France, in a
pact called the Triple Entente, was in the
process of strengthening these bonds by
negotiating for an Anglo-Russian Naval Convention, which would effectively strengthen
the Entente's position against the Triple
Alliance, composed of Austria, Germany,
and Italy. Rowan was studying the possible
effect of the naval negotiations on the
delicate balance of power in Europe and
trying to estimate whether they would increase the antagonism between Austria and
Russia, and the complexities of the situation
were beginning to make his head swim. He
found his sister's impulsive interruption

timely, for he was badly in need of diversion.

"What have you got there, Lucy? More finery?" he asked good-naturedly, running a hand across his face to smooth out the frown lines of his tiredness.

Lucinda ripped her package open with reckless haste and held up the frock for Rowan's inspection. "It's my court dress," she enthused. "Isn't it beautiful!" Tucking the dress around herself, she waltzed around the room, a vision in white duchesse satin with an overskirt of mousseline de soie, embroidered in silver and pearls.

When Rowan had made the appropriate complimentary response, Lucinda turned to Alexa. "Now show him yours," she demanded.

Alexa's heart sank. If she opened the box and removed the court dress from its tissue-paper wrappings, the brown-paper parcel would be in plain sight. It was only too obvious that it was not a product of Madame Lucille's, and if Rowan's eagle eyes spied it, he would be sure to demand an accounting and then . . . Alexa swallowed hard . . . then there would be the devil to pay!

"My frock is almost the same as yours," she protested quickly. "It differs only in detail," she pointed out with a sickly smile, trying to put a damper on the younger girl's enthusiasm.

"Oh, Alexa, it's not *exactly* the same!" Lucinda pouted. She grabbed the box, heedless of her cousin's restraining hand.

"Rowan *wants* to see it. Don't you, Rowan?"

She began tugging at the strings with which the dress box was tied and Alexa caught her breath in alarm, but Rowan, who was in no hurry to get back to the intricacies of international diplomacy, unwittingly came to her rescue. Shuffling his papers into a neat pile, he closed his roll-top desk and suggested that the girls might like to go upstairs and change into their new finery in order to model it for his benefit.

"That's a wonderful idea!" Alexa exclaimed. She rescued her half-open dress box from Lucinda and firmly shepherded her young cousin towards the door, even as she breathed a sigh of relief for her narrow escape. Her guilty conscience made her feel sure that Rowan was endowed with extraordinary powers of vision, similar to these newfangled X-ray machines and that if he took a good look he would be able to see right through dress box and wrapping paper to the enclosed parcel and then through its wrapping to the petition, beginning, "It is the respectful and loyal request of the W.S.P.U. that Your Majesty . . ."

Lucinda, bewildered by the speed with which Alexa was propelling her from the room, protested plaintively, "But . . . but won't it bring bad luck for Rowan to see us all dressed up beforehand?"

"That only applies to brides, you goose!" Rowan heard Alexa retort as she shepherded his sister from the room. He chuckled and

settled back in his big easy chair before the
fire to wait for the fashion show.

Alexa looked very much like a bride,
dressed as she was all in virginal white, he
thought when, a few minutes later, the girls
came downstairs in full fig, even to the
Prince of Wales plumes affixed to their head-
dresses. And on the afternoon of the great
day itself the thought crossed his mind again
that Alexa would make a beautiful bride.

He himself looked quite correct in a frock
coat and pin-striped trousers, for he was
deputizing for his Foreign Office superior,
Sir Edward Grey, at a diplomatic reception
scheduled for later in the day. He must set
off for the palace in a few minutes himself,
but first he had summoned the girls downstairs to present them with their ornaments
for the great occasion. For Lucinda he had
the traditional pearl necklace, and for Alexa,
whose vivid coloring and personality
demanded something a little more striking,
there was a brooch set with pearls and
diamonds. The diamonds, he thought absently, sparkled no more brightly than her
eyes.

He fastened the necklace of pearls round
his sister's slender throat. Excitable Lucinda
whirled and threw her arms around her
brother's neck and kissed and hugged him
exuberantly. "Oh, Rowan, they're beautiful!
Beautiful!" she burbled and landed another
smacking kiss on his mouth. "You're ab-

solutely the most wonderful brother a girl could have! Thank you . . . thank you!"

Rowan eyed his young sister with affectionate amusement. At that moment she seemed very young and childish compared to Alexa. "You're quite welcome, my dear, but don't crush your frock," he cautioned, stepping out of her exuberant embrace.

Lucinda ran to the gilt-edged mirror that hung on the far wall to admire herself, and Rowan turned to Alexa. Her slender fingers were trembling so that she could not fasten the clasp of the brooch to her bodice.

"May I help you?" he said courteously and, taking the brooch out of her shaking hand, bent to pin it to the bodice of her gown. Inevitably his hand brushed her breast. Was it his imagination or did that soft swelling mound swathed in closely fitted mousseline de soie rise and fall a little faster at his touch?

Alexa raised great limpid eyes to his. "It's lovely, Rowan. Thank you," she whispered.

"Mustn't forget your bouquets," he said lightly, handing one to each of the girls. He had chosen and arranged the flowers himself. For Lucinda there was a bunch of pink roses, for Alexa a bouquet of varicolored orchids.

Alexa again murmured her thanks. Her subdued air of suppressed excitement and the trembling of her hands surprised him. Somehow he had not thought that suffragette Alexa, so willful and heedless of tradition, would be in the least susceptible to pre-presentation jitters.

"It'll all be over quite soon," he said by way of encouragement. He bestowed a brotherly kiss on the twittering Lucinda, then, after a moment's hesitation, bent and bestowed an equally brotherly kiss on Alexa.

So cool, so brotherly was the kiss that it left Alexa feeling vaguely dissatisfied, though she could not have said why this was so.

Rowan also felt dissatisfied but *he* knew the reason for it. As his firm, masterful lips brushed Alexa's soft, trembling mouth he realized, with a sense of shock, that she, in her youth, beauty and innocence, represented an infinitely delectable temptation to a man.

Was this, he wondered, why he had found himself avoiding her of late? Because he felt confused by the bewildering array of emotions that she engendered in him? There were, he ruefully acknowledged, times that she exasperated him to the point that he would like nothing better than to wring her pretty neck! And yet, at other times she seemed to embody in one small person all that was soft and vulnerable and sweet with feminine allure. He found himself wishing he could extend the kiss, explore the warm recesses of her red-lipped mouth, and he straightened up hastily before such desires could get the better of him.

"I must be on my way," he said a bit

thickly. "It won't do to be late for the reception, you know." He hesitated. "You're looking very much 'en beaute,'" he added rather formally. "Both of you."

Rowan had barely stepped out of the house when a little maidservant came in search of her. "Please, miss," she reported, "Lady Salter wants to see you upstairs right away. It's most urgent, she says."

Alexa sighed, wondering if she were about to be read a final lecture on the importance of behaving with decorum and propriety. It was a theme that lady never tired of. She had never quite forgiven her, Alexa knew, for the disruption of that first dinner party at Nun's Farthing. As she ran lightly up the stairs to answer the summons, she found herself fingering Rowan's pearl-and-diamond brooch as if it were a talisman.

Lady Salter was magnificently arrayed in a purple satin court dress and glittering diadem. Her stance, shoulders back, head erect, hands clasped behind her back, emphasized her well-developed bosom which jutted forth like the prow of a ship.

"You wanted to see me, Aunt Hermione?" asked Alexa meekly, hesitating in the doorway. Lady Salter was Rowan's aunt and no relation to Alexa, but she had instructed the girl to address her thus.

"Come in, Alexa," she said grimly. "And close the door behind you."

Alexa obeyed. Only Lady Salter would have the effrontery to invite one into one's own bedroom, she thought with resignation. She looked forward to the day when she would be out from under Lady Salter's thumb. How like Rowan to saddle her with such a termagant, she mused.

"*Now,*" said Lady Salter in an awful voice as the door closed behind Alexa, "you can tell me *what*, pray, is the meaning of *this*!" And she whisked the petition to the king out from behind her back and waved it under a startled Alexa's nose.

Alexa blanched. She could not believe her eyes. How had Lady Salter come by that precious packet of papers—the suffragette petition to the king? She had kept it locked away in a secret compartment of her escritoire and worn the key on a chain round her neck. Then she remembered that just before Rowan had summoned her and Lucinda downstairs she had gotten the petition out to have ready to hand when they left for the palace. Ah, yes, she remembered it now! When the summons came, she had hastily thrust the packet back into the drawer and in her haste had evidently neglected to turn the key.

But nevertheless, her privacy should have been respected. Mama, she knew, would never have stooped so low as to go through her papers or even to snoop in the little red-leather diary that she wrote in every day, whether she had anything interesting to record or not.

Alexa drew herself to her full height,

which fell several inches short of Lady
Salter's and was therefore far less imposing.
"You had no business going through my
things!" she cried. "You had no right
to . . . to snoop!"

An ugly flush, which clashed horribly with
her purple satin ensemble, spread across
Lady Salter's craggy features. "I was not
snooping!" she retorted angrily. "I came
here to see if you were presentable. The
drawer was hanging open in a very untidy
fashion," she said in self-justification. "And
when I went to close it, the top sheet of paper
caught in it and crumpled. I took it out to
smooth it—not to read it—but my eye inevitably fell upon . . ." Belatedly realizing
that she was justifying her conduct to this
harum-scarum chit of a girl, she broke off
abruptly.

"That is not the point, Alexa." Lady Salter
regrouped her forces and went on the attack.
"The point is this. *Why* are you in possession
of this . . . this document?" She rattled the
offending petition. "And what do you intend
to do with it?"

"I should have thought that was fairly obvious."

Lady Salter's breath whistled through her
large, horsy teeth. "Just as I thought!" she
exclaimed, her judgment vindicated. "You
do intend to make a scene at the palace!
Why, you wretched ungrateful little hussy!
Well, let me tell you that—"

Lady Salter's tirade was interrupted by a

timid rap at the door. Lucinda opened it and
poked her head in. "Alexa ... Aunt Hermione, it's nearly time to go," she reminded
them. "Chalmers has the Rolls drawn up out
front and—"

Lady Mary's head appeared round
Lucinda's. "It's getting very late, Hermione.
Don't you think we should be going soon?"
she said, drawing on her elbow-length gloves
as she spoke.

"Ah, Mary. I'm glad you're here. Come in. I
want you to see for yourself, with your own
eyes, exactly what mischief your daughter is
engaged in." She thrust the petition at Lady
Mary who entered the room trailed by a
curious Lucinda. "Just read this! I'm sure
you will agree with me that *something
drastic* must be done about Alexa!"

Lady Mary scanned the first page of the
petition, her face turning pale. "The respectful and loyal request of the W.S.P.U. ...."
she whispered. "I don't understand, Alexa.
What ... what does this mean?"

"It means that your willful, irresponsible,
ungrateful chit of a girl is planning to make
her family a laughing stock, Mary," retorted
Lady Salter grimly. "She means to take advantage of her court presentation in order to
present this ... this outrageous proposal to
the king himself. Is that not true, Alexa?"

"I planned to present the petition to the
king. Yes, I'm afraid it's true, Mama," Alexa
said quietly.

Lady Mary sank into an easy chair as if her

legs would no longer support her. "Oh, Alexa, how *could* you?" she wailed.

"How perfectly thrilling!" Lucinda squealed. "Please, may I read it, Cousin Mary?" she asked, taking the document from Lady Mary's limp fingers and mumbling over it, half aloud.

"Alexa is not going to do any such thing," pronounced her aunt majestically. "Alexa will not be given the opportunity to *disgrace the family* any more than she has already done!" Lady Salter drew herself up to her full imposing height. "Because I, for one, am not going to be responsible for foisting such an undisciplined, ungrateful wretch on Society. I refuse to sponsor her debut," she thundered.

"Oh, Aunt Hermy, you can't be so cruel!" Lucinda burst out, sheets of typescript dropping from nervous hands and fluttering face down onto the carpet.

"I most certainly can!" Lady Salter retorted. "Mary," she declared grandly, "as of this moment I wash my hands of the girl!"

"Oh, where are my smelling salts?" moaned Alexa's mama.

"If Alexa can't go to the palace and be presented, well, then, *I* won't go either!" Lucinda's lips trembled but she set her pretty face in a mulish expression.

Lady Salter rounded on Alexa. "There, girl, see what you have done," she fairly shrieked. "Your poor dear mama in a fainting fit . . . your cousin throwing away her whole future . . . !"

Alexa snatched at her mother's reticule and rummaged through it for smelling salts. "Mama, you are *not* going to faint," she said strong-mindedly. She found the restorative and waved it under her mother's nose. "And, Lucy, you *must* have your court presentation. You've been looking forward to it for weeks. It means so much to you," she argued. "And it doesn't mean anything to me. Truly it doesn't. Only," she added wistfully, "I had hoped to do something for the Cause."

Lady Salter made a rude noise.

Mama, taking a deep draft from her vinaigrette, added her persuasions to Alexa's. "Yes, Lucinda, you must go. You must not be deprived of your debut because of this naughty, naughty child of mine. I could never forgive myself—or Alexa. I shall stop at home with her. You go along with your Aunt Hermione, child, and do the family proud."

"Oh, please, Mama. Go along with Lucinda," her daughter begged. "You are dressed for the occasion and ready to go." Indeed, Mama was looking extraordinarily pretty in dove-grey satin, Alexa reflected. "You've been looking forward to it too. You know you have," she said persuasively.

"Looking forward to seeing *you* make your court curtsy," her mother said pointedly.

"Yes, well . . ." Alexa busied herself tucking the vinaigrette back into her mother's reticule. "There, you have your smelling salts in case you come over faint again," she said encouragingly. "And I would rather be alone now. Truly I would." Over her mother's head she caught Lucinda's commiserating eye and telegraphed a signal to her. *"Go!"* her eyes flashed. In an undertone she added, "You must go, Mama. Lucinda's really very nervous. She needs you."

"Indeed I do, Cousin Mary," Lucinda came loyally to Alexa's aid. "I feel quite sure that I cannot get through it without you and Aunt Hermy to support me." She contrived a small joke. "Why, I might even need to share your vinaigrette."

"Oh, very well." Alexa's mother stood up, smoothing her faded blond hair which was elaborately frizzed for the occasion. She started towards the door, then paused to look back wistfully at her daughter. "Oh dear, Alexa, whatever will Rowan say? And whatever is to become of you?"

"I'm very sorry, Mama," Alexa offered. And she was. Sorry that she had been found out. Sorry that her scheme had been foiled before it could come to fruition.

"Come, Lucinda," ordered Lady Salter. "It grows late and we must affix your train." She swept her charge from the room, saying over her shoulder to Alexa, "As for you, miss, your Cousin Rowan shall hear of this!"

Alexa was sure that Lady Salter would put the worst possible construction on it to Rowan. She found that thought troubling her more than she had thought it might. She dis-

covered, with some surprise, that it
mattered to her what Rowan thought. She
wanted to maintain his good opinion of her.

Well, she should have thought of that
before, she supposed. It was too late now.

In her enthusiasm for her project she had
given no heed to its inevitable repercussions.
Rowan would be furious, she knew. He
would add his recriminations to those of her
mother and Lady Salter. It would be worth
it, of course, if she had succeeded in accom-
plishing something for the Cause. But as it
was . . .

All this fuss! And it was all for nothing! It
was so galling! Her shoulders drooped disconsolately. Listlessly she stooped and
began picking up the typewritten sheets that
Lucy had scattered over the carpet. She
smoothed the crumpled sheets with a heavy
sigh.

The room was deathly quiet now that
everyone had gone. The ormolu clock ticking
away on the mantelpiece was the only sound
to be heard. She wandered to the window
and brushed back the curtain, waiting and
watching.

Presently she saw the two older women
and Lucinda come out of the house. Saw
Chalmers get out of the driver's seat and
come round to open the passenger door. Saw
him stoop and help Lucinda arrange the
folds of her heavy train. Mama and Lady
Salter got in and Chalmers closed the door.

Biting her lip, Alexa watched them drive away with Chalmers at the wheel. She closed the curtain. Well, she thought, that was that.

She had told everyone that she didn't care about being presented. And she didn't. Not all that much. But she wouldn't have been human if she hadn't felt a small pang of envy for Lucinda, for whom life would always be so simple, and she had to admit to herself that it hurt to see everyone drive away and to be the one left behind.

She went to the mirror, heavy-hearted, and began to take the Prince of Wales plumes out of her hair. She had outsmarted herself, Alexa reflected. She wouldn't have a debut now, yet she wouldn't be able to help the Cause either. Oh, it wasn't fair, she thought angrily. If only Lady Salter hadn't snooped! It was all her fault!

Alexa scowled into the mirror, lost in thought. If only there were something she could do . . . something to get the better of Lady Salter, horrid old dragon that she was.

Being thwarted had always had the effect of putting Alexa on her mettle. It did so now. Thinking furiously, she jumped up from the dressing table and checked the door, which swung open at her touch. It was fortunate that Lady Salter had not thought to lock her in her room, she reflected.

Her eyes began to sparkle and a wicked little grin tugged at her lips. She wasn't beaten yet! Not by a long chalk!

She went back to the dressing table and, picking up her discarded plumes, replaced them in her headdress at a jaunty angle. Frowning a little at her reflection, she smoothed her hair, bit at her lips and pinched her cheeks to redden them and dusted a little rice powder over her nose. Then she got up and yanked at the bell pull. When Violet appeared in answer to her summons, she said imperiously, "Call a cab for me, Violet."

"A . . . a cab, miss?"

"Yes," said Alexa firmly, knowing but not caring that tongues would soon be wagging in the servants' hall. "Call a cab and then come back and help me with this . . . this confounded train."

"Very well, miss." And Violet, a well-trained servant, bobbed a little curtsy and did as she was bid.

If the cabbie was startled to see a slip of a girl in full court dress, with a heavy train looped over her arm, a wilted bouquet in one hand, a sheaf of papers in the other, come running down the steps of Number Twenty-two Cadogan Square, he concealed it well. "Where to, miss?" he asked cheerfully.

Alexa tossed the precious petition and the bouquet into the cab and scrambled in after them. "The palace!" she cried. "And hurry, please!"

Unfortunately, Lady Salter had her ticket,

but Alexa explained to a somewhat skeptical palace official that she had been delayed, that her mother and aunt were somewhere ahead of her with the tickets. "It's Lady Hermione Salter and Lady Mary Traherne," she specified. "I am Miss Alexa Traherne." And after the official had checked his lists, she had no further difficulty obtaining entry to the palace. A second harried official gave her directions through the labyrinthine passages when she explained that she had become separated from her sponsor.

It was all amazingly easy, much easier than she had thought it would be. Lady Salter and Lucinda were far ahead of her, and she was not acquainted with any of the other debutantes who crowded into an anteroom with her and with whom she queued up in a slow-moving line along the grand staircase, and then into the drawing room.

And then . . . then . . . *her* name was called and she found herself automatically sinking down in an exquisitely graceful curtsy. She had a hazy impression of a glittering uniformed figure with a spade-shaped beard who must be His Majesty. She dipped another curtsy to the regally imposing Queen Mary, standing at his side, and dipped again to a handsome young man, the Prince of Wales.

Alexa took a deep breath. Her heart was pounding like a wild thing, threatening to leap out of her chest, but her voice, when she spoke, was clear and ringing. "Your Majesty, please ... please read this petition!" she begged, thrusting it at George V as she spoke. "And, oh, please, sire, put a stop to force feeding!"

Chapter 8

Alexa was back at Nun's Farthing in the deepest disgrace. That alone would not have mattered to her overmuch if only she could bask in a sense of achievement and fulfillment. But she did not.

It had all been, she thought wearily, rather anticlimatic. She suffered from a sense of letdown and depression and she was wretchedly convinced it had all been for nothing.

Her dramatically presented petition to the king had not, so far as she knew, had the slightest effect on the treatment of the suffragettes. Summonses had since been issued against Mrs. Flora Drummond, the so-called "general" of the movement; Mrs. Dacre Fox, and Miss Grace Roe. And those suffragettes already imprisoned were still being forcibly fed.

Probably, Alexa thought gloomily, the king

had not even *read* her petition. At the
moment she had presented it to him and
begged him to put a stop to force feeding, a
terrible hush had fallen over the room. His
Majesty had stared at her blankly and said,
"Dear me, what are things coming to?" Or
words to that effect. She couldn't be quite
sure because as he spoke, courtiers had
come running up from all directions. Sir
Douglas Dawson, Comptroller of the Lord
Chamberlain's Department, had grabbed for
her and clutched at her skirt, ripping a part
of the overskirt away and leaving a large
piece of mousseline de soie fluttering at the
king's feet as he dragged her away.

They had taken her to a small anteroom,
Alexa remembered, and a few minutes later
Rowan had appeared, tight-lipped with fury.

Rowan had seen it all. He had been button-
holed by Izvolsky, the Russian Foreign
Minister, a wily diplomat who, in Rowan's
opinion, never let his right hand know what
his left hand was up to, and had despaired of
extricating himself in time to see his sister
and cousin make their curtsies to the king.
At last he made his excuses to Izvolsky, who
was pressing the urgency of the Anglo-
Russian Naval Accord—demanding an assurance that Rowan could not give him—and
made his way to the drawing room barely in
time to see his sister make her curtsy.

Very prettily done, he thought approvingly. But . . . where the devil was Alexa? She
was nowhere to be seen. Had she become

separated from Lucinda and their sponsor, Lady Salter? She must have gotten lost in the crowd. He groaned. Trust Alexa to bollix things up! he thought uncharitably. Spying her mother in the crowd, he wended his way through the press of people to Lady Mary's side.

"Cousin Mary," he hailed her. "Where the deuce is Alexa?"

"Rowan!" Ignoring his question, she beamed at him. "Did you see Lucinda? Wasn't she lovely? Absolutely a picture of the perfect debutante! So sweet, so charming, so innocent..." Lady Mary gushed. "You must be very proud of her."

"Very much so," Rowan agreed impatiently with all his cousin's vaporings. "But I did not see Alexa," he said pointedly. "Where the devil is—?"

"It's very hot in here, don't you think?" Lady Mary interrupted him, fanning herself vigorously. "Perhaps if we stepped out for a breath of air?" she suggested, laying her hand on Rowan's arm.

"If you feel the need of it, Cousin Mary," he said politely. He had the feeling she was evading his questions, that she did not, for some reason, want to talk about Alexa.

He had barely begun to pilot her through the throng when Alexa's name was announced. Lady Mary gasped and stopped stock still. "Oh, dear, oh, dear," she murmured, craning her head for a good look.

Rowan, who was half a head taller than anyone in the room, had a bird's eye view. He felt his heart swell with unexpected emotion as he saw Alexa, floating light as thistledown toward the king. She was so tiny, so petite, so graceful as she made her obeisance. Lucinda, he mused, had had the ordinary prettiness of any attractive young girl on the threshold of womanhood, but Alexa was quite something. She seemed radiantly beautiful, lit up with an inner glow that signified her excitement, he supposed. Her delicate bone structure and translucent skin gave her a deceptive air of fragility that was enormously appealing even though he knew perfectly well it was at variance with her character. For Alexa, he suspected, was as tough as old boots even though, in her debutante finery, she had the appearance of a fairy-tale princess.

His eyes narrowed speculatively. What the devil was she up to now? It looked like she was ... by God, she *was* ... thrusting something ... papers of some kind ... at the king! Rowan cursed under his breath and instinctively tried to move closer but Lady Mary was clutching his arm, holding him back and whimpering softly, her face paper-white.

And then Alexa's clear bell-like tones drifted to them—" Your Majesty ... Stop ... force feeding!"

"Good God!" Rowan ejaculated as Alexa's

mama gave a little moan and sagged, a dead weight, on his arm.

As soon as Lady Mary recovered from her faint, Rowan left her in the charge of a sympathetic court functionary and went in search of Alexa. It took him a few minutes to determine where she had been taken, which was fortunate, he afterwards reflected, as it gave his temper time to cool from white hot to a gentle rolling boil. If he could have gotten his hands on her in those first few minutes, he would cheerfully have throttled her!

As it was, he burst out the moment he saw her, "You little fool! Do you have any idea what you've done!"

"Struck a blow for the Cause, I hope!" Alexa retorted defiantly. She felt uncommonly glad to see Rowan, even if he *was* going to browbeat her. She had been thrust into this small but elegantly appointed reception room and left severely to herself for what seemed like hours, though probably it was only a few minutes, as if . . . as if she were the carrier of some highly contagious disease, she thought indignantly.

"The Cause . . . the Cause be damned!" Rowan roared. Conscious that his voice might very likely penetrate to other rooms, he lowered it a decibel or two and said scornfully, "It's not the Cause, Alexa, it's *you*! You thrive on attention. You flaunt yourself in order to attract the maximum amount of it!"

"That simply isn't true!" she flared. "I don't want to attract attention for *myself*, Rowan. It's all for the Cause. Mrs. Pankhurst is trying to make women's suffrage a major national issue and I want to do my part to bring that about." She went on rather desperately, "It's a matter of conscience, don't you see? *You* would have the courage of your convictions, wouldn't you? So why shouldn't I be allowed to stand up for mine? Why should it be forbidden me simply because I'm a woman?"

This struck a chord. In spite of himself, Rowan was touched. He could appreciate the force of her argument. She was, he supposed grudgingly, fighting an unpopular battle in the only way she knew how as bravely as any soldier. Indeed, at this moment she closely resembled a battle-worn soldier, clothed in pathetic dignity and bedraggled finery, her court dress ripped and torn, her once-jaunty Prince of Wales plumes hanging at half-mast.

"I'm very much afraid that you've only succeeded in making yourself notorious," he said heavily. "You've thrown away your chance for a good marriage and a wealthy husband, Alexa. Willfulness, strong-mindedness, rebelliousness—those are not qualities men prize in a woman."

"I don't care," Alexa said quickly. "I would not want to be any man's doormat."

Rowan shook his head. "You might as well say you've thrown your whole life away," he said gloomily, "by following the dictates of your conscience." If indeed that was what had prompted her action, and he was by no means convinced of that.

Her excitement and elation were by now seeping away and she was feeling exhausted. "Could we go home now, please, Rowan?" she asked.

He gave her his arm. "Very well, I'll see you home. We can talk again later and decide what's best to be done."

More recriminations followed—the reproaches of Mama and Lady Salter and even Lucinda who had belatedly realized that her own chances for making a good match might be damaged by her cousin's quixotic behavior.

When the seemingly bottomless well of reproaches had at last run dry, Alexa was allowed to go to bed and sleep the clock around. In the morning, a family council of war was held and it was decided—with Rowan casting the decisive vote—that Alexa must go down to Nun's Farthing and rusticate out of the public eye. In time, her social regeneration might be attempted, but "Not by me," said Lady Salter firmly. "I wash my hands of the gel."

"I believe we know your views, Aunt Hermione," said Rowan tiredly. Not only had his aunt expressed them, loudly and forthrightly, within the family circle, but she had also gone so far as to issue a statement to the newspapers to the effect that "the unfortunate incident was deeply deplored by the whole family." She had also made it plain that *she* was not related to "the perpetrator of this outrageous insult to His Majesty."

Rowan had been appalled when he learned of it, thinking it better that the family maintain a dignified silence, though he knew the papers would not. Indeed, his own usually restrained morning paper had devoted a leading article to Alexa's prank, labeling her (Rowan cringed) "the Militant Debutante."

He acknowledged grudgingly that the papers had been bound to have a field day with it, but Aunt Hermione need not have added grist to their mill.

Women, Rowan decided, were, individually and collectively, the very devil and the sooner he got Alexa down to Nun's Farthing the better it would be, before she could get an inflated sense of her own importance, decide that she was some kind of heroine, and—God forbid!—issue her own statement to the press.

And so Alexa found herself back at Nun's Farthing. Since Rowan had whisked her away from Cadogan Square before she had even had a chance to glance at the morning papers, she had no real notion of the commotion she had caused. In the clear light of a new day, it seemed to her that her gesture was no more than a pebble cast upon the waters which made not a ripple and sank without a trace. Once again, her well-meant attempts to stand up for her beliefs had achieved nothing. She was a failure!

And the attempt, futile though it was, had cost her dearly. She had forfeited her chance to "come out" in Society. But, more than that, she had forfeited Rowan's good opinion of her, and that, for some inexplicable reason, hurt her horribly.

Why it should do so puzzled her. If asked, she would have denied it vehemently. She would have said she didn't give a fig for his opinion, pompous overweening brute that he was! And yet, deep in her heart she knew that she *did* care. It mattered very much what he thought of her.

She had warmed to the glow of admiration in his eyes when she had appeared before him in her court dress. And then when he had pinned on her brooch and brushed his lips to hers, she had thought . . . she had felt . . . it was as if something had sparked between them, a tiny flickering flame that was almost immediately extinguished.

She wished suddenly, passionately, that he would see her as a woman—a beautiful, desirable woman—rather than as a silly little troublemaker. But not, she reminded herself, at the cost of her ideals. She had to be true to herself, hadn't she? She wasn't about to turn herself into a silly simpering Society miss to please Rowan—or any man alive!

One thing she could take satisfaction in, she reflected, was that she had certainly scotched Rowan's plan to marry her off. No man would want her now, for men, as Rowan was fond of reminding her, did not want women who had ideals and opinions and minds of their own. No indeed, what a man wanted was a silly little doll who would bat her eyelashes at him and tell him how wonderful he was a hundred times a day! Someone who would ensure that his life ran smoothly, ignore his peccadilloes, and turn a blind eye to his amours. Just as Mama had had to do with Papa all those years. Just as any woman who married Rowan would have to do, Alexa supposed, her lips drawing into a thin, tight line. No, she had no regrets about spoiling her chances on the marriage market, despite whatever Rowan or anyone else might say.

But, as it happened, her chance to make an advantageous match was not so remote as either of them supposed.

Rowan had taken Alexa and her mother down to the country and motored back after luncheon, a dispiriting meal during which Lady Mary, relieved of the restraining presence of Chalmers had given free rein to her lamentations. Even Rowan could find it in his heart to spare some sympathy for Alexa, for by the time he was ready to leave, Lady Mary's soft-voiced plaints were beginning to grate on *his* iron nerves.

Well, she had made her bed, now let her lie
on it, he thought irritably. She had had her
chance and had chosen to throw it away! He
had done all he could for her. More than
could reasonably be expected of him,
actually!

Back at Cadogan Square, he shuffled
through the day's mail which was presented
to him on a silver salver by his very correct
town-house butler, Flemings. A note from
Lady Wyndham caught his eye and he slit it
open with a sigh. The note, written on expensively scented stationery, was yet another
invitation to tea. He scowled down at it,
wondering if it was going to be necessary to
forsake tact and diplomacy and have it out
with Frances once and for all, for despite
numerous hints that their affair was over,
she had not abandoned her pursuit of him.

He crumpled the note and sat down at his
desk to compose a curtly worded refusal
when Derek Cathcart was announced.

His hand on the bell pull, Rowan said, "Ah,
Derek, I was just about to send for a brandy-
and-soda. Will you join me?"

"Thanks, old man. I could use one," Derek
admitted.

Rowan cocked a quizzical black brow at
his friend. Cathcart was far from his usual
cheerful self. It was obvious that something
was preying on his mind.

When their tray of drinks had been
deposited and Flemings had made a soft-
footed retreat from the room, Rowan said

encouragingly, "Well, what is it? Come
along, out with it, Derek. Are you in Dun
territory again?" The Guards was an
expensive regiment, as he well knew, and
Cathcart had from time to time borrowed
small sums from his friend to tide him over
until his next quarter day's allowance was
paid in.

"What? Oh, nothing like that." Derek
looked as though he rather wished it were.
He lifted his brandy-and-soda to his lips and
took a gulp of the fiery liquid. "The fact of
the matter is ... well, I popped in earlier,"
he said awkwardly. "They told me you had
taken Alexa and her mother down to the
country. Er ... being sent to Coventry, is
she?"

Rowan's lips tightened. It was none of
Cathcart's business what disposition he had
made of Alexa. Oh, he knew Derek had a
tendresse for the chit but ...

"And if she is? What of it? I really cannot
see what else I can do with her, considering
the exhibition she made of herself yesterday," he said stiffly.

"Don't you think you're being rather hard
on the girl?" Derek interposed. "Oh, I know
all about what happened at court ... bound
to, the way it was splashed all over the newspapers." He grinned nervously. "Must have
been quite a sight. Damned if I don't wish I'd
been there to see it for myself."

"See here," said Rowan tiredly, "if you're
here to plead Alexa's case, I must tell you

that you'll be wasting your breath. She'll have to forfeit her Season—this year at least. I want to keep her out of the public eye until the smoke clears."

But Cathcart shook his head. He knew his friend's implacable determination too well to suppose that anything he could say would change his mind. "You've got the wrong end of the stick, old man. That's not why I'm here . . . that is . . ." He paused, fortified himself with a large gulp of brandy, and said, "The fact of the matter is . . . I'm here to make an offer for Alexa."

"Make an offer for her!" Rowan repeated blankly. It was the last thing he expected and his astonishment was such that he blurted out the first thing that came into his head. "Good God, man, have you taken leave of your senses!"

Derek looked aggrieved. "Well, I must say, that's hardly the tone I expected you to take!" he protested.

Rowan frowned, gathering his scattered wits together. It was, he felt, incumbent upon him to warn his young friend off. True, this was exactly what he had hoped for when he had first evolved his plan of introducing Alexa into Society. But that, he told himself, had been before he realized the lengths to which she would go. He groaned within himself. He had deliberately brought the pair together . . . thrown them together . . . with just such an end in view, and now . . . why, that willful little flibbertigibbet would spell ruin for Derek's career. And if he couldn't see that for himself, he, Rowan, would have to spell it out for him!

"If you're offering for her out of some misguided sense of chivalry..." he began cautiously.

"No such thing," Derek cut in. "Alexa's a beautiful girl, full of fire and spirit. Why, any man would be proud to have her for a wife. I was," he admitted, "going to wait until she'd had her Season. It's hardly fair to sweep a girl off her feet before she's had a chance to look around her and see what's what. But since she won't be having a coming-out ball and all that . . . well, it puts a different complexion on things . . ."

Rowan sighed heavily. Love, it appeared, was blind. "Good God, man, don't you realize she'll be the ruin of your career!" he snarled.

Derek was startled by his friend's vehemence. "Oh, come now. That's a bit harsh, don't you think? This presentation business will be a nine-days wonder for a while, but by the time our engagement is announced in the *Times*, it will have all blown over. Alexa," he prophesied, "will be the toast of the regiment!"

"And the earl?" Rowan pursued ruthlessly. The Earl of Sandhaven was Derek's father. "Have you thought what he'll say when you bring home a suffragette bride?"

"Father'll come round," Derek assured his friend. "Alexa will win him over. And it's not as though I'm the heir, you know," he pointed out. "What's more, Mama has already met her and likes her. Says she was just such a romp when she was a girl."

"You surprise me," said Rowan dryly.

"Oh, yes, Mama is of the opinion that marriage and, er, motherhood will settle Alexa down. She'll make an exemplary wife!" said young Cathcart enthusiastically.

"Indeed." Rowan did not allow his face to express the skepticism he was feeling. It was obvious that he might as well save his breath to cool his porridge. The poor fool was not to be dissuaded, and indeed, he asked himself moodily, why should he make the effort? Alexa had been a thorn in his side for weeks now. This was a golden opportunity to get her off his hands once and for all. If young Cathcart was so besotted he could not see what he was letting himself in for by saddling himself with a wife like Alexa, well, that was his lookout.

Derek drained his glass. "Well, do I have your permission to pay my addresses to Alexa?" he asked impatiently.

"She is of age," Rowan reminded him. "She must make her own decision."

"Oh, quite. But tell me confidentially, old man, do you think she'll have me? Only a second son, you know. And most of my mother's money will go to my brother to keep up the estate."

"Such a consideration won't enter Alexa's head," Rowan assured him truthfully. She was not the woman to marry for money or

social position, he knew. And he also knew
that she was fond of Derek. But, more
important, this was likely to be her first,
last, and only chance to marry well and if she
had the brains of a gnat, he thought cynically, she would leap at it. At the same time he
wondered why he found the thought so
depressing.

But Alexa did not leap at it. She refused
Derek gently but firmly. If she had had any
notion that a proposal was in the wind, she
would have found some way to forestall it,
she thought unhappily, in order to save both
Derek and herself embarrassment. But she
had not. It came as a bolt out of the blue.

He had come down to Nun's Farthing on
the weekend and she had welcomed him
warmly, for she was very lonely. After the
excitements of London, life in the country
was dull and Mama's tearful reproaches
very hard to bear. She missed Lucinda's
companionship . . . why, she even missed
Rowan! He had, at least, been a worthy
opponent to pit herself against, she thought
moodily.

Derek was not Rowan, of course. There
was no comparison. But he was amusing and
cheerful and carefree (or so Alexa thought).
He made a pleasant, undemanding companion and she was glad to see someone,
anyone, who was not censorious. Who
accepted her as she was. She revealed her
pleasure in seeing him so openly that it gave

Derek quite the wrong impression and unwonted high hopes.

Even Mama perked up to see a new face and, after tea, gave her permission for an unchaperoned stroll in the rose garden, for she too had hopes!

There could hardly be a more romantic place for a proposal, thought Derek. He could not, of course, know that Alexa had vivid memories of a similar stroll in that same garden with Rowan. And while the topic of their conversation had been matrimony, it had had a very different purpose.

Derek took so long in getting to the point that at first she didn't grasp what on earth he was talking about. When she finally began to get the drift she was appalled. A wave of hot and then of cold passed through her, leaving her knees weak and her hands unsteady. To conceal their trembling, she picked a rose blossom and began plucking at the petals, letting them drop and scatter round her feet.

"But I . . . I can't marry you, Derek," she gasped. "I . . . I don't love you . . . at least, not in that way," she added diplomatically, for, tender-hearted as she was, she could hardly bear to hurt his feelings by refusing him.

"You could learn to!" Derek persisted, not unduly downcast, for didn't a woman always say "No" when she meant "Yes"? It would hardly be proper for her to accept him outright, he reflected, without first expressing a little maidenly coyness, a demure hesitation and reserve, becoming to a young woman of her station in life.

"I daresay this has come as a surprise to you," he hazarded. "I expect you'd like a little time to think it over."

But Alexa was already thinking furiously. It was a temptation, she had to admit. She was fond of Derek—very fond—and was not fondness as much as could be hoped for in a Society marriage? There were, she knew, any number of debutante brides who drove away from the wedding ceremony with husbands who were almost strangers to them, having been forced into marriage for money or social position.

Derek would make a kindly, good-natured husband, she was sure of that. And he was young and handsome enough to satisfy the heart of any girl—very, very far from the fat unattractive old man she had feared Rowan would foist upon her.

Moreover, if she did not marry, what *was* she going to do with her life? Marriage, she was realistic to see, was one of the few options open to her. It would give her independence (of a sort) and an establishment of her own. While life as Mama's unmarried daughter would be bleak, she was well aware, offering her nothing more important to do than arrange the flowers and wind Mama's knitting wool and listen cheerfully to her unceasing complaints.

There were, of course, a few unmarried women who had succeeded in breaking out of this mold. But the women of her own social class and position who had done so were few and far between.

All the same, she just could not bring herself to marry for security. There should only be one reason for marriage, Alexa considered. That you loved the man so terribly that you could not visualize life without him. And, fond as she was of Derek Cathcart, he simply did not fit into that category.

"I have thought it over, Derek," she said steadily. "I'm very fond of you and . . . and I shall always treasure your friendship but . . . but I cannot marry you."

The simple statement had the ring of finality, and Derek was nonplused. "Are you quite sure of that, Alexa?" he pursued. "Your people would approve of the match, I know. In fact, Rowan said—"

"Rowan!" Alexa's temper flared dangerously. "What has Rowan to do with this?"

"Well, naturally I approached him first and he gave me to understand that you—"

"Oh, he did, did he?" Alexa interrupted. The light of battle kindled in her eyes. "Rowan," she declared indignantly, "takes a good deal too much on himself if he undertakes to answer for me!"

The nerve of the man, Alexa fumed, when a disappointed Derek had hastily taken himself off and she was alone again. How dared he presume to manage her life for her! As if . . . as if she were a . . . a child or . . . or an imbecile . . . incapable of deciding such matters for herself!

And to think she had actually been missing the brute! *Missing him*! She decided, with a toss of her red head, that it just went to show the lengths to which she had been driven by desperation! It was because she was so lonely and bored, shut away down here with only Mama for company, she told herself. And because Rowan could be such a delightful companion when he chose—he was so witty and well-traveled, so knowledgeable about foreign affairs, that went without saying, of course—so charming and agreeable . . .

But only so long as he got his own way! Cross him and see how far you got, Alexa raged in the privacy of her own room. Then he could be a demon. She didn't miss him! One might as well experience a yearning to be with Frankenstein . . . or Count Dracula . . . or Jack the Ripper!

Ooh! she was burning with rage and resentment. Her temper was up, her adrenaline flowing so that she was unable to be still but paced back and forth across the carpet. Marry her off, would he? She would show him!

On her third peregrination across the room, she paused by the mantelpiece, her fingers curling round a little Dresden china shepherdess. She squeezed it as if it were Rowan's neck and then hurled it as far as she could.

It hit the far wall and shattered into

smithereens which drifted down onto the
carpet. Oh, it did her heart good just to hear
it smash! She had never liked the ornament
anyway—the shepherdess was a silly, simpering miss—just the sort of female they
were all trying to mold her into. But she,
Alexa Traherne, did not fit the mold. And she
never would! Never . . . never . . . never!

Her feelings somewhat relieved, she knelt
and gathered up the shards of broken china
and deposited them in the dustbin before her
ladies' maid came in to dress her for dinner.
Life, she reflected, had really been so much
simpler when she and Mama had lived in
London with only a little maid-of-all-work to
do for them. At least one had not had to keep
up appearances in front of the servants.

It was too much to hope for that Mama
would not notice and comment upon Derek's
abrupt   departure.   "Such   a   pity,"   she
lamented, "that dear Derek had to go back to
London tonight."

"Yes, wasn't it," said Alexa noncom-
mittally, her eyes on her plate.

"And after I ordered cook to prepare a
special dinner for him," Mama mourned.
"And there are fresh-picked strawberries
from the garden and Devonshire clotted
cream. It really is too bad."

When the main course had been brought in
and the servant had retired, Mama said, "It
was rather a long drive to make for such a
short visit, was it not?"

Alexa agreed that it was.

Mama carefully cut and impaled a piece of spring lamb on her fork. "You and Derek didn't have words, did you, Alexa?"

"Words?"

Mama sighed. "Well, he did make rather a precipitous departure. I thought that perhaps—"

Alexa was tiring of this cat-and-mouse game. And it was useless to try to keep Derek's proposal from Mama, she reflected. She was bound to find out about it sooner or later.

"Derek came down for a specific purpose, Mama. He . . . he asked me to marry him but," she added quickly, "I refused him."

"Refused him!" Mama dropped her knife and fork with a clatter. "Oh, you foolish . . . foolish girl!" she shrilled, all her bright hopes for her daughter cast down.

"But I don't love him, Mama," Alexa said desperately.

"Love! What has love to do with it?" Mama exclaimed. "It is time and past time that you grew up and faced facts, Alexa. Skivvies and housemaids may marry for love, but people of our station in life cannot. Not as a rule, that is," she amended, mindful that her own had been a love match. Reggie Traherne had swept her off her feet, charmed her family and friends—and been a thoroughly unsatisfactory husband! She went to some pains to point this out to her daughter.

"Derek is a fine young man, well-born and personable," Mama concluded. "I can see no objections to the match, Alexa. Especially in view of the fact that you have quite spoilt your chances by your deplorable behavior at court. You should be thanking your lucky stars that he will have you!" she said in exasperation.

"But I have already refused him, Mama," Alexa pointed out, hoping that that would put an end to the matter.

Her mother sighed, then brightened. "Perhaps that can yet be remedied." She pursed her lips—a bad sign, Alexa knew, indicative that her gentle mother was digging in her heels and would not be deterred. She thought for a minute, then nodded decisively. "I shall speak to Rowan. It may be that he can bring you to a sense of your responsibilities and what you owe to your family. Heaven knows I cannot!" she exclaimed, seeing her daughter's sulky stubborn expression. "And for your young man ... well, a tactful hint that you only refused him out of maidenly modesty and reserve would do wonders."

Alexa sprang up from the table so quickly that her chair toppled over backwards. "I cannot sit here any longer and . . . and listen to this, Mama!" she cried. "Believe me when I tell you that nothing . . . nothing . . . that you—or Rowan—can say will change my mind. I will not marry without love, not even if you and Rowan do succeed in bringing Derek up to scratch again." Her hands clutched at the back of her chair as she righted it, the knuckles turning white. "Never . . . hear me, Mama . . . never will I marry without love!" And with that ringing declaration she turned and ran from the room, leaving her mother staring at the remains of the festive dinner she had ordered for Derek in the fond hope that it would be a feast of celebration.

Alexa took refuge in her bedroom and resumed her frantic pacing, even more distressed than she had been earlier on. She felt as if the jaws of a trap were closing around her.

She had no doubt whatsoever that Mama would appeal to Rowan to "bring her to her senses." And if Rowan had set his mind on this marriage, as Derek had implied, why, then, he would find some way of bringing it off. Was she strong enough to hold out against him? She thought not. Recalling his dark, swarthy face set in lines of implacable determination, she knew, with a sinking of her heart, that she was not strong enough to stand against him, for Rowan was the strongest man she had ever known.

Sinking down on her bed, she gave way to sobs. What on earth was she going to do now?

Chapter
9

It was not in Alexa's nature to weep and wail over her fate. At least not for long! Action was what she preferred and the more direct, the better! So she dried her eyes and bathed her tear-swollen face in cold water and, by the time her maid had come in to turn down the bed for the night, she was quite calm and even cheerful again for she had determined on a course of action and was bent on carrying it out.

If she couldn't fight the good fight and expect to win, there was only one alternative, she thought coolly, flight. She would go up to London and lose herself so thoroughly in the heart of that vast, bustling metropolis that no one would be able to find her.

She was not altogether without resources, she reflected. She had a little money of her own—only a few pounds, but it was suf-

ficient for a first-class ticket to London.
Mama had long since impressed upon her
that a lady could not travel other than first-
class.

Once she got there, one or another of her
suffragette friends would take her in—she
was sure of it. Maybe even the Pankhursts?
Hadn't Mrs. Pankhurst taken into her home
Annie Kenney, the mill girl, who had since
become one of the Movement's most valuable recruits?

But at the moment Mrs. Pankhurst had
enough on her plate without giving refuge to
uninvited guests who popped up on her door-
step. Especially not one who was likely to
bring wrath down upon her head, as was
only too likely to happen if Rowan caught up
with her. As he would be sure to do, she reflected, if she sought sanctuary in such an
obvious place.

Christabel was still in France, as far as she
knew. But there was Sylvia, Mrs. Pankhurst's younger daughter, who, not content
with being merely a suffragette, was also a
Socialist who lived and worked among the
poor working-class people in London's East
End. Yes, she thought, she could take refuge
with Sylvia. It was so far from her normal
milieu that Rowan would never think of
looking for her there.

She would go tomorrow, she decided,
while Mama was taking her afternoon rest.
She would leave a note for her, pack a small
bag, and ride Gypsy to the station where she

could catch the 2:12 up to London. The station master, an old friend from her childhood, would take charge of the little mare, she was sure, until such time as a groom could be sent from the stables to retrieve her.

It all went according to plan. Alexa experienced a little trepidation, however, at finding herself, for the first time in her sheltered life, in the East End. She had not thought such places could exist, she mused, looking around her wide-eyed. The streets were so narrow and mean. Even on this bright spring day they were dark and depressing, for crowded, ramshackle buildings towering overhead filtered out the sunlight. It was, she thought uneasily, another world from the world she knew. The world of Mayfair and Belgravia, Park Lane and Cadogan Square.

And the people! Pasty-faced, poorly clothed and underfed. At least they *looked* hungry, she thought, from the safety of her cab—no doubt they *were* hungry—and her heart contracted with compassion. Particularly for the children who hung around the street corners or clustered on the stoops of grimy brick tenements, too listless to play. They were horrifying to her—seemingly stunted little dwarves or gnomes who wore, to her country-bred eyes, an unhealthy pallor along with their rags.

But some of the street children, despite their poverty, seemed to possess an astonishing zest for life. One such, an impudent, dirty-faced little ragamuffin, came running up as she alighted from her cab. "Carry your bag, lady?" he suggested.

Alexa nodded, since her hands were fully occupied in hoisting her skirts ankle-high to keep them clear of the refuse and filth that littered the street. She followed the boy, who identified himself, when asked, as "Erbert, miss," up the steps of the tenement and gave him a coin for his trouble. He flashed a gamin grin at her when he saw the denomination of the coin and volunteered that he was available to run errands at any time of the day or night. "I runs 'em regular for Miss Sylvia," he added.

Sylvia was at home, for which Alexa was thankful, but, alas, she did not appear as glad to see Alexa as Alexa was to see her. "See here, my dear, if you're running away from home, you'd do well to entertain second thoughts," she said bluntly. "There's no place for fine ladies hereabouts. If you stay, you must be prepared to buckle down and do some real work—dirty work," she added quite fiercely.

"I'm not afraid of work!" Alexa cried indignantly, burning to be useful and stung by the implication that she only wanted to play at being Lady Bountiful.

Sylvia softened. "Well, I daresay you could help with my milk distribution scheme," she said grudgingly, for, not content with raising the consciousness of working women, Sylvia was actively trying to promote their health and well-being. "At the moment I have my hands full organizing my Women's May Day march."

"Possibly I can help with that too," Alexa suggested. And so it was arranged that Alexa should stay with her friend, at least for the time being.

Sylvia was the more sympathetic when she learned that Alexa was fleeing from an unwanted marriage, arranged for her by her cousin, for by now she had convinced herself that Rowan had somehow engineered the whole thing, even Derek's proposal!

"He sounds the worst kind of brute," Sylvia commented darkly.

"Ye-e-s," said Alexa, a bit dubiously. It was, she found, one thing for her to denounce Rowan as a brute—an ogre—a monster of selfishness—but quite another to hear someone echo her own vociferously expressed opinions. Oddly enough, it made her feel like springing to his defense.

It was, she mused, very odd indeed. It was unconscionable of Rowan to force her into an unwanted marriage, willy-nilly. Of course it was! And yet . . . yet, could she really blame him all that much? Marriage was the only career considered suitable for a young woman of her station in life. And everything Rowan had done—arranging for her presentation and coming-out into Society, introducing her to Derek Cathcart and other eligible young men, even promoting a

marriage between Derek and herself (and
Derek was, admittedly, a highly eligible
suitor)—all this was meant for her ultimate
benefit and welfare, was it not? Alexa was
too fair-minded not to admit this, if only to
herself.

Down through the centuries, women had
traditionally found their happiness and fulfillment in marriage. Could she really hold it
against Rowan because he harbored the
traditional and, to her mind, old-fashioned
view of women's role in life? Of course she
could not! The old ways had passed the test
of time, she supposed, and the new views,
which she held, of a woman's expanded role
in society were largely untried and had yet to
be proved.

She sighed. If only Rowan could be
brought to see that she could not be content
with woman's traditional role—that she
needed more than a husband and a home to
find her happiness and fulfillment.

She pondered ways and means as she went
about her new duties, donning a cap and
apron to help out with the babies at Sylvia's
milk depot, assisting her in getting out the
monthly issue of *The Women's Dreadnaught*,
a suffragette publication aimed at East End
women, and helping her to organize the
Women's May Day march. She was overjoyed when Sylvia promised that she could
be among the twenty-odd women who would
chain themselves together and march in the
procession.

But while Alexa, once her initial rage and resentment had passed off, was thinking more kindly of Rowan, he was not reciprocating.

This time he really would throttle her! Rowan thought savagely, slamming down the telephone receiver. He had just held a prolonged and painful conversation with a tearful and semihysterical Lady Mary, who informed him, between sobs, that Alexa had done a bunk.

Running away from home surpassed all her previous pranks, Rowan reflected. It was not only irresponsible, annoying and embarrassing, it was potentially dangerous. The thought of what could happen to a beautiful, naive, penniless young woman alone on the streets of London made his blood run cold. Not that he held with her mother's hysterical fears that Alexa would be accosted by procurers or white slavers. Indeed, any white slaver that tangled with Alexa was likely to find that he had bitten off more than he could chew, Rowan thought sourly. But this opinion he kept to himself, not wishing to exacerbate Lady Mary's already frazzled nerves.

In any event, he reassured himself, she wouldn't be along for long. She would go to her suffragette friends. But which one? He had obtained a partial list of them from her mother, as well as the names and addresses of those authors for whom she had done

typing on her previous sojourn in London.
Alexa, he was sure, was bound to take refuge
with one or another of these friends and
acquaintances.

He would track her down, Rowan thought
grimly, pocketing the list, and when he found
her, God have mercy on her! *He* would not!

But he did not find her. Not that day nor
yet the next. Or the next. Alexa had, to all
intents and purposes, vanished without a
trace.

He scoured the city, his temper rising as
his anxiety level soared, tracking down the
leads that Lady Mary had provided him. But
all they yielded him was sore feet, an in-
creasingly irascible disposition, and the sour
taste of defeat in his mouth. No trace of
Alexa could be found.

It was a pity, he reflected, that that fellow
Sherlock Holmes was only a figment of Sir
Arthur Conan Doyle's fertile imagination. He
could put to good use the services of the
world's most famous consulting detective,
he mused.

In fact, he was on the way to the offices of
a firm of private investigators when a notice
chalked on the pavement caught his eye.
Knowing that it was the habit of the militant
suffragettes to post notices of their
demonstrations, marches and rallies in
chalk on the city pavements, he paused to
read it. This particular notice was an
advertisement of a forthcoming rally in
Victoria Park.

Rowan was jubilant. If Alexa was not already in Holloway, she would be there. And so, by God, would he! His jaw tightened. He would apprehend her and then whisk her down to Nun's Farthing where her mama was well-nigh prostrate with worry. It was where she belonged.

But would she stay on there? Rowan chewed it over in his mind and came to the conclusion that she would. According to the note she had left her mother, fear of being forced into an arranged marriage had precipitated her flight. The damned little fool! Hadn't he promised her—well, as good as promised—that he would not force her into a marriage of convenience!

On the surface it had appeared that a match between her and Derek Cathcart would be ideal, but he could see now that young Cathcart was not the man for her. He was not the man to tame Alexa's fiery spirit, that was obvious. She had done well to refuse him, Rowan considered, and as soon as he had an opportunity to reassure her on that point, all would be well. It had better be! His grey eyes glittered ominously. He was not going to take any more nonsense from the chit. Of that he was sure!

On the day of the great rally, the park and the streets adjacent to it were alive with people of all descriptions. Women swarmed everywhere—women clothed in white with sashes of purple and green and revolutionary red, for the East End Federation of

Suffragettes had a distinctly socialist tinge.
There were even a few men who sported the
suffragette colors, for the East End Federation was open to men as the W.S.P.U. was
not. Rowan had heard that they had further
organized themselves in a "People's Army"
for the purpose of repelling police brutality,
though he himself was of the opinion that
such belligerency would be more likely to
invite brutality and rough treatment than to
repel it.

Plainclothes policemen were as easy to
spot as those in blue uniforms who swarmed
everywhere, some on horseback, others on
foot.

But even more menacing than the police
were the rowdier elements in the crowd.
Rough working men who resented the
efforts of the suffragettes to lead their
women astray, out of the kitchen (where
every right-thinking man knew they
belonged) and into the polling booths (where
they had no business at all). Such men,
Rowan knew, were well used to knocking
their women about and would have no
inhibitions about laying rough hands on the
suffragettes whom they regarded as the
enemy. Worse still were the inevitable
hangers-on who collected on the fringe of
every crowd, idle toughs and bully boys who
had come armed with rotten eggs and
squashy tomatoes and overripe fruit. The
rally, thought Rowan worriedly, had all the
earmarks of turning into a full-scale riot

before very long. He wished he could find
Alexa and get her out of here fast, before the
storm broke.

His eyes searched the crowd, his great
height and breadth of shoulder giving him a
definite advantage amidst the closely
pressed throng of human beings. He spied a
ginger-haired street urchin who was
obviously acting as courier between several
different groups of suffragettes and their
sympathizers. As the boy darted hither and
thither among the crowd, Rowan's eyes
followed him to where a group of some
twenty suffragette women were chained together.

Rowan's eyes narrowed. Yes, there was
Alexa, second from the left, and her clear
bell-like tones, ringing out to summon the
lad, confirmed the evidence of his eyes.

He had begun to work his way towards her
when one of her companions—Sylvia Pankhurst, though Rowan did not know it and
would not have cared had he known—began
to harangue the crowd.

Before he could shoulder his way through
the mob, plainclothes detectives had set
upon the women in an effort to break the
links of their chain. Rotten fruit and
tomatoes began flying through the air,
pelting suffragettes and detectives alike.

Dodging flying missiles, the police and the
line of chained women swayed back and
forth in a kind of grotesque dance, until the
men succeeded in breaking the chains that

linked the women together and began
leading them away to a waiting Black Maria.

Rowan, kneeing, elbowing, and ruthlessly
gouging his way through the surging crowd,
saw an elderly woman next in line to Alexa
trip and fall to her knees. Two detectives
bent low, grabbed the old woman under the
arms, and began hauling her roughly away.

Alexa, screaming like a banshee,
belabored the stooping detectives about the
head and shoulders with her tiny fists. One
of them dropped the old woman's arm, rose
to his full height, and backhanded Alexa
across the face—a blow that sent her reeling
backwards into the crowd.

Rowan saw red. That was Alexa they were
manhandling! His willful, wrongheaded,
aggravating—but utterly enchanting—
Alexa!

With a low growl he sprang into action.
Grabbing the plainclothesman by the
shoulder, Rowan spun him around to face
his punishing fist. The man staggered and
went down even as his companion, who had
dropped the old woman into the dirt, came to
his aid, advancing on Rowan. Rowan dealt
with this second adversary summarily,
feeling the seams of his own jacket give way
with the force he packed into his punishing
blow.

And then the mob surged forward, barring
his way to Alexa who knelt over the old
woman's prostrate form, trying to protect
her aged body with her own youthful one,

making sure that she would not be trampled upon by the mob.

Using his head and powerful shoulders as a battering ram, Rowan burst through the ruffian mob but two or three of the toughs still barred his way. One burly brute swung clumsily at Rowan, who ducked. But the fist of a second man crashed into his face and he reeled, tasting blood as his full lower lip split open like a ripe melon.

By God, he thought exultantly, he had not been in such a skirmish since serving as a young subaltern on the Northwest Frontier, a dozen years or more ago. Well, he had learned some tricks from the wily Afghans and he would put them to good use against this gang of London street toughs.

His blood well up, he uttered a low growl and burst into a wild melee of flailing fists. Seizing a couple of ruffians by their shirt collars, he knocked their heads together. Another man charged him with the bellowing of an enraged bull, but Rowan skipped nimbly aside and whirled to face still another opponent. Out of the corner of his eye he caught a glimpse of Alexa. She was on her feet, fighting desperately to protect her elderly friend. That pitiful old woman, Rowan thought angrily. Had these brutes no respect for her grey hairs!

He redoubled his efforts, occasionally catching a brief incomplete view of Alexa who was kicking, biting, and scratching like a wildcat, more than holding her own. Where

had she learned that trick? he marveled as
he saw her knee a man in the groin. He heard
the fellow groan, saw him double up with
pain, and then his attention was claimed by
an opponent. Rowan moved to tackle him
rugby fashion and lost sight of the girl.

The police had rallied round in force and
were laying about them impartially with
their billyclubs, and the mob began to melt
away. There was a lull in their immediate
vicinity, though the battle still ebbed and
swirled around them, and Rowan took advantage of it to check on Alexa. To his great
relief, she appeared remarkably unscathed
by her adventures. She was kneeling by the
older woman and imploring her to answer.
"Please, Mrs. Frobisher, are you all right?"
she whimpered.

The old woman moaned and, with Alexa's
help, managed to sit up. "Yes. I believe I am
all right, my dear," she murmured weakly.

Alexa cast a look around her, rather
wildly, hoping to spot someone—anyone—
who could give her a hand. Her eyes fell
upon a pair of expensive black boots that
had once been polished to a high gloss but
which were now sadly scuffed. The eyes
traveled slowly upwards past immaculately
tailored trousers, encasing sturdily planted
masculine legs, past the narrow lean-hipped
waist, upwards to his powerful torso and
broad shoulders topped by a swarthy face,
arrogant in its hard-boned masculinity.

As her gaze had traveled slowly upwards,

her heart at an equal rate was sinking downwards. Oh, God, no! She prayed. It couldn't
be . . . but it was . . . !

"Rowan!" she burst out. And then, more
doubtfully, "Rowan?" She could hardly
believe her eyes. Maybe, she thought hopefully, it was an apparition, a trick of her
disordered senses brought on by the blow
she had sustained earlier on. Because if it
wasn't, she would just as soon crumple up
on the pavement and play dead—anything to
avoid his wrath. She wasn't up to it—not just
now she wasn't.

"Rowan?" she said again, experimentally.

Alexa surveyed him doubtfully, not yet
convinced. How could this battle-scarred
warrior be her stuffy, pompous cousin? The
sleeve of his jacket was almost torn away, he
wore a purplish bruise high on his cheek-
bone, one eye was swelling shut which gave
him a rather rakish appearance, and blood
was trickling in a steady stream out of the
corner of his normally well-shaped but now
grotesquely swollen mouth.

It was this that convinced her. Apparitions
don't bleed, she told herself with a shiver,
and this man was real—as real as the wrath
that was sure to come!

But, miracles of miracles, Rowan was
grinning—a rakish lopsided grin, it was true,
but a grin nonetheless. And when she summoned the courage to look into his normally
hard grey eyes she found a matching twinkle
in them.

Suddenly, to her surprise, Rowan, who was feeling extraordinarily lighthearted and lightheaded—it was the sheer relief, he supposed, of finding Alexa apparently safe and sound—executed a flourishing bow and said gaily, "Rowan Traherne at your service, madame! Knight Errant Extraordinary and Slayer of Dragons!" With the toe of his boot he prodded disdainfully at one of the recumbent forms sprawled untidily at his feet. "Or at least Maimer of Ill-Mannered Louts!" he amended.

For the first time Alexa really grasped the implications of the scene around her. At the time she had been too actively engaged in the struggle to defend herself (and Mrs. Frobisher) to be more than vaguely aware of the tall, broad-shouldered man fighting at her side. She had caught only glimpses of him in the heat of battle and had supposed, without giving it any thought, that he was one of the Movement's male sympathizers, a "People's Army" man perhaps, who had come to her rescue.

She stared blankly at the bodies sprawled about in varying degrees of discomfiture. One or two were out cold; another man sat up, holding his head and moaning loudly; another clutched at his stomach and retched into the gutter while his companion in misfortune prodded experimentally at a loosened tooth with a grimy forefinger and spat out a mouthful of blood.

Alexa transferred her awed gaze to Rowan.

She could hardly believe that it was he who had wreaked such havoc among the street toughs and bully boys.

"You . . . you did this!" she exclaimed, looking around her wonderingly. A thrill of primitive emotion engulfed her—the emotions of a woman who knows that a man has fought for her and emerged victorious! Quickly she lowered her eyes in confusion, not wishing him to read the too blatant message they contained.

"I did," he confirmed her assessment of the situation. "And now I suggest we make ourselves scarce. When these minions of the law come to," he pointed to the two detectives who were beginning to stir, "I want us to be long gone. Hopefully they'll busy themselves taking charge of those ruffians and forget about looking for us." He extended a hand to help Alexa scramble to her feet, then brushed her cheek with gentle fingers. "You're not hurt, are you, Alexa?"

"I'm quite all right," she said a bit unsteadily, for the touch of his hand caressing her face unsettled her more than she was willing to admit. Then she caught at his hand, turning it over to examine the knuckles which were swollen and battle-scarred. "Rowan . . . your   hand . . . it's bleeding."

"Just a few scratches," he said lightly and added whimsically, "Next time I come looking for you, Alexa, I'll remember to equip myself with knuckle-dusters."

Alexa managed a smile at this sally, then looked down at Mrs. Frobisher, who had lapsed into semiconsciousness. "Rowan, what shall we do about Mrs. Frobisher?" she said anxiously.

Rowan frowned and hunkered down by the elderly woman, running gentle hands over her to ascertain if any bones had been broken. She moaned and opened her eyes.

Satisfied that she was not seriously injured, he spoke to her soothingly. "Can you put your arms around my neck?" he asked.

The woman nodded, weakly endeavoring to do so. "Are you one of us, young man?" she whispered as he scooped her into his arms.

Rowan hesitated for a fraction of a second, then answered in the affirmative. That he did so was not solely for the old woman's benefit, he knew. The events of the day had been a revelation to him.

It was not, he mused, that he was opposed in principle to the franchise of women. No, it was the tactics of the militant suffragettes that he found objectionable, and that was primarily because he feared for Alexa who had been drawn ever more tightly into their net. He did not, he told himself as he followed her out of the park, want to see her get hurt—to wear herself out in a futile attempt battering her head against the entrenched bastions of masculine privilege and prejudice.

As this poor woman had done. He looked

down with compassionate eyes at the frail female form cradled in his arms. Women like this Mrs. Frobisher had been agitating for the vote in a quiet and ladylike manner for forty years or more. It was not until the W.S.P.U. had burst upon the scene that they had come anywhere near achieving their goals. But at what a price! To court the abuse of louts and ruffians who enjoyed the privilege of citizenship that women were denied merely because of their sex! If the truth were known, Rowan thought morosely, it was women who were more likely to exercise the privilege in a responsible fashion than those hooligans who, more often than not, staggered to the polling booths the worse for drink.

He grunted his disdain for them, and Alexa, who was trotting along by his side, taking two steps to his one to keep up with his long strides, misinterpreted it and said encouragingly, "It's not far now. There's a doctor's surgery just round the corner. He's sympathetic to the Cause and he'll look after Mrs. Frobisher."

"She should go into hospital," Rowan remarked, for his elderly charge had fainted again.

But Alexa shook her head. "I don't think there's anything seriously wrong with her. She's only just out of Holloway and is weak from hunger-striking and force feeding. She told me so." Alexa looked up at him worriedly. "She ought not to have been at the

rally at all. If the police pick her up
again ... I'm afraid she won't be able to
stand another spell in gaol."

"Very well, lead on, Macduff."

Alexa skipped nimbly ahead of him, taking
a circuitous route to avoid encountering
those officers of the law who were busy
bundling suffragettes and hooligans alike
into police vans.

The medical man confirmed Alexa's diag-
nosis—that his elderly patient had sustained
no serious injuries but was merely weak and
worn-out from previous ordeals. He
prescribed a lengthy stay in one of the rest
houses the suffragettes maintained for
released hunger-strikers and good-naturedly
agreed to make the arrangements to convey
her thither in an ambulance.

He then insisted on attending to Rowan's
cuts and bruises, cleaning and disinfecting
his wounds and, where necessary, binding
them up.

"And how about you, young lady?" The
doctor eyed her keenly. "You look a bit the
worse for wear yourself."

Alexa denied it instantly. "I'm fine," she
assured him. "Just a trifle stiff and sore
and," she looked ruefully down at her frock
which was stained with great splotches of
ripe fruit, "a bit grubby. That's all."

But Rowan grasped her by the shoulders
and gently steered her into the examination
room he had just emerged from. "No arguments, Alexa," he said firmly but pleasantly.

"We'll just have Dr. Lomax check you over, as long as we're here."

"Oh, very well," she grumbled. "Though I assure you it's quite unnecessary."

But when she emerged from the surgery a few minutes later she was carrying a small jar of ointment and the physician was giving her low-voiced instructions as to its use.

Rowan's keen grey eyes surveyed her anxiously. "You *do* have an injury, then?" he commented.

Alexa flushed. "Nothing to speak of. Just a bruise," she said evasively.

Rowan's brows rose. Though Alexa presented a disheveled appearance, her face a little puffy from the blow she had sustained and her bobbed hair tangled and disordered, on the whole she appeared to have come through the ordeal remarkably unscathed.

Her color deepened when she saw his enquiring gaze. "Just here," she murmured uncomfortably, her hand brushing her bodice. "One of those men ... he ... he grabbed my ... breast and ..." her voice trailed off in embarrassment.

Rowan's face darkened. "Come along," he said curtly. "I'll see you home."

He had already summoned a cab, and Alexa trailed after him unhappily to where it was waiting by the curb. Oh, dear, she thought they had been getting along so well and now he was on his high horse again! She wished she had not mentioned her bruises to him—she had not meant to but he had wormed it out of her. She didn't want or expect his sympathy, she told herself indignantly, but he needn't act as if it were all her fault. She supposed he thought it was only what she deserved—that she had brought it on herself.

With a grim expression on his face, Rowan stood back politely to let her precede him into the cab and she crawled in reluctantly and rather stiffly for she was sore and aching all over after her exertions. He snapped, "Number Twenty-two Cadogan Square," at the driver and got in beside her, slamming the door after him, and they set off. Alexa slid along the seat until she was in the farthest corner, as far from him as she could get, and took refuge in silence.

Rowan *was* infuriated, though not, as she thought, with her. Dammit, he thought, if he could get his hands on the man who had assaulted Alexa, he would flay him alive! He hoped that it was one of the men who had already had a taste of his fists.

But more to the point, she was, he realized, laying herself open to just such abuse—or worse!—by her continued association with the militant suffragettes. Given her current course—her headlong rush into danger—it was no more than could be expected. Somehow, he mused, he *must* find a way to sever her connections with them once and for all! He may have revised his opinion of the suffragettes, but that didn't mean he wanted to see Alexa tangled in their snares. He didn't even mind acquiring a few bruises in the Cause himself—in fact, he had found the skirmish in the park quite exhilarating—but he could not stand by and see the woman he loved abused and . . .

The woman he loved! Suddenly Rowan's quiet, well-ordered world rocked to its foundations. His heart began to labor painfully, he heard a high thin ringing in his ears, and all at once there seemed to be not enough air in the cab for him to breathe properly.

He tugged at his necktie and loosened his collar studs. Great God Almighty, he thought in a daze, he couldn't be in love with the chit! In love with the impudent little minx who had turned his hitherto placid, well-regulated life upside down! It simply wasn't possible!

But there it was . . . against all reason and logic and prudence, he loved her! He wanted to make her his own, to love her and cherish her and protect her against the world and all.

But Alexa, he reminded himself, didn't want loving or cherishing. Not his—or any man's. What she valued was her freedom—her vaunted independence. If only, he mused, he could find a way to tame her restless spirit . . . to make her his own . . . to bind her to him with the silken chains of love.

Rowan brooded over the seemingly irreconcilable differences between his needs and

Alexa's all the way back to the Cadogan
Square house without coming to any very
satisfactory conclusions. One might as well
love a Vestal of ancient Rome, he thought
gloomily, a Vestal vowed to virginity in the
service of the Goddess, as love a suffragette
so devoted to the Cause and enamored of her
own personal freedom as Alexa!

Chapter 10

"I won't go back to Nun's Farthing! And . . . and I won't marry Derek Cathcart, either!" Alexa announced defiantly. It would, she thought, be as well to establish at the outset that these two points were non-negotiable.

Rowan blinked. What with one thing and another he had almost forgotten about Alexa's rejected suitor. On the point of reassuring the chit that he was not going to pressure her into a marriage of convenience, he hesitated—thinking rapidly—for she had given him a little idea.

Immediately upon their arrival at the Cadogan Square house, they had gone their separate ways. He had gone upstairs to bathe and change while he gave Alexa over to the ministrations of Lucinda's ladies' maid.

Violet had risen to the challenge with

admirable aplomb, running a hot bath for her charge and quickly altering a frock belonging to her mistress to fit that lady's much more slender cousin, for all of Alexa's own clothing was down in the country. But even the well-trained Violet could not help showing her dismay at the state of Alexa's hair. "Oh, miss, whatever have you got in your hair?" she exclaimed, trying and failing to comb out the snarls and tangles.

Alexa pulled one of the sticky strands down to eye level to examine it. "Er . . . umm . . . I think it's egg," she pronounced. "And the red stuff . . . that's tomato juice."

A scandalized Violet had given her a shampoo.

And now, feeling much refreshed, her tawny-bronze bobbed hair curling damply about her face, she was ensconced in that supremely male preserve—Rowan's study— and they were going at it hammer and tongs. She had, she reflected, grown so used to being called on the carpet that it abashed her not a whit. She was ready and willing to spit defiance at him!

But she found his silence and his steady thoughtful gaze unnerving, and when she repeated, "I won't go back home! And I won't marry Derek Cathcart!" she was a shade less strident in her tone.

Rowan roused himself from his brown study. "You will do as you're told!" he thundered.

He had no intention whatsoever of forcing

her into marriage with his friend. Even before the stunning realization that he loved her himself had hit him like a ton of bricks, that had not been his intention. Recalling his dismay when young Cathcart had applied to him for permission to pay his addresses to Alexa, Rowan shook his head. Now he understood why he had tried to warn Derek off. He hadn't been thinking of the younger man's best interests at all! He had been deceiving himself—he could see that clearly now. Even then he must have wanted to keep Alexa to himself, though he couldn't bring himself to admit it. Lord, how could he have been so blind!

No, the last thing in the world he wanted to do was force her into marriage with Derek Cathcart. *But*—it occurred to him that if she thought he might . . . well, it just might give him some leverage with her. A bargaining point. Not for nothing was Rowan a diplomat! He could pretend that he was set on the match and then magnanimously yield in exchange for her promise to go straightaway down to the country. He would accompany her, take a few weeks leave from the Foreign Office, and spend the summer wooing her!

Rowan had a very healthy estimate of his own worth; he knew quite well that he was possessed of considerable charm when he chose to exert it. But Alexa was a challenge the likes of which he had never encountered. All the fire and passion of her nature was given up to an ideal. Could he awaken her to the joys of love and passion between a man and a woman? He thought that he could . . . yet a little niggling doubt remained.

Well, first things first. He must persuade her to go down to Nun's Farthing, if only to prevent the London police from picking her up, if for no other reason. That was essential.

"Surely you can see what an excellent match it would be for you, Alexa. Not only that, your mama has quite set her heart upon it. She is gravely disappointed that you refused his offer."

"But I *did* refuse him," Alexa protested. "I know Mama has some quite ridiculous notion that you could use your influence with him . . . to bring him up to scratch again, I mean." She leaned forward in her chair, her eyes imploring. "But you won't will you, Rowan? It would only cause untold embarrassment for us all. Because . . . because I should only refuse him again." She took a deep breath. "I won't marry any man unless I love him with all my heart. I . . . I told Mama so . . . and . . . now I'm telling you. I will only marry for love!" she declared in ringing tones.

"Don't excite yourself, Alexa," he soothed her. "I imagine Derek would not want an unwilling bride—"

"Of course he would not!" Alexa interrupted.

"And your mother and I can hardly drag you kicking and screaming to the altar—"

"Of course you cannot," said Alexa in

relief, feeling a bit more sure of herself. Though she knew perfectly well that it was not unheard of in their social set. Why, only a few years ago, the beautiful Consuelo Vanderbilt had been pressured into marriage with the Duke of Marlboro, by her strong-minded American mother. The bride had wept throughout the ceremony, it was said, and the unhappy marriage had ended in a divorce that rocked British Society. Alexa knew that she could consider herself lucky not to be forced to follow in Consuelo's footsteps.

"It's a pity, really . . ." Rowan shook his head. "There's no denying it would be an excellent match . . ." he said regretfully.

Alexa trembled.

"Suppose we leave it like this . . ." he said meditatively. "If, in exchange for my promise that neither your mother nor I will exert any pressure on you to change your mind, you would be willing to make one small concession . . ."

Alexa looked at him suspiciously. "And that is . . . ?"

"To motor down to the country with me and remain there quietly in seclusion. To forgo any more suffragette demonstrations or rallies—at least for the time being," he added hastily. "Your mama is frantic with worry over you, Alexa," he said with perfect truth. "It would ease her mind to have you with her for a time at least. And while I'm there I'll have a word with her—convince her

that the matter is to be dropped." He looked
at her quizzically. "What do you say?"

Alexa thought it over. It seemed an
eminently reasonable concession to make.
To go home for a while in order to ease
Mama's mind. That was not such an unrea-
sonable stipulation, she decided with some
relief. She had expected to wage a long and
bitter battle with Rowan on this issue of her
marriage. Really, he had given way surprisingly easily, she reflected. But now that
she had his word that he would not harass
her himself, nor allow Mama to badger her,
well, that put quite a different complexion
on things. She knew she could trust him to
keep his word; once given it would be
inviolate.

Rowan felt a small but distinct twinge of
conscience at the palpable relief he saw
mirrored in Alexa's lovely eyes. In the trade-
off he had suggested, he had nothing to lose
and everything to gain! But it was for her
own good, he reminded himself virtuously.
She must be got out of London and away
from the suffragettes at all costs.

"Very well," she agreed with a sigh. "I'll
go back down to Nun's Farthing. But can't
we stop by my . . . er . . . my lodging house
first so that I can pick up my belongings?"

Congratulating himself on the success of
his stratagem, Rowan was feeling relaxed
and expansive and ready to placate her. "I
don't see why not," he agreed easily. "By the
way, where you have been staying? I've

scoured half London looking for you."

"The wrong half, I expect," Alexa said lightly. "I've been with Sylvia Pankhurst . . . in the East End!"

Had he known that Alexa had taken refuge in the East End he would not have agreed so readily to returning her there, thought Rowan sourly. Rather inexpertly he drew up to the curb—he was a man more at home on the back of a restive steed than he was behind the wheel of a motorcar, but Chalmers had begged leave to go visit his ailing mother and so Rowan was, perforce, acting as his own chauffeur, a role he did not relish in the slightest. But at least, he reflected, it would give him ample opportunity to enjoy a quiet chat with Alexa as they motored down to Nun's Farthing.

If, indeed, there was anything left of the Rolls by the time they emerged from the house that was the headquarters of the East End Federation of Suffragettes. He eyed with disfavor the crowd of grimy street urchins who swarmed about the vehicle, their eyes popping out of their heads.

But when he voiced his misgivings to Alexa she said blithely, "Not to worry. We'll leave Herbert in charge." She beckoned to the same ginger-haired street urchin who had caught Rowan's eye at the demonstration. He tossed a coin to the lad and warned him to stand guard over the vehicle.

The boy's freckled face split into a broad

grin as he snatched and pocketed the coin.
"Sure thing, guv'nor."

"I'm glad the police didn't pick you up,
Herbert," Alexa observed as she descended
from the Rolls.

"Who, me?" The lad hooted. "Not likely,
miss. I knows when to take to my heels, I
do!"

"And Miss Sylvia . . . and the others?"
Alexa enquired anxiously. "Have you
heard . . . ?"

"In quod, miss. All of 'em except you and
the old lydy what was chained next to you.
Miss Sylvia . . . she announced that she was
going on a 'unger and thirst strike till the
prime minister 'imself agrees to receive her
and a . . . a deputation of suffragettes," he
volunteered.

Alexa's face fell. "Oh, dear, I was afraid of
that," she murmured despondently. Implor-
ingly, she looked up at Rowan. "I . . . I don't
suppose *you* could . . . could speak to Mr.
Asquith on her behalf?" she suggested dif-
fidently. She did not really expect an affirmative answer but he surprised her.

Rowan took one look into her lovely
anxious eyes and acknowledged himself
forever lost. "Very well," he said recklessly.
"If it means so much to you, I'll have a word
with the P.M."

"You *will*?" Her eyes glowing like stars,
Alexa threw her arms about him. "Oh,
Rowan . . . !"

"I can't promise that my opinion will hold

any weight with the Prime Minister,
though," he felt obliged to warn her. Not
nearly such an effect that her impetuous
embrace was having on him, he thought
wryly. He wanted to crush her softly
rounded form against his broad chest, to
press feather-light kisses on the lids of her
star-bright eyes, to capture those soft,
trembling lips with his own—but he was
acutely aware, as she evidently was not, of
their audience. Several pairs of youthful
eyes were gawking at them with unabashed
curiosity—not to mention numerous unseen
spectators who were doubtless peering at
them from the windows of surrounding
tenements. They were presenting a vastly
entertaining spectacle, he was sure. But even
worse, he was ruefully convinced that Alexa
did not share the powerful emotions which
gripped him—that her impulsive embrace
was no more than an expression of gratitude
and youthful enthusiasm.

But in that, he was wrong. Oh, it had begun
that way. But as she flung herself into his
arms and they automatically closed round
her to steady her, she found herself beset by
a host of totally unexpected and utterly
bewildering emotions. She found herself
reveling in the hard strength of his body and,
at the same time, was shockingly aware of
her own femininity. He was solid—so strong,
she thought dizzily, like a rock to cling to.

But what was she thinking of? She,
Alexandra Traherne, was no helpless,

hapless, clinging sort of female! She didn't
want or need any man's strength to lean on!

Her hands slid down his chest and, in spite
of herself, she thrilled to the feel of his heart
beating beneath her palms, even as she
pulled herself away and stepped out of the
shelter of his arms.

"I . . . I do beg your pardon," she said a
trifle breathlessly. "I . . . I can't think what
came over me. The . . . the excitements of the
day, perhaps . . ." she faltered.

"Undoubtedly," said Rowan dryly,
straightening the tie that Alexa had knocked
askew.

Blushing in confusion, she turned and led
the way up the steps of the house that was
headquarters for the East End Federation of
Suffragettes.

It was full of women hastily destroying
confidential papers and potentially compromising documents in imminent expectation of a police raid, and Rowan, who
thought those expectations only too likely to
be fulfilled, warned Alexa to make haste
with her packing before they found themselves swept up in a police dragnet.

It did not take her long to collect her few
belongings, but her protracted farewells to
her comrades in arms put him in a fever to
be off. He contained his impatience, however, for he could see that she had formed a
strong attachment to these toil-worn and
hard-pressed women. But at last he caught
her eye and said, half-humorously but with a

steely undertone, "My dear, if we are not to spend the night as, er, guests of His Majesty, we must be on our way."

She was forced to acknowledge the truth of this, at the same time realizing that being caught up in a police raid on suffragette headquarters would do Rowan's career no good at all and would undoubtedly go far towards dissipating his newly acquired tolerance for the Cause. So she handed the infant she had been dandling in her arms back to its mother, advising her, "You'd best go along too, Bessie. If you're thrown into Holloway, who'll look after little Davey?"

"True enough, miss," the other woman agreed. "Not but what I wouldn't go willingly if it would help the Cause, but, as you say, who would look after my little ones?" She called to an older child who was quietly sitting in a corner amusing himself with a piece of chalk and a bit of slate, and after a word of farewell to two or three other women who still remained at their task, went out, her toddler clutching at her skirt and her baby on her arm.

They followed after the little family, Alexa looking back over her shoulder a trifle wistfully. "I feel like a soldier deserting his post," she mourned. "There is so much to be done here. These women have such a harsh life and—"

"You have other responsibilities, Alexa," he reminded her. "Your mama, for example." He could not but admire her

passionate desire to help those less fortunate than herself—indeed, he reflected,
her warm and generous heart was one of the
reasons he loved her. And, in the role he ul-
timately envisioned for her—that of beneficent lady of the manor—it was entirely
appropriate that she should evince care and
concern for the unfortunate . . . misery and
misfortune were not limited to city-dwellers
and to alleviate distress was a time-honored
preoccupation of people in their position. It
was noblesse oblige. But at the moment
there were more pressing concerns.

He took her by the arm and propelled her
along to where their vehicle, proudly
guarded by Herbert, was awaiting them.
"You and the toff better 'op it, miss," he
advised cheekily, just as a police van came
careening around the corner.

Rowan was more than ready to "hop it,"
but Alexa balked. On the point of stepping
into the Rolls, the door of which Herbert was
holding open for her, she gasped, "Oh, no!
I . . . I've got to go back! I forgot
my . . . something very important!"

"Go back?" Rowan ejaculated. Had she lost
her mind? Didn't she realize the police
would be rounding up everyone in the
house? "You most certainly are not going
back!" he snarled, retaining his grip on her
arm.

"I must!" She wrenched herself away from
him and darted back to the headquarters
house, calling over her shoulder, "Wait for

me right where you are. I won't be a minute.
I promise."

How could she have forgotten her precious
brooch? she wondered as she pounded up
the stairs. She took it with her everywhere
but she hadn't been wearing it today, of
course. It would never do to flaunt pearls
and diamonds in the East End—and particularly not at a street rally! It was her most
cherished possession—prized because
Rowan had given it her—and she was not
going to leave it behind, not if she could help
it!

When she came running down the steps a
few moments later and scrambled into the
Rolls, she was carrying a small jeweler's
case which Rowan could not help but
recognize. "Do you mean to say you went
back for that . . . that trumpery bauble?" he
growled, thoroughly out of patience with
her. The police were tumbling out of the van,
blowing their whistles, and she had
narrowly escaped being picked up.

"It's not a trumpery bauble!" she panted,
clutching her hat, as with a horrible grinding
of gears they got under way. But her
pride—or something else—forbade her to
admit to him that she attached any senti-
mental value to his gift. "It's my only piece
of good jewelry," she said repressively.
"I . . . I brought it up to London with me in
case . . . in case I ran short of funds, thinking
I could always pawn it for ready money."

Something flickered in Rowan's grey eyes.

"How commendably foresighted of you!" he grated.

"Yes, it *was*, wasn't it?" she remarked coolly, tucking the case away out of sight in her overnight bag. Seeing that his face was like a thundercloud, she wondered if she hadn't gone a trifle too far in implying that she treasured his gift only for its inherent monetary value. Oh, dear, why had she let her terrible tongue run away with her? Resolving that she would not let it do so again, she lapsed into silence.

Rowan, too, was silent, devoting all his attention to negotiating the London traffic, in which horse-drawn vehicles still predominated though motorized vehicles, most of them less luxurious than his Rolls, were represented as well. There would come a time, he supposed, when the motorcar would totally replace the horse, at least in the city and its environs. It was not a time he looked forward to with enthusiasm. Oh, he could see their advantages in increased speed and sheer mobility but he privately regretted their necessity. Compared to the beauty and grace of a fine piece of horse-flesh, motorcars were noisy, chugging monsters that emitted foul-smelling exhaust and petrol fumes.

Alexa loved horses as much as he did but he could not suppose that she would agree with him. She would laugh at him—call him a fogey if he expressed such a point of view. She was enamored of all that was modern, forward-looking, progressive—without counting the costs or the losses along the way.

Left to her own devices, Alexa was lost in her own thoughts. It was the first chance she had had to ponder over the events of this event-filled day. She began to wonder what on earth had prompted Rowan to come to her rescue at the rally. Chivalry? Deeply ingrained family loyalty? Kindness of heart? Well, whatever it was, there was no doubt that he had a disconcerting way of popping up just when she needed him the most. He seemed to have a sixth sense about these things, she mused.

She would like to think that she didn't need him at all—him or any man—that she could manage very nicely on her own, thank you! But she was beginning to suspect that such was not the case. Without his timely intervention she would surely have been trampled or badly beaten by that mob of ruffians. Without his intervention she would have spent at least one uncomfortable night in Holloway. Why, he had even promised to intervene with Mama on her behalf.

There was no doubt in her mind that he would keep his word, though she was puzzled by his strange about face. It seemed curiously out of character. Well, no matter. The important thing was that Mama listen to him (she always did) and refrain from plaguing her about her lost chances to make a good match.

It was a pity, she reflected, that she could not be so obliging as to fall in love with Derek. It would have been so very suitable. He was eligible, well-born, handsome (though much less so than Rowan). And what was more to the point, he was good-natured and easygoing and would have made a complaisant and fondly indulgent husband. Just the sort she could lead about by the nose!

But she had no regrets. She *could* not give him her heart, and, failing that, she *would* not give him her hand!

Good heavens! It . . . it couldn't be because . . . because she had already fallen in love, could it? Fallen head over heels in love with Rowan?

Oh, no, no, surely not, she thought feverishly. Why, the very idea was absurd.

To begin with, he had such inconvenient and old-fashioned views on the role of women—views which he did seem to be modifying, to be sure, but still . . .

And then there was his overpowering, domineering personality—he was ever seeking to dominate her and she would not be dominated!

Besides, nothing could come of it. Because there was Lady Wyndham. And before her there had been a string of other sophisticated Society ladies, she had heard. And she could never tolerate playing second fiddle to another woman. She was not like her Mama who had borne so patiently with Papa's foibles and follies!

And what about the plans she had recently made for her future? Plans which were very dear to her heart but in which no man—and especially not a man like Rowan—could play a part.

No—it was inconceivable that she could be in love with him—and if she had been so foolish as to do so, the very best thing for her to do was root that love right out of her heart before it brought her untold grief and misery. Not for nothing had she watched Mama suffering from Papa's neglect and even cruelty! She had learned a lesson then that she would never ever forget. Never would she let herself be trapped in a similar situation, she vowed. It was better to maintain one's self-sufficiency—to walk forever alone—than to break one's heart over a man that other women found irresistible!

Which brought her to the single most important reason why she could not—must not—be in love with Rowan. That he did not love her! And he never would, she decided moodily, because he could have virtually any woman he wanted—some of the most beautiful and desirable women in London—merely by snapping his fingers. Her, she was miserably convinced, he saw only as a tiresome, troublesome little chit for whom he had an exaggerated sense of responsibility.

Well, she would relieve him of that responsibility as soon as she could. It fitted in

nicely with the plans she had been for-
mulating for her future—a future that did
not include Rowan and suddenly seemed to
her intolerably drab. But she could find self-
fulfillment, of a sort, in her project; it had
the advantage of rendering her independent
of family ties; it would provide her with
plentiful mental and physical challenges that
would, in time, enable her to forget this
foolish fancy she had conceived for him.

All she had to do was assure him that she
had set her heart upon the scheme and convince him of its feasibility. Doubtless, she
mused, he would raise objections at first but
when he realized that she was in earnest and
that it would relieve him of his family
obligations towards her, he would come
round.

She resolved to broach the subject to him
at the very first opportunity.

It came sooner than she had expected.

They stopped for a meal at a country inn in
a charming village halfway between the city
and their destination. Despite her pertur-
bation of mind, Alexa ate heartily for she had
skipped her luncheon and missed her tea.
Rowan, too, did full justice to the refresh-
ments provided—a crusty cottage loaf,
spread with fresh butter; ham and cheese
and pickles, followed by rhubarb tart and
several cups of freshly brewed tea.

At last Rowan sat back, comfortably
replete, and watched her demolish the last
rhubarb tart with amusement in his eyes.

"And this is the lady who yearns to go on hunger-strike," he chaffed her gently with mock wonder. "I've seen half-starved troopers tuck away less."

"Not by choice but for the Cause," Alexa reminded him, chasing crumbs around her plate. "I never said I didn't like my food!"

She eyed him thoughtfully over her mug of tea. He was well-fed, relaxed and expansive, and in good enough humor to tease her . . . now was the perfect opportunity to sound him out. Strike while the iron is hot, Alexa, she told herself nervously.

She put down her cup and said hesitatingly, "Rowan . . . I . . . there's something I'd like to discuss with you."

"Hmm?" He was fishing a cigar from its gold monogrammed case and looked up at her quizzically. "Oh, do you mind . . . ?"

"No . . . no. Go ahead and smoke. I rather like the aroma, actually," she said ingenuously. And she did. The aroma of fine cigars which often clung to his clothing was one she had come to associate with him and seemed to enhance his innate masculinity.

She waited until he had applied a light to the tip of the cheroot and had taken a puff.

"Well?" he said encouragingly.

She took a deep breath. "I . . . I've been wondering . . . that is . . ." she said haltingly, "how long do you expect me to stay down at Nun's Farthing?"

The question was not unexpected and he was ready with an answer. "As long as is necessary for you to ease your mama's mind," he said promptly. The implication that her visit need not be prolonged should satisfy her, he considered, yet was sufficiently vague to suit him. For himself, he was quite determined that she should stay down in the country until he had won her heart.

But he was not going to give away too much too soon. If the little chit had any inkling of the true state of affairs, she would do her damndest to wind him round her little finger! Involve him ever deeper in the Cause that was so dear to her heart, and God only knew what else. Just because he loved her didn't mean he was going to relinquish the upper hand! Or regain it, once lost, he thought ruefully.

So he said mildly, "The summer can be quite pleasant in the country, Alexa. I'm taking a leave of absence from the Foreign Office to spend a few weeks at Nun's Farthing. And once the commotion over your presentation has died down, I see no reason why you and your mama should be deprived of some of the pleasures of the Season. Ascot, perhaps? And the Regatta at Henley. Would you like that?"

Would she not? Alexa bit her lip. It was a tempting prospect, spending long lazy summer days down at Nun's Farthing with Rowan and enjoying the delights of Royal Ascot and the Regatta, of which she had heard much but never seen. But such shared pleasures would inevitably bind her to him and increase the heartache when the time came to part. As part they must. For she had to look to her future and so did Rowan. One of these days he would be bringing a bride home to Nun's Farthing and how would she feel then? An unwanted third party—a spinster cousin. The thought was intolerable.

She summoned all her resolve and said politely, "It . . . it sounds very pleasant, Rowan, but . . . but you see I have made other plans."

His brows rose even as his face darkened. "May I ask what they might be?" he said with resignation. He had a notion that her plans and his would not coincide at all.

She drew a deep breath and plunged in. "The . . . the thing is, Rowan, while I was staying in the East End I . . . I became aware of . . . of how much misery there is in the world and . . . and I want to do my bit to alleviate it. But . . . but . . . I also realized how little I know . . . how poorly prepared I am to deal with it—"

"Indeed!" Rowan's dark face was inscrutable. This was most unlike Alexa, who did not, he thought, suffer from false modesty. But if a brief stay in the East End had served to convince her that she could not right the wrongs of the world singlehandedly, so much the better. But what was she getting at anyway?

"Cut the cackle and come to the horses," he said impatiently.

Flustered, she blurted out, "I have decided that I need training. I . . . I want to train as a nurse!" There—it was said. She eyed him warily.

"A *nurse*!" Rowan choked over his cigar.

"It's a perfectly respectable profession these days!" she said defensively. "And has been so ever since the days of Florence Nightingale!"

"Good God, Alexa!" he burst out in irritation. "What will you think of next? First you want to emulate the Pankhursts and now you fancy yourself a latter-day Florence Nightingale!"

"But it's all of a piece, don't you see?" she said reasonably. "The suffragettes' aim is to better the lot of women by obtaining political equality. But you object to my involvement with the Cause. And . . . and perhaps you are right. Perhaps acquiring the vote will not materially alter the lives of women. There is so much that needs to be done. And I can do it—some of it—by becoming a nurse!" Seeing his face darken, she added desperately, "I must *do something* with my life Rowan! And . . . and I am not likely to marry, as you and Mama have been at pains to remind me."

"Not to marry well, perhaps," he retorted unkindly. "I daresay a poverty-stricken curate or a struggling young medico might not be put off by an inveterate do-gooder such as yourself!"

"Well, there, you see!" she said

triumphantly. "How much more appealing I would be to such a one if I had proper training."

Rowan sighed. "I will think about it, Alexa. And now," he crushed out his cigar and stood up, "we must be on our way."

As he followed her out, her reflected, not for the first time, that winning Alexa's heart would be the most difficult challenge he had ever faced. How much easier it would be, he mused, if his rival were merely another man like himself—a man of flesh and blood. But Alexa was in love with no other—she was in love with an ideal. Could he woo her away from it? he wondered. Only time would tell.

Chapter 11

As it happened, the fates conspired to give him a helping hand.

The sky, which had been lowering all afternoon, had come on to drizzle while they were at their meal and they dashed back to the Rolls through a spattering of raindrops. Another woman might have made a fuss at getting a wetting, Rowan reflected, as they ducked into the vehicle, but Alexa merely laughed, delightedly turning her face up to the misty rain like a thirsty flower. But not, he thought ruefully, a sweet old-fashioned variety of flower—oh, no, not Alexa—she was one of the new, thoroughly modern hybrids.

Take this new maggot she had got into her brain—that of training for a nurse, a profession for which, in his opinion, she was totally unsuited. She simply did not realize the dedication and self-discipline such training would require—he was convinced of that.

But he knew her quite well enough by now to be assured that direct opposition to the scheme would only serve to strengthen her resolve. Once she made up her mind to pursue a certain course of action, she possessed, he knew, a determination and strength of will fully as strong as his own.

It was not, he mused, that he wanted to clip her wings altogether. Merely that he wanted to protect her from all that was unpleasant or distasteful. A gently bred young woman such as Alexa should not be exposed to the seamier side of life—to ugliness and illnesses and human mortality.

But it would not be easy to turn her aside from this new scheme, and perhaps the best he could do was lend his countenance to it in the hope (if not the expectation) that after a few weeks of drudgery she would give it up as a childish whim. In time perhaps some more satisfactory solution to the problem would present itself. In time he could prevail upon her to see him in the light of a sweetheart, a lover, rather than a tiresome, naysaying older cousin.

The rain had not abated and now, above the pattering of raindrops on the roof, sounding like impatiently drumming fingers, a new sound could be heard—the rumble of thunder. Alexa glanced at him nervously and almost imperceptibly slid along

the seat in order to be closer to him, but he
was too preoccupied to notice.

They were still a goodish distance from
home when the heavens opened up and the
sky spilled down torrents. Rowan slowed his
vehicle to a crawl, then opened the window
and craned his head out, for the torrents of
rain splashing down on the windscreen
severely limited visibility.

He was making fair progress, giving all his
attention to the road ahead, when a loud clap
of thunder resounded, heralding an even
more horrendous downpour. With a squeak
of alarm, Alexa clutched his arm and the
vehicle slewed sideways, its wheels spinning
on the slimy road surface.

Rowan disengaged his arm from Alexa's
desperately clutching fingers. "What in hell
did you do that for?" he barked as their
vehicle went into a skid.

"Do what?" Alexa squeaked.

"Oh, never mind!" With a muttered curse,
Rowan fought to regain control of the car.
And then, in a flash, as in a flash of lightning,
it came to him how he might turn this near
accident to good account and he relinquish-
ed his regained control and allowed the
vehicle to slide gently into the drainage ditch
at the side of the road where it sank to the
fenders.

Because the vehicle was tilted at a slight
angle, Alexa found herself slithering to the
far side of the seat. Rowan caught at her
before she could bruise herself against the

door. "Wh-what happened?" she gasped.

"It appears," said Rowan quietly, "that we're stuck."

"St-stuck?"

"In the mud," he confirmed. "No doubt about it . . . we're stuck."

"Well . . . aren't you going to . . . to *do* something?" she asked, her voice rising.

What, he wondered, had happened to women's equality? Obviously, the onus of *doing something* had been squarely placed on his admittedly broad shoulders.

"What do you suggest I do?" he enquired with deep interest.

"We-e-ll . . . um . . . shouldn't you . . . ah . . . get out and . . . and push?"

"In case you haven't noticed," he pointed out, "it's raining!"

"Don't tell me you're afraid of getting wet!" she retorted. She turned her back on him sharply and peered out the window on the passenger side, but dusk had come on early and the window was streaked with rain and she could see nothing. "Maybe if we *both* got out and pushed . . ." she suggested hopefully.

"My dear, we are already in so deep it will take a team of draft horses to pull us out. I may have more than my share of physical strength but not, alas, as much as a good team of shires. And as for the puny bit you could contribute . . ." He laughed softly. Seeing her downcast expression, he added consolingly, "If I remember rightly, tomorrow is market day. I daresay a farmer or two will be along at the crack of dawn hauling his produce to market and we can enlist his aid."

"*Tomorrow*!" Alexa gasped. "But . . . but we can't stay here all night!"

"I don't see what else we *can* do," Rowan said reasonably. "Unless, of course, a farmer with a good strong team should happen along sometime during the night. But I shouldn't pin my hopes on that if I were you," he said kindly.

He slid down in his seat and tipped his hat over his face. "I don't see why we shouldn't be quite comfortable. We're well-fed and won't starve by morning, and in any case I have some chocolate we can share and my pocket flask. And the Rolls is warm and dry and sufficiently roomy for us to stretch out." He suited his action to his words, easing his long legs out from behind the wheel.

Alexa eyed him askance. "But isn't there *anything* we can *do*?" she cried, in a fever of impatience to take action of some kind, no matter how futile.

He rolled a lazy-lidded eye at her. "It's been quite a strenuous day," he observed mildly. "If I were you, I should have a nap." And with that, he pulled his hat down over his face even further and composed himself for slumber.

"A . . . a nap!" Alexa stared at him in consternation. How *could* he be so calm . . . so blasé . . . so insouciant! Didn't he realize they were stranded?

She ground her teeth in frustration. There must be something she could do . . . there must be!

She eyed her companion disdainfully. How *could* he be so poor-spirited? His attitude was perplexing in the extreme. Ordinarily, Rowan was not a man to take setbacks so calmly. He was not one to bow to circumstances, any more than she.

Puzzling over it, she frowned. Why, it was . . . it was almost as if he were enjoying their predicament!

Well, she was not! And she was going to do something about it or die trying! She opened the car door a fraction, thereby letting in a gust of rain and wind.

Rowan opened a lazy eye and said lightly, but with a hint of steel in his voice, "Going somewhere, Alexa?"

"Yes," she said fiercely. "I'm going to summon help." With a toss of her head, she added, "Since you are so . . . so poor-spirited!"

He reached a long arm across her and shut the passenger door firmly against the driving wind and rain. "Don't you have sense enough to stay in out of the rain!" he grated.

"We . . . we . . . just can't stay here all night!" she retorted desperately. "Even . . . even though we are cousins, it . . . it is in the highest degree improper . . ." she blurted.

Rowan threw back his handsome head and laughed long and loud. "Don't tell me that *you*, of all people, Alexa, are worried about the conventions," he said mockingly.

Her face reddened. On the surface, her sudden concern for the proprieties must appear absurd, she realized. But it cloaked a very real disinclination to spend a night alone with him in the close confines of the vehicle. It was . . . it was *too* close . . . too confining.

She shifted uncomfortably in her seat, feeling somewhat overwhelmed by his sheer physical presence. All of her senses were intensely aware of him. Her nerve endings tingled with that awareness; an awareness that kindled strange, fiery feelings within her; feelings she was almost entirely unacquainted with. For almost the first time, she saw him as a magnetic and disturbingly masculine man and herself as a woman capable of being aroused to passion, and she didn't know how to cope with it.

Except that she mustn't let him see how she felt. Goodness, no! Because, of course, he didn't see her as a woman at all. Not, at any rate, as a passionately desiring and desirable woman. Oh, no! He saw her only as his tiresome, troublesome little cousin. And that being the case, he naturally didn't see anything improper in their spending the night together, stranded as they were.

He was looking at her with a quizzical expression, and, embarrassed, she mumbled unhappily, "You ... you're quite wrong, Rowan. I ... I have never defied the conventions out of bravado or ... or to satisfy a whim but ... but out of conviction and ... and for a purpose!" Which was not exactly accurate but ...

"Well, it is *my* conviction that no good purpose can be achieved by dashing around in the dark getting drenched to the skin," he said briskly. "No farmer in his right mind is going to leave his snug fireplace on a night like tonight to come to our assistance when tomorrow morning would do as well. I suppose we *might* be able to find more comfortable accommodations—a farmhouse or a village inn—but we would surely get soaked in doing so. It hardly seems worthwhile. As for the proprieties," he added, "I daresay some way can be found to satisfy them." A curious little smile played about his lips as he spoke.

Alexa looked unconvinced, but a sudden loud clap of thunder followed by a burst of rain dispelled all argument, even as it sent a convulsive shiver quivering through her slender frame.

Rowan frowned. "Are you feeling chilly?" Despite her almost instantaneous denial, he stretched a long arm into the rear seat and drew forth a lap robe which he unfolded and proceeded to tuck round her solicitously.

The damp *did* get into one's very bones, he mused, pouring a tot of brandy into the cap of the flask and handing it to her. "Here, drink up. It's for medicinal purposes," he said encouragingly.

But Alexa, remembering her former disastrous experience with strong drink, refused it. A few weeks ago, under the influence of a few sips of brandy, she had become pot-valiant and accused him of being stuffy and pompous, and then he . . . he . . . she shook her head in refusal, fearing to become loose-lipped again. What she might not blurt out under the influence of a capful of the potent liquor, she shuddered to think.

"I'm not cold and I don't need any medicine," she said pettishly.

But he held the cap to her lips and insisted that she swallow a sip or two, claiming that it would ward off a chill.

"If you're not chilled, why are you shivering?" he demanded with inexorable logic as little tremors of nervous apprehension quivered through her in response to another ominous rumble of thunder. The rumble, at first a deep, heavy, reverberating sound, turned into a deafening clamor almost directly overhead, very nearly drowning out Rowan's words.

It was Alexa's undoing. "Be-because I'm f-frightened!" she wailed, casting reticence to the winds and herself into his arms. A streak of lightning split the sky, illuminating the interior of the vehicle, and she burrowed her head against his broad shoulder in an attempt to shut out its glare.

His arms closed round her automatically,

his big hands patting her back and stroking her hair soothingly. "Frightened!" he ejaculated in amazement. It was inconceivable to him that indomitable Alexa could be so terrified of natural phenomena like thunder and lightning. Other women . . . lesser women, yes, but not Alexa!

"But you used not to be," he said, puzzled, for he remembered Alexa as a naturally courageous, not to say downright foolhardy child, who rejoiced in being out in all kinds of wind and weather.

"I never was . . . until . . ." she paused, deeply ashamed of herself for revealing such a childish fear to him . . . ashamed that such fears had the power of reducing her to a quivering bowl of jelly. She sniffed against this shoulder that was so broad, so comforting.

"Yes . . . go on . . ." he said encouragingly.

"It happened when I was perhaps eight or nine," Alexa said haltingly. "Papa had brought a shooting party down for the weekend. I begged to be allowed to go out with the guns but, of course, it wasn't allowed."

"I should think not!" said Rowan with feeling. He knew what these big shooting parties consisted of—the slaughter of hundreds of pheasants, specifically raised for the purpose and driven out of their coverts by beaters while loaders stood by, loading guns for the gentlemen sportsmen—guns which often grew too hot to handle as the day wore on. He himself had a quick, keen eye and was accounted a

superior marksman who usually brought
home a full bag, but he avoided such parties
whenever possible for he considered it tame
sport.

Alexa ignored his interruption. She was
lost in thought . . . in memory.

"After lessons with Miss Pringle, I . . . I
ran away. She . . . she thought I was with
Nanny, and Nanny, I suppose, thought I was
still in the schoolroom. But I was lured by
the sound of the guns and I wanted to see
what was going on. I . . . I wanted to see what
it was all about and . . . and I did." Alexa
shuddered. "All those poor dead birds,
Rowan, staring with their glassy eyes. And
the noise! Close up, it was deafening."

He nodded, knowing it was not unusual for
members of a shooting party to suffer a
temporary loss of hearing after a day spent
in the field.

"It was . . . it was horrible! I was terribly
frightened by the thunder of the guns . . . and
the sky seemed to be raining death and destruction. One of the birds came down quite
near me and I . . . I stooped and picked it up.
It was quite dead; its head was hanging limp
yet its claws kept opening and shutting . . .
by some reflex action, I suppose." Alexa
shuddered in his arms. "It was dreadful.
I . . . I dropped the bird and ran . . . ran away
as fast as I could."

"I don't understand how it was that no one
saw you," interjected Rowan with a frown.

"I suppose because they were all looking

up at the sky. And you must remember that I
was skulking about trying not to be seen. In
any event, by that time I was so frightened
and confused by the booming of the guns
that I ran deep into the woods. All I could
think of was getting away from that place of
noise and death and killing. I ran on and on,
losing all sense of direction, but I couldn't
get away from the thunder of the guns."

"You ran in circles?" guessed Rowan.

"Possibly," she agreed. "But in time, I
realized that the booming noise really *was*
thunder. That a storm had blown up and I
was lost and all alone." She shivered convulsively, though whether at the recollection
of a long-dormant childhood fear or at the
reverberating drum roll of yet another heart-
pounding clap of thunder, he could not
know.

"There's nothing to be frightened of,
Alexa," he said reassuringly, stroking her
bright hair with a gentle hand. "You're not
alone any more, my dear."

Indeed she was not. As his big hand
caressed her face, his fingertips lightly
toying with the lobes of her ears, her cheeks
flamed with color. She had never before
known that it was possible to be as aware of
another human being to the very ends of her
nerves as she was of Rowan at that moment.
Though as to whether or not there was any
need to be frightened—of that she was not so
sure!

"What happened after that?" he prompted

her.

Alexa marshaled her wool-gathering thoughts. "Oh, I . . . I wandered around for what seemed like hours, though it was probably only a few minutes. Finally I stumbled onto a little hut used by the gamekeepers to raise partridge chicks. I took shelter in it just before the storm broke, huddling there out of the rain. When it was all over, one of the keepers found me and took me back to Nanny. She'd got the wind up by then and had sent all the estate workers out looking for me. I . . . I told her I'd gone for a walk in the woods and got caught in the storm. It's odd but I never told her or anyone else about going out with the guns and the dead birds and all . . ." Alexa sighed. "I've always tried to conceal my irrational fear of thunder; it's so silly, just as if I were a simpering Victorian miss," she said with sudden self-disgust. As if only aware of it for the first time, she tried to squirm out of his embrace, but his arms held her fast. "I . . . I'm afraid I've made an awful fool of myself," she murmured.

"Not at all," Rowan said promptly. "Everyone has something he or she fears, Alexa. Some special fear peculiarly horrifying to that individual, for one reason or another. Perhaps yours won't seem quite so overpowering now that you've brought yourself to share it with me." He glanced assessingly at the sky. "In any case, this particular storm seems to be moving off. I

daresay we won't see or hear any more fire-
works tonight. It'll probably settle down to a
steady, soaking, all-night rain. If I were you,
I'd try to relax and get some sleep," he
advised. "Everything will look brighter in
the morning."

"Will it, Rowan?"

"Bound to," he assured her optimistically,
hoping that his optimism was not un-
justified. He had an inkling that when she
learned exactly what he had in mind for her,
she would go straight through the roof! It
was, he supposed, a trifle unscrupulous of
him to take advantage of the plight in which
they found themselves, but he was not the
man to let a few scruples stand in the way of
what he wanted—and he wanted Alexa!

Looking down at her bright head which
drooped against his shoulder like a battered
flower on the delicate stem of her slender
neck, he felt overwhelmed by a passionate
spasm of protective tenderness. She didn't
love him—not yet—but he was convinced
that he could teach her to do so—his prickly
little rose that was not without her thorns.
She was such a feisty little thing—so fiercely
determined to prove and maintain her independence—but she needed him. He was convinced of that! And, one day, she must
acknowledge it.

Alexa leaned drowsily against him,
thinking it was unlikely that she would be
able to follow his excellent advice and go to
sleep. Rowan had a disconcerting way of

bringing her untried senses to life, she
mused, peeping up through her thickly
curling lashes at his darkly handsome
profile. She felt acutely conscious of the
virile appeal of his hard male body which
cocooned her in an invisible and extraordinarily comforting warmth—a warmth
that presently lulled her into a kind of
drugged euphoria. His broad shoulder was a
remarkably comfortable pillow, she thought
sleepily, with a little secret smile of
satisfaction. Gradually, as the steady rhythm
of his breathing and the regular beat of his
heart replaced the now-distant rumble of
thunder, her lids began to droop. Before
long, it combined with the steady pit-pat of
rain on the roof to lull her to sleep.

Violet shadows rimmed her closed eyes,
the circles darkened by the crescent
shadows cast by her long, curling lashes.
Her exhaustion was also marked by the deep
rise and fall of her breathing.

Rowan curved his long arm around her
slender waist, drawing her ever closer to fit
the curve of his body, and buried his face in
her bright and shining hair, inhaling deeply
of its sweet, clean fragrance. Paradoxically,
now that she was asleep he found himself
longing to waken her from slumber, to
arouse her with a thousand warm-lipped
kisses and caresses, to stoke the banked fires
of his own suppressed passion. But he was
equally loath to break the spell he had
himself induced.

Before long, she would be his, wholly and completely, he reminded himself. He had only to contain himself with patience and fortitude until . . .

With a smothered smile, he bent and brushed featherweight kisses, light as a benediction, over the lids of Alexa's closed eyes, and then, settling back in the seat, composed himself for slumber.

The last to fall asleep, Rowan was the first to awaken, perhaps because a shaft of strong sunlight was streaming across his handsome face and closed eyelids, perhaps because the arm and shoulder with which he was supporting her recumbent form had gone numb.

Alexa slumped against him, still deep in dreamland, and he sat up carefully, trying not to disturb her, as he carefully withdrew his arm from around her and rubbed it briskly to restore the circulation.

Despite his caution, the brisk movements of his arm swinging to relieve the pins-and-needles sensation startled her, and her whisky-colored eyes popped open in alarm. "Wh-where am I?" she mumbled, looking around her in bewilderment.

"It's all right." He spoke soothingly. "It's just the morning after . . . we went off the road last night. Don't you remember?"

Alexa blinked and knuckled her sleepy eyes like a child. Rowan eyed her thoughtfully. "I wonder if you have any notion how sweetly defenseless you look when you are asleep?" he teased.

She had not, and, like many other people, was inclined to be a little pettish when suddenly awakened. Nor did she relish the thought of his finding her vulnerable. And as memory came flooding back, she flushed with shame, remembering her self-revelatory confidences of the night before.

Sitting up with a sudden jerk, she snapped, "No more so than anyone else, I trust!" Desperately, she wished that she had been the first to awaken. She felt terribly ill at ease, groggy and disoriented, and was sure she looked a fright. Distractedly, she smoothed her tangled hair into a semblance of order with her fingers, sneaking a glance at Rowan out of the corner of her eye. Plainly, she thought with resentment, he was one of those tiresome people who wake up all at once and all of a piece and totally in command of himself. Whereas she, even on the best and brightest of mornings, when she waked up properly in her own bed, was an utter wreck until she'd had her first cup of tea.

But there seemed no prospect of early morning tea today, and she squinted in the bright sunlight and snarled, "Are you always so cheery so early in the morning?"

Her crankiness seemed to amuse him. A provoking grin split his swarthy face and, filled with an extraordinary sense of well-being, he said recklessly, "Invariably. But that need not worry you. I shan't expect my wife to be. You can lie in as late as you wish and I'll bring you a cup of tea or coffee as a pick-me-up . . . when we're married!"

Alexa's sleepy eyes went round and wide. "M-married!" she gasped. "Wh-what d-do you mean . . . m-married?"

Chapter
12

"Married!" Her voice was still husky from sleep—or was it that her heart had leaped into her throat? Whatever the reason, the word came out in a tortured squawk. She cleared her throat and tried again, as if she had never heard the word before and felt under a compulsion to try it—to taste it on her tongue—"Mar-married!"

There was a long, tension-fraught pause. Finally, "You . . . you must be joking," she essayed feebly.

Rowan stiffened. "It is scarcely a matter that lends itself to levity, Alexa," he reproached her with a hint of his former pomposity. "Surely you realize that you have been hopelessly compromised."

"C-c-compromised?" she stuttered.

"Beyond redemption," he said flatly. "We spent the night together quite unchaperoned.

Your reputation, which, may I remind you, is not altogether spotless, will be in tatters after this—er—episode. You will be utterly ruined. I am offering you the *amende honorable.*"

"But . . . but we were stranded through no fault of our own!" she all but wailed. "It . . . it was unavoidable. There was nothing we could do to prevent it. You . . . you said so, yourself!"

"I also said that some way would be found to satisfy the proprieties," he reminded her. "And this is the only way."

"B-b-but . . ." Alexa began.

Rowan shushed her, lifting his head and listening intently. His keen ears detected something that Alexa was too bemused to notice—the far-off jingle of a horse harness.

"Aha! Just as I predicted—a rescuer!" he remarked with satisfaction and, pushing open the door, slid out from behind the wheel.

Alexa scrambled out after him. "B-but . . . but . . . Rowan . . ."

"Not *now*, Alexa," he said in the offhand way one addresses an importunate child. "Can't you see I'm busy?"

She stared after him indignantly as he slogged up the muddy lane to hail the driver of a team of dapple-greys that hove into sight, conveying a load of live produce to market, judging by the cackles, squeals, and grunts that emitted from the crated occupants of the wagon bed. Absently, she watched as Rowan and the drover engaged in a brief colloquy. Then she saw Roman leap lithely onto the wagon and it proceeded down the road to the spot where their more luxurious vehicle was bogged down. Both men jumped down and set about attaching a tow rope to the stranded Rolls, not without many a chuckle at their plight from the ruddy-faced farmer.

But she saw all this as if in a daze, for her mind was seething with activity and much more concerned with her own far more precarious plight.

Amende honorable, indeed! she thought with a sniff. If only . . . if only Rowan had *asked* her to marry him instead of *telling* her in that high-handed fashion . . . why, she would be the happiest girl in the world, she thought disconsolately. If only he had breathed one little word of tenderness . . . of love.

But he didn't love her. Of course he did not! He had a certain regard for her—felt a certain sense of responsibility for her because she was his cousin, and that was all there was to it. He was grimly determined to do the right thing by her—like a . . . a conscientious second footman who had got a housemaid In Trouble, she thought with shame.

But Rowan hadn't got her In Trouble. In point of fact, nothing had happened last night. Well—almost nothing. To be sure, they had slept in each other's arms but it had been totally innocent. Alexa might not know much about the intimate relationships of men and women but she was not totally naive. She was quite sure that there was more to intimacy than that, though everyone, she thought discontentedly, had conspired to keep her innocent, or rather, ignorant of the facts.

Nevertheless, by the tenents of the society in which they lived, she would be ruined if word got out about their spending the night together unchaperoned, whether anything had happened or not. Rowan was quite right about that, she acknowledged gloomily. Even marriage would hardly restore her reputation—yet marriage was her only protection.

It didn't seem fair to Rowan, she pondered. To let him pull her chestnuts out of the fire. To salvage her reputation for her. She was quite well aware that she was not the wife he would have chosen had circumstances not forced his hand. He needed a wife who would never put him out of countenance by her impulsive or indecorous behavior as she had so often done. He needed a wife who was loving and dutiful and submissive.

She could not quite see herself as becoming dutiful and submissive, no matter how hard she tried! And as for love . . . oh, dear, she had never meant to fall in love with anyone, least of all Rowan, but she had! And now that he was offering her marriage—

though for the wrong reason—could she
bring herself to refuse him?

She very much doubted that she had the
strength of will to oppose him, especially
since it was so much against her own in-
clination. Because, in spite of their differences, she wanted to be his wife more
than she had ever wanted anything in her
life. She wanted him to be the one to introduce her to all the unmentionable mysteries
of marriage; she wanted to fall asleep in his
arms as she had last night and she wanted to
wake up in them every morning of her life.

Oh, it would be inexpressibly sweet—if
only he loved her, she thought wistfully. If
only he didn't feel obliged to marry her in
order to protect her good name—which was
his name too, and no doubt the reason he felt
so strongly on the subject.

Well, even if he didn't love her as she
wished he would, she was quite sure of one
thing—that she could trust him never to hurt
and shame her as Papa had shamed Mama. If
Rowan kept a mistress he would not flaunt
the other woman in her face—he would be a
model of discretion. And she, on her part,
must never burden him with her love or hang
on him in an unseemly fashion as if . . . as if
they had made a love match.

It was ironic, she thought, that she, who
was so determined to marry only for love,
would do so . . . while the man she loved was
marrying her only because he felt duty
bound!

"Wool-gathering, Alexa?"

She started in surprise, so deep in thought that she was scarcely aware that the drover's sturdy team had performed its rescue mission and was clip-clopping down the road while their own mud-caked vehicle was once more on terra firma, its motor idling in readiness to continue their journey.

She turned a white, pinched face to Rowan, whose heart smote him at her evident distress. It was, perhaps, a scurvy trick he had played on her but, he rationalized with a shrug, it was for her own good. And they were in too deep now to back off. Gossip spread like wildfire and he knew their rescuer could be relied on to spread the word of their plight in market and pub. By nightfall everyone in the district would know they had spent the night together.

When they were under way again, he said, "I gather you've been giving some thought to our—er—our predicament."

"Yes," she said tonelessly. "I have."

"And . . . ?"

"Yes." She turned her head to look up at that hard, swarthy but handsome face, so firmly set. "Yes. I will marry you, Rowan."

He had not expected capitulation to come so easily and he very nearly sent them slewing into the ditch again.

Mama was overjoyed and bewildered by turns, but, on the whole, much too relieved that her tempestuous daughter's future was

settled at last to question their decision. She
happily went about making wedding plans,
aided and abetted by Rowan, who displayed
an eagerness to put his neck in the matrimonial noose that positively astonished
Alexa. She was puzzled but put it down to the
man's usual unflagging zeal to achieve that,
or any goal he had set for himself.

Rowan went so far as to suggest that he
obtain a special license so they could
be married immediately—a suggestion
promptly vetoed by Mama because of its
unseemly haste. It would take at least a
month to make arrangements and equip
Alexa with a trousseau, she argued, and in
that time the banns could be read in the
normal fashion.

In the end, the wedding date was set for
June 28 and an announcement sent to the
Times. Thereafter, Rowan rolled like a
juggernaut over opposition or delays as he
encountered them, involving himself in the
wedding plans to a degree that was unusual
in a bridegroom. Alexa found herself swept
along with the tide, caught up in a whirlwind
of preparations so that she hardly knew
whether she was on her head or her heels.
She was unusually subdued, whisked along
by the plans Rowan had set in motion, too
dazed by it all to know whether she was
happy or unhappy. She felt benumbed—in a
trance.

Occasionally, when pressed to make a
decision, she emerged from the fog that en-

veloped her, as when Mama and Rowan were debating the merits of two rival candidates who claimed the honor of giving the bride away. In the normal course of events, that honor would have fallen to Rowan as her nearest male relative on her father's side of the family, but as that was, of course, out of the question, the choice fell between gouty great-uncle Humphrey and her eccentric and dipsomaniac cousin Geoffrey, both from her mother's side of the family.

Mama opted for Uncle Humphrey (despite his limp) while Rowan felt that Cousin Geoff represented the lesser of two evils. "He's presentable enough until the champagne starts to flow and that won't be till *after* the ceremony," said Rowan with brutal frankness.

Mama sighed. "Which do you prefer, dear?"

"Neither of them," replied Alexa with a flash of her old spirit. "I will give myself away!" she declared.

Mama looked helplessly at Rowan whose eyes were twinkling with merriment. "Entirely appropriate for a suffragette bride," he commented approvingly.

"Oh, dear," sighed Mama. "It will be such a . . . a peculiar wedding, one feels. No one to give the bride away and only one bridesmaid—Lucinda."

"If Lucy isn't enough I shall ask some of my suffragette friends," threatened Alexa. "Annie Kenney, the Lancashire mill girl, perhaps. And Sylvia Pankhurst . . . if she's out of prison in time."

Mama subsided.

With the wedding preparations well in hand, Rowan decreed that it was time to attempt Alexa's social regeneration. That her own folly had deprived her of her "coming-out" ball and its attendant gaieties was no reason to deprive her of the pleasures of "the Season" or to deprive himself of the pleasure of escorting his beautiful bride-to-be to certain select social functions.

He chose Royal Ascot as *the* social event most likely to appeal to horse-loving Alexa. It was the classic flat-race meeting of the season, but more than that it was a social occasion of great elegance—a colorful fashion parade in which Society ladies vied with each other to make an appearance dressed in the highest possible fashion. If this was too frivolous an occasion to suit high-minded Alexa, she could, Rowan reflected, salve her social conscience by reflecting upon the prosperity that the fashion-conscious brought to couturiers, dressmakers, seamstresses and milliners.

It did not, however, take any particular persuasiveness on Rowan's part to convince Alexa to put aside her scruples and accompany her fiancé to Ascot. The four-day-long extravaganza was the perfect occasion to bring out her dis-used debutante finery. Moreover, she anticipated a distinctly feminine pleasure in flaunting the great square-cut emerald set with diamond chips that adorned the third finger of her left hand.

Thoughtfully, she twisted it on her finger this way and that to catch the sun's rays, delighting in its sparkle. Rowan had gone up to town specially for it and had slipped it onto her finger one evening as they were strolling together on the stone-flagged terrace in the moonlight.

She had turned away from him to bend and sniff the sweetly scented gillyflowers that sent up their alluring fragrance from beds bordering the terrace. While she was thus occupied, Rowan plucked from his breast pocket a small velvet-covered jeweler's box and thumbed the catch open.

"Ooh!" Alexa, who had swung round to offer him a blossom to tuck into his button-hole, stopped short, her eyes widening. "Oh, Rowan . . ." she whispered. "It's . . . it's beautiful! I never saw anything half so beautiful!"

Her hand was half-upraised to offer him the delicate little gillyflower. He relieved her of it, tucked it in as a boutonniere, and then slipped the ring onto her finger.

"It's a perfect fit!" she marveled, holding out her hand, fingers spread wide, to catch the gleam and glitter of the gemstones in the moonlight. "However did you know the right size?"

"Your mama," he explained with tender

amusement, watching as she turned and twisted her hand to catch the light. On impulse, he caught the little hand and carried it to his chest where her fingers splayed out over his immaculate white shirt and dinner jacket. Beneath the material, Alexa felt the strong, steady rhythm of his heartbeat, and her own heart began to throb.

"I claim the privilege of a betrothal kiss, Alexa," he murmured huskily and bent his head to meet the soft sweet lips she turned up to him even as he drew her into the circle of his arms. Her gently rounded curves melded to the contours of his hard, muscular frame as she felt his hands explore the hollows of her back and waist. His touch, so firm and persuasive, made the blood course through her veins like a river in spate. It emboldened her to wind her arms inside his jacket and around his broad, muscular back.

They clung together, hip to thigh, chest to bosom, lips conjoined. The kiss was gentle yet masterful, his tongue which tasted faintly of old brandy and fine cigars, tracing the soft fullness of her lips and then probing them open to explore the soft recesses of her mouth.

Alexa uttered a soft little whimper of surprise and wholly pleasurable shock as she awakened to feelings that were hitherto unexperienced. The wholly unexpected feelings left her weak and shaky in the legs; her usually lissome limbs felt weighted down with a kind of delicious languor; she felt engulfed in lassitude and yet . . . yet, at the same time, her pulses pounded like a ship pounding through heavy seas.

Her breasts felt soft and swollen, though tingling at the tips, and instinctively she pressed them into Rowan's broad chest as if to ease their aching heaviness in him. She thrilled to the feel of him, to the male hardness that half-frightened, half-exulted her.

Rowan's head swam; to him, Alexa's innocently provocative allure was infinitely more intoxicating than the finest French brandy. As he crushed her yielding body into his own and moved his mouth lingeringly over hers, devouring its softness, she returned his kisses with an eager, if unpracticed, abandon that stirred him profoundly. Raising his head, he uttered a grown as his knee instinctively teased her thighs apart.

Though her eyes widened her her breath caught in her throat, Alexa did not pull away—instead, she locked herself into his embrace, spreading her legs slightly to accommodate him, feeling a swelling wave of excitement ripple through her as, for the first time, she experienced the male response to sexual arousal through the layers of clothing that separated their throbbing flesh.

Rowan made a noise deep in his throat, his hands slid down her waist and hips to cup her buttocks as he ground his body into hers, almost overcome by the purely primitive need to sweep her into his arms and carry her off to the nearest sofa ... bed ... divan ... there to divest her of her clothing and make her wholly his own.

But, of course, he could do no such thing.

The scent of crushed gillyflower drifting up between them belatedly brought him to his senses. With a smothered groan, he said huskily, "Come, Alexa. It's growing late and we *must* go in. I should take you back to your mama." With utmost reluctance, he stepped back, still half-supporting her with one arm, and straightened his disordered clothing.

Alexa made a half-whimper of protest. She felt drowsy, drugged with a whole host of new and delightful sensations that she didn't want to end. She wanted ... she wanted *more*, so much more. Oh, she wanted his kisses and caresses to go on and on forever.

Rebelliously, she smoothed her hair and twitched her own clothing straight though there was little she could do, she feared, about her flushed face, overbright eyes, and kiss-swollen lips. But Mama, when Rowan led her daughter through the French doors and into the drawing room, was too taken up with that official symbol of betrothal—the ring—uttering little oohs and ahs of admiration—to notice Alexa's disheveled appearance—or, if she did, she was too tactful to comment on it.

Alexa was pondering on that evening now as she stood on the terrace and twirled the heavy ring upon her finger, delighting in the play of sunlight on its jeweled facets. As well as a symbol of betrothal, it was, she supposed, a symbol of her own imminent subjugation to a man—a state she viewed with mixed emotions.

On the one hand she yearned quite shamelessly for his kisses and caresses and, yes, even for his ultimate physical possession of her. Even in remembrance she could feel the potency of those kisses, and little shivers of desire raced through her at the memory.

But, on the other hand, she dreaded the thought of subordinating her proud spirit to that of any man—even Rowan. Twisting the ring around and around on her finger, she wondered if it were a weakness to take such pleasure in a . . . a symbol of bondage!

But marriage needn't necessarily spell bondage and servitude, she reminded herself. There were some women, notably her mentor, Mrs. Pankhurst, who hadn't found it so. Emmeline Pankhurst and her late husband, Richard, had worked together as partners and equals, not only to improve the lot of women but for all those less fortunately circumstanced than themselves. Perhaps . . . perhaps she and Rowan could do the same one day.

Feeling his eyes upon her, she gave a start of surprise and blushed, self-conscious to be caught at playing with her ring. He smiled at her, his grey eyes gentle with tender amusement and understanding.

"Ready, Alexa?" he enquired. "Your

mama and Lucinda are in a fever to be off.
Lucy in particular is sure that we're going to
miss the Royal Procession if we don't get
under way."

Alexa gazed at her fiancé admiringly. He
was elegantly attired for Ascot in an
expensively cut grey morning coat, broad
ascot tie, knotted so that its broad ends were
laid flat upon each other, pin-striped
trousers, and the grey topper that was de
rigueur for gentlemen attending the race
meet. Alexa smothered a smile, remembering the story of the barmaid who had once
protested to her gentleman protector, "You
'aven't been to Ascot. A toff 'asn't been to
Royal Ascot unless 'e 'as a topper on 'is
'ead," she'd scoffed.

"How . . . how very handsome you do look,
Rowan," Alexa murmured naively, taking his
arm. At that moment she was suddenly convinced that if it were her fate to marry and
be forever subservient to a dominant male
animal, it was well that that man be Rowan
Traherne!

"I might well say the same for you, my
dear." Rowan eyed her with unmistakable
approval. His pretty fiancée was stylishly yet
demurely dressed, as befitted a jeune fille, in
wheat-colored chiffon and cream lace. On
her head she wore a fetching broad-brimmed
concoction with broad chiffon ties that met
under her pointed little chin.

He tucked her hand into the crook of his
elbow. "Come along now. We must be off

before my eager little sister flies into a fit of impatience. Have you your hanky to wave at the Royals?" he enquired.

Alexa nodded, straightened the elaborate concoction that adorned her red head, and produced an enormous chiffon hanky, whisking it saucily under his nose so that he caught a whiff of the lavender in which it had been stored. "It was my grandmama's and is a family heirloom," she explained.

They were not, as Lucinda had feared, late for the Royal Procession that set off from Windsor Castle bound for Ascot heath. The lead carriage, containing the king and queen, was, as always, drawn by four Windsor Greys, a special breed of horse brought to England with the first Hanover kings. Subsequent carriages contained other members of the royal family.

The Royal Procession entered through the Golden Gates and proceeded down the course for about six furlongs. Seated at the back of each landau was a coachman in a top hat and velvet livery while postillions in green velvet jackets and billed caps rode the horses, two to each team.

It was a magnificent, never-to-be-forgotten sight, and Alexa and Lucinda cheered themselves hoarse along with the rest of the multitudes and waved their chiffon hankies enthusiastically as the procession turned into the Royal Enclosure. The oldest of the Old Pensioners who served as attendants in the Royal Precincts had the honor of

stepping forth to open the coach door for
Their Majesties. The old retainer wore a
long, befrogged black velvet coat and a black
satin topper with gold ribbons and gold silk
trim around it. He looked almost as elegant
as the king himself, thought Alexa with an
irreverent giggle.

Rowan misinterpreted the cause of her
mirth. "Are you thinking of your debut,
Alexa?" he said sternly. "I want no such
shenanigans today, should we encounter
Their Majesties in the Royal Enclosure."

Alexa, for once, looked suitably subdued.
She hung her head with a blush. Had she
ever been so silly, she wondered, as to think
that she could affect the course of history?
"No, Rowan, of course not," she mumbled,
suitably squelched.

After the splendor of the Royal Procession,
the racing meet itself seemed almost anti-
climactic, even to horse-loving Alexa though
she was properly shocked to overhear a lady
standing directly behind her complain to her
escort, "Dear me, it's all over so quickly,
isn't it, Nigel? Shall we go home now, my
love, or shall we stay around and wager a
pound or two?"

Alexa hazarded a pound or two herself,
betting on the fillies and regularly losing her
small wagers, much to Rowan's amusement.

The second day of the race meeting was
Gold Cup Day at Royal Ascot and everyone
who was anyone turned out for it. And on the
informal acres of the heath thousands of

ordinary spectators milled around, enjoying a glorious afternoon, betting a bob or two and watching their "betters" parade around in formal dress. They looked a good deal more comfortable than their upper-class counterparts, mused Alexa. She noted that Rowan's topper had left a red mark on his forehead, and her own "Paul Poiret" designer gown was uncomfortably warm in the glorious summer weather while the pin that anchored her frivolous tulle bonnet to her head was pricking her scalp unmercifully.

Under Mama's indulgent eye, the two young couples, Rowan and Alexa, Lucinda and her faithful swain, Dabney Cathcart, strolled about the velvety green lawns of Ascot, enjoying the fashion parade and chatting with chance-met friends and acquaintances. Together they watched the Gold Cup Race from the family box, rented only for the four-day extravaganza and leased in perpetuity to the family, but instead of lunching there, as they had on the previous day, Rowan escorted them to the huge Chautauqua-like tent erected by his London club, the Carlton, for a luncheon party. As he had picked a winner for the Gold Cup Race, he was treating them all to oeil-de-perdrix, pink champagne.

Alexa was sipping her champagne gingerly, wary of the bubbles—and of the alcoholic content—when in swept Lady Wyndham, dressed in the height of fashion, with a luncheon party of her own.

Ignoring the members of her own laughing, gesticulating party, she latched onto Rowan with a frankly possessive air that took Alexa aback.

"Rowan . . . my dear . . . it's been an age . . . simply an age!" she prattled affectedly. "Where *have* you been keeping yourself?" Her cold blue eyes affixed themselves upon Alexa with a basilisk stare that sent shivers down the girl's spine. "And this, so I'm told, is the little bride-to-be." She laughed in a tinkling artificial manner that grated upon Alexa's nerves. "Lord, all of us who know him were taken quite by surprise that Rowan chose a bride for himself out of the schoolroom—and a member of his own family at that!"

She made it sound vaguely incestuous and Alexa was indignant. "We are only very distant cousins," she said stiffly. "And at one-and-twenty, I can hardly be considered a schoolgirl!"

Lady Wyndham tinkled again. "You mustn't mind my speaking frankly, my dear—after all, Rowan and I . . ." she laid a hand on his arm possessively . . . "are such very old friends."

Alexa lifted her chin. "Oh, quite!" she retorted. "Very *old* friends!" she added pointedly.

Lady Wyndham's plucked brows rose. So, the whey-faced chit had claws, had she?

"Champagne, Frances?" Rowan interjected, signaling to a liveried lackey.

"Ah, yes. Champagne to toast the winner!" Frances Wyndham helped herself to a glass of the bubbly liquid from a proferred tray. "Do you remember, Rowan, when we were at Longchamps race course in Paris and . . ." Linking arms with Rowan and launching into a spate of "do-you-remembers," she drew him away, adroitly detaching him from his own party—and from Alexa.

The incident rather spoiled the day for Alexa, though she did her best to keep her chin high and her spirits up. She would *not* pout and sulk like a spoilt child, she told herself, just because . . . because Rowan chose to . . . devote himself to his former mistress rather than his bride-to-be.

So she maintained an appearance of outward calm and high spirits, but inwardly . . . inwardly she was seething . . . and even when Rowan rejoined his party she viewed the rest of the day's events with a decidedly disinterested and lackluster eye.

Rowan had booked a table at the Savoy in London for Cup Night. It was perhaps the smartest, gayest night of the London Season, and Alexa, who had been looking forward to it with high anticipation, tried desperately to throw off her black mood and participate fully in the festivities. She knew she was looking her best in a silver lamé gown, more daringly cut than her debutante finery, with silver and gold lamé slippers to match.

The scene that met her wondering eyes at

the Savoy was one of unparalleled luxury
and opulence. Everyone else was also
dressed in his or her best, the gentlemen in
formal black and white, the ladies glittering
with jewelry and gorgeously gowned in rich
fabrics bright as peacock feathers.

Rowan skillfully threaded his way
between the tables with Alexa on his arm,
carelessly nodding to friends and acquaintances. Among them Alexa recognized such
notables as Prime Minister Asquith seated
with his witty, sharp-tongued wife, Margot,
and their brilliant eldest son, Raymond; the
Winston Churchills; Lady Mary Elcho,
Rowan's neighbor in Cadogan Square, who
was squired by her devoted friend of many
years, Sir Arthur Balfour. The younger set
was represented by Lady Diana Manners,
escorted by Rowan's associate at the Foreign
Office, Duff Cooper; the Tree sisters,
daughters of London's most famous Shakes-
pearean actor; the Grenfell brothers; the
Charteris family, and many others of the
rich and famous and well-born, the gay and
the gifted. There was the enticing aroma of
good food, the sound of music, the popping
of champagne corks, and the pleasant hum
of conversation as everyone greeted old
friends, chatted and joked and sipped
champagne.

Alexa felt her volatile spirits begin to rise
in such a festive atmosphere. She glanced
over her shoulder to exchange a laughing
remark with Lucinda, who followed after on

the arm of her escort, Dabney Cathcart, but when she caught a glimpse of Lady Wyndham at an adjacent table, the laughter died on her lips.

Was the woman going to follow them everywhere? Alexa wondered despairingly. But presently, under the stimulus of music and food and wine and lively conversation, her common sense reasserted itself. After all, their social set was comprised of a limited number of individuals; they were bound to run into Frances Wyndham from time to time; she, Alexa, must learn to put a good face on it. And surely, surely, she told herself, Lady Wyndham would not be so bold ... so forward ... as to intrude on this very special evening.

But she did.

The evening was well advanced and Alexa and Lucinda had gone to one of the retiring rooms to freshen up. When they returned to their table, they found that Frances Wyndham had ensconced herself there and was talking in a low-voiced tone of intimacy to Rowan, whose face was as black as a thundercloud.

As Alexa reseated herself, Frances Wyndham glanced up with the tinkling laugh that so grated on Alexa's nerves.

"Ah, my dear," she purred. "I was just telling Rowan that I quite forgot earlier today to ask what you two would like for a wedding present. Something suitably intimate, surely, since he and I are such good friends."

Alexa suppressed the impulse to shriek that the only thing she wanted from Her Ladyship was for her to leave her, Alexa's, fiancé *alone*! For once, she controlled her errant tongue and muttered something properly banal.

"What . . . no suggestions?" said Lady Wyndham mockingly. "Well, no doubt I shall think of something." She rose in a graceful swirl of skirts as a handsome but rather willowy young man approached the table with a diffident air. "Ah, here is my escort come to claim me." She raised a protesting hand. "No . . . no . . . I simply mustn't linger any longer," though nobody had asked her to do so. "I must be off. Au revoir, mes cheries." And then she was gone, leaving the air reeking of a heavy cloying scent . . . and a bad taste in Alexa's mouth.

They themselves left a short while later, for Frances Wyndham's intrusion had put a definite damper on the evening. Rowan had lapsed into abstraction, Alexa and Lucinda, after exchanging eloquent glances, had fallen silent, and young Dabney Cathcart, who had been table-hopping while the girls were freshening up and had thus missed the exchange, was clearly bewildered by new undercurrents he could sense but not understand.

Back at the Cadogan Square house, Alexa and Rowan, by mutual unspoken agreement, left the drawing room to Lucinda and her smitten swain to conduct their courtship under Mama's watchful eye and repaired to Rowan's study for a nightcap, for as an engaged twosome they were allowed more freedom than the younger couple.

Rowan rang for a brandy-and-soda. "And you, Alexa?" he asked, when the servant appeared. "A glass of wine perhaps?"

"I would prefer a cup of tea," announced Alexa who felt it was incumbent upon her to keep a clear head at all costs. "That is, if it isn't too much trouble, Flemings, at this time of night," she added courteously.

"Not at all, miss. There's always a pot kept going in the servants' hall."

But when Flemings had brought the tea tray, Alexa let the steaming beverage grow cold as she, fidgeting with her cup and spoon, tried to summon up the courage to speak to Rowan.

He drained his brandy-and-soda almost in one gulp, then looked at her quizzically. "Your tea is getting cold, Alexa," he reminded her.

She looked down at her cup as if surprised to see it in her hand. "So it is." Mechanically she lifted it to her lips and sipped the tepid brew. Over the rim of the cup she said, "You . . . you've known Lady Wyndham rather a long time, haven't you, Rowan?"

"Rather a long time . . . yes," he agreed.

"She's very beautiful." Alexa remarked, seemingly inconsequentially.

"She is indeed."

Alexa traced the rim of her teacup with a thoughtful forefinger. "And . . . and the two of you are . . . were . . . very good friends," she persisted.

Rowan frowned, choosing his words with care. "When, at some time *in the past*"—he put particular emphasis on the phrase—"a gentleman and a lady have enjoyed a particularly close friendship, it is better, Alexa, for her own piece of mind, that his betrothed should not enquire too closely into that relationship."

"Oh . . ." Alexa bit down hard on her lower lip, then, after a short pause, lifted a brave face to her betrothed. "Just . . . just so long as that relationship is . . . *is* in the past, Rowan."

"You have my word on it, Alexa. It is."

Her troubled eyes met his for a long, breathless moment, and then, satisfied by the honesty and integrity she saw in his, hers fell away.

Embarrassed suddenly by her own temerity, Alexa hastily set down her teacup and said breathlessly, "I . . . it's growing late and . . . and I'm tired. I . . . I think it's time to say goodnight."

"Perhaps you're right. It has been a long, eventful day," Rowan agreed. He pressed a tender kiss on her brow—much as he might have kissed Lucinda, thought Alexa rather forlornly, and saw her to the door.

To ensure that he had spoken the truth and

nothing but the truth to his fiancé, Rowan went up to town after Ascot week to have it out once and for all with his former lady-love. He wanted to make sure that he was off with the old love before taking on the new.

It was, he reflected somberly, too much to expect that Frances and Alexa should meet on any very cordial terms. On the whole, he thought that his usually tempestuous fiancée had been remarkably forbearing in coping with Frances's gibes and sly hints and innuendoes. It was up to him to see to it that these provocations should cease forthwith!

As Rowan had expected, the interview with Lady Wyndham was an exceedingly unpleasant one. Frances railed at him like a fishwife, heaping scorn upon his head for his "bourgeois" values and mentality. "Never think that I will welcome you back with open arms," she sneered, "when you have grown tired of the role of uxorious husband . . . when you have grown bored with that . . . that whey-faced chit!"

The notion of his ever growing bored with Alexa brought an involuntary smile to Rowan's lips—a smile which only served to enrage his erstwhile mistress even further. "Get out!" she shrieked. Looking wildly around for a weapon, she picked up an exquisitely enameled cloisonné vase with the evident intention of hurling it at him along with a stream of bitter invective, and Rowan made his departure, satisfied that he had made his point. He was done with Frances

once and for all and, having made that
abundantly clear to her, he sped homeward
to Alexa with a light heart—a free man at
last.

Despite Rowan's declaration of good faith,
Alexa had been troubled ever since Ascot
Week. Lady Wyndham's sly innuendoes and
barbed shafts had met their mark and
revived all of Alexa's distrust of men in
general and of him in particular.

That sexual fidelity could not be expected
of a gentleman in the circles in which they
moved, Alexa knew well. Nor was it required
of women either, once they had met their
wifely obligations and produced an heir and
a spare for their husbands, just so long as
they remained reasonably circumspect.

But Alexa knew in her heart that she could
never live by a social code which, while
giving lip service to family and fidelity,
encouraged discreet husband-swapping. Discretion, circumspection and, above all, dis-
loyalty, were just not in her nature. Nor
could she accept infidelity in the man she
loved and to whom she would give her heart
and body.

That Rowan was physically attracted to
her, she knew quite well. He was not, she
brooded, marrying her *solely* to protect her
good name and reputation from vicious
gossip mongers. But she was equally sure
that he did not love her as she longed to be
loved. And, that being the case, how could

she hope to hold him once desire had been satiated?

She could not, she thought with a wistful sigh, expect Rowan to curb his sexual appetites—to be a faithful husband. You really could not expect *men* to be faithful, she mused sadly, mindful of Papa's treachery. Especially not a man as sexually magnetic, as magnificently male, as Rowan.

As usual, whenever doubts or worries nagged away at her, Alexa sought her refuge in the stables. Old Saunders, who had been head groom ever since she could remember, had collapsed one day of a stroke and had then taken his promised pension and gone into retirement. The stables did not seem the same without him.

Saunders's replacement as head groom was a man she instinctively disliked. Though hard-working, efficient, and respectful to Rowan, there was a sly expression of veiled amusement in his eyes whenever he looked at her—an expression that made her uneasy.

As was her routine, she made the rounds of the stalls, patting each animal and giving it a sugar lump. She lingered longest by the stall of Shaitan, Rowan's magnificent black stallion. Deep piles of clean straw were heaped in the stall muffling the stallion's impatiently drumming hooves and his jet-black hide was impeccably groomed, but he seemed to Alexa to be unusually restless.

"Has Shaitan not had his exercise today?"

she asked rather sharply.

"No, miss, that he has not," the groom responded with scarcely veiled insolence. "As you should know, the master's away and I've had my hands full today what with young Lucas going off to his sister's wedding and Brock being given leave to go visit his old mum." The head groom's tone implied criticism of Rowan who had authorized these unnecessary absences.

The powerful animal arched his proud neck and tossed his thick mane as he racked restlessly around the loose box, nostrils flaring. He was the epitome of strength and equine beauty. It would, mused Alexa, be poetry in motion to ride him.

She eyed the great stallion thoughtfully, sorely tempted. In Rowan's absence, this was a golden opportunity for her to ride the Black—something she had been itching to do ever since she had returned to Nun's Farthing. But she had refrained for fear of getting old Saunders into trouble. It would have cost the old man his place to contravene Rowan's express orders and mount her on the Black.

She had, however, no such compunctions regarding Jeffers, the new head groom. As a matter of fact, she had argued against promoting him to the position, but Rowan had informed her in no uncertain terms that while she might do as she chose in the household, the stables and the stable staff were *his* province.

This sweeping assumption of masculine authority and prerogatives had put her back up at the time, just as the remembrance of it served to do now.

A wicked little smile playing around the corners of her mouth, she edged closer to the loose box and offered the stallion a sugar lump.

He took it regally, a sovereign accepting the homage of a subject. The velvety muzzle tickled Alexa's sugary palm as with her free hand she stroked the stallion's gleaming sweat-streaked neck.

"This animal needs exercising, Jeffers," she said authoritatively. "He frets under too close confinement."

The groom heaved a long-suffering sigh. "I'll see to it, miss, before the day's out," he promised her.

"No," Alexa said authoritatively. "*I* will." She tossed her red head, her mind made up. "Saddle the Black for me," she commanded imperiously.

The smirk vanished from the head groom's face, to be replaced with an expression of alarm. "Now, miss," he said, "you know I can't do that. The master left strict orders about who was to ride Shaitan and who was not." Seeing the mulish expression on Alexa's pretty face, he added rather desperately, "If I mount you on the Black, the master will turn me off without a reference. I can't do it!" he exclaimed.

"And *I* will see to it that you are dismissed

if you do not!" Alexa retorted swiftly. The man was young and capable, she reasoned. He would have no difficulty in obtaining another situation.

The groom hesitated, caught between a rock and a hard place. His master had issued strict orders regarding Shaitan, it was true. But everyone in the household, from Peacham, the butler, down to the lowliest skivvy or stable boy knew that the master was besotted with love for Miss Alexa, who was shortly to become the mistress of the manor.

Sullenly, the man moved to do her bidding.

Riding Shaitan, Alexa discovered, was like riding the wind. Perched on his broad back, in the breeches to which Rowan had long since become resigned, she felt like a centaur, that mythological creature, half man, half horse. Or, in this case, she thought with a giggle, half horse, half woman!

For Shaitan, accustomed to Rowan's firm hands on the reins and heavy muscular frame bestriding him, carrying this puny female creature was very nearly like running free. Unlike Gypsy, he needed no touch of the crop to spur him on to greater and greater speed. He flew and Alexa flew with him, the wind in her face, blowing back her cropped reddish hair. Going full-tilt, she laughed aloud, exulting in Shaitan's speed and power, feeling freed of all earthly burdens, all cares and concerns.

Down the grassy lane they flew, pell-mell over a brook and a low stone wall, across the field and then another till they came to the downs. And there the wild gallop they enjoyed when Alexa gave Shaitan his head finally cleared all the cobwebs from her brain and left all of her worries far behind.

Feeling refreshed and exhilarated, she turned her face towards home at last, instinctively employing the same route back that she and Rowan always followed on their early-morning rides, through the Home Farm woods, across the pasture, then through the park to the manor house.

It was a route that detoured around the five-barred gate where Alexa had come a cropper early in the spring. But, catching a glimpse of that gate out of the corner of her eye, she again fell prey to temptation—and succumbed.

What a thrill it would be to sail over that gate on Shaitan! she mused. What a fitting climax to her glorious ride—a ride only too likely never to be repeated, if Rowan had anything to say about it.

This was her chance! Her only chance!

Impulsively, she turned Shaitan towards the gate.

Chapter 13

Rowan felt exuberant as he drove through the gates of Nun's Farthing, a free and unencumbered man now that he had formally broken with Frances.

His first thought was of Alexa. Lord, he must have it bad, he thought ruefully as he sped along the beech-lined drive. He had seen her only this morning at breakfast and already he was hungry for the sight of her again.

In the courtyard, he turned the Rolls over to Chalmers who had not chauffeured him up to town on this most delicate of errands, and went in search of Alexa.

She was not in her room; her maid had not seen her since luncheon time. Nor was she in the garden as he might have expected on this most beautiful and sunny of June days.

Her mama was seated at a delicate Louis

Quinze escritoire going over the wedding guest list. She looked up with an abstracted air when Rowan came in through the French doors. "Alexa?" she said vaguely, in response to his impatiently worded question. "Why, I believe she went down to the stables, dear," and went back to her lists.

Rowan felt the first premonition of alarm. He had glimpsed Gypsy in the paddock when he pulled in, but of Alexa there had been no sign.

Impatiently he strode to the stable block. Jeffers was instructing one of the under-grooms in the proper application of hot packs and fomentations to a hunter's fore-leg. Both men straightened and touched their caps at Rowan's approach. Seeing his master's dark face, Jeffers's heart sank. He was going to be in for it and no mistake and all because of a flighty red-headed flibberti-gibbet, he thought resentfully.

"Have you seen Miss Alexa?" Rowan barked in his parade-ground voice.

"N-no, sir." Jeffers's first instinct was to deny it. "That is . . . she was here, sir. Some time back." He floundered miserably on. "She . . . ah . . . she took out one of the horses and—"

"Which one?" Rowan snapped.

The groom's adam's apple bobbed convulsively.

"Well, speak up, man!" But Rowan's glacial grey eyes had already swiveled to Shaitan's empty stall. He let fly with an oath that all but muffled Jeffers's mumbled response.

"Er . . . Shai . . . Shaitan, sir."

Rowan rounded on his head groom in a black fury. "I left express orders that Miss Alexa was not to be mounted on the beast!"

Jeffers found his voice at last. "If I may say so, sir, Miss Alexa is a headstrong young woman, and determined to have her own way," he defended himself.

Rowan ignored the man's excuses. His body was rigid with anger and apprehension, his grey eyes narrow slits of rage. "Saddle one of the hunters for me," he ordered.

The undergroom leaped to obey him while Jeffers stood, sweat beading his face, attempting to answer a rapid-fire volley of questions as to how long the young mistress had been gone and which direction she had taken. When the undergroom trotted up with a saddled horse, Rowan sprang into the saddle and clattered off down the path Alexa had taken, leaving Jeffers to wonder if he would be given the sack and inwardly cursing all flighty flibbertigibbet females.

The headstrong little fool! Rowan fumed to himself, giving the placid hunter a vicious cut with his crop. Shaitan was too much horse for her to handle, as he had warned her any number of times. He was strictly a man's mount. If Shaitan had taken the bit in his teeth there was no telling what might happen.

His heart filled with dread, Rowan

followed the path Alexa had taken, his sharp eyes scanning fields and woods for sight of her.

He had not far to look.

Rowan experienced a distinct sensation of déjà vu when he came upon the five-barred gate, the limping horse trailing its reins, the white-faced girl sprawled out prone on the grass.

"Alexa!" Rowan dug in his heels and galloped up to where she lay, then slid from the saddle in one lithe bound, prudently wrapping his mount's reins around the top bar. "Alexa!"

He knelt beside her, his heart pounding with fear. She lay as still as a corpse and nearly as pallid. For one heart-stopping moment he thought that she *was* a corpse! But, picking up one of her limp wrists, he detected a faint pulse beat and that gave him hope.

He chafed her wrists and loosened first the stock at her throat and then her tightly buttoned shirt and jacket so that she might breathe more easily. The frilly chemise thus revealed seemed oddly at variance with her boyish costume and caught at his heart as did the slender bared throat and fragile collarbone. He ran a hand round them anxiously to ensure there was no damage and breathed a little easier to find that there appeared to be none.

Pulling the frilly chemise downwards, he laid his head against her chest to listen for her heartbeat. To his intense relief, it came, faint but regular, to his listening ear.

The tickle of Rowan's thick black hair against her chin and on her partially bared chest roused Alexa from her stupor. Uttering a little whimper, she raised her head and, squinting a little, opened her eyes. Her first conscious sight was of Rowan's anxious face bent over her. The tender light in his eyes told her that she was infinitely precious to him.

"Oh . . . Rowan . . . what . . . what are you doing here? Wha-what happened?" she murmured groggily.

"You took a spill." Alexa struggled to sit up but he forestalled her. "No. Don't move. Just lie still till I make sure nothing's broken." He ran anxious, questing, but nevertheless expert hands over her body. Assuring himself that nothing was broken, he gave her the support of his strong arm beneath her back. "Does it hurt anywhere special?" he asked urgently.

"Only my ankle. A bit. I . . . I think it got twisted under me." She bent over to tug at her boot, unconsciously revealing an expanse of soft white bosom that took Rowan's breath away.

"Oh!" Following the direction of his gaze, she flushed and drew the jacket more tightly around her. It was only common sense for him to have loosened her clothing, she told herself woozily, but the warm light of approval in his eyes assured her that she was pleasing to his sight and this knowledge sent her unsteady pulses to fluttering wildly.

Averting her eyes from his, she murmured, "I . . . my . . . my ankle feels like it might be swelling. Can you . . . can you get my boot off?" she begged.

Rowan tugged gently at it but a sickening stab of pain shot through Alexa and she lay back with a little moan.

"The boot will have to be cut away," Rowan said practically. "We must get you back to the house, Alexa."

"Wh-what about Shaitan?" asked Alexa, suddenly remembering the stallion. "I . . . I tried to lift him too soon, I think. At any rate, there was some sort of fumble at the gate and I pitched over his head. Is . . . is he hurt, Rowan?"

Rowan gathered her against his shoulder, one arm under her knees, and carried her to his patiently waiting mount. "Damn Shaitan!" he growled. "It's you I'm concerned about, Alexa!"

It was music to Alexa's ears.

The doctor, hastily summoned from the village, assured his anxious patient and her betrothed that the ankle was not broken nor even severely sprained and that two or three days of rest and quiet should put it right again. "You'll be able to float down the aisle, Miss Alexa, when the great day comes," he jested. "That is, if you stay off horses."

"She will," promised Rowan grimly. "I'll

see to it myself."

Alexa greatly enjoyed her short con-
valescence. It was a delightful novelty to be
pampered by Rowan who insisted on
carrying her in his strong arms from room
to room and from sofa to bed, refusing to
allow her to put her foot to the floor until the
doctor gave his permission. She loved to
twine her arms about his neck and lay her
head on his broad shoulder as he swept her
into his powerful embrace, holding her a
little more tightly than was strictly
necessary, to convey her wherever her fancy
dictated.

She particularly thrilled to his touch at
evening's end when he transported her from
the drawing-room sofa to her bedchamber.
Soon—very soon—he would not be leaving
her to Mama's ministrations. Soon he would
be sharing a room—a bed—with her. Alexa
looked forward to that time with a delicious
sense of half-fearful, half-eager anticipation.
And she knew that Rowan was looking
forward to it too—his eyes, when he laid her
on the bed and bade her goodnight with a
tender kiss, under Mama's indulgent gaze,
told her so.

Before long, Alexa was on the mend, her
old saucy self again, no longer content to
play the invalid. Her doctor's timely remark
about the "great day" now rapidly
approaching had raised the vexing question
of just which aisle Alexa was to float down.

It had originally been planned that the

wedding would take place in London, but when Alexa had belatedly discovered that she would be expected to promise to "love, honor, and *obey*" her future husband, she stirred up such a hornet's nest that, for a time, it looked as if the wedding might not come off on schedule.

Neither the clergymen at fashionable St. George's in Hanover Square nor the equally fashionable St. Margaret's, Westminster, were disposed to alter the wording of the wedding service at the behest of a defiant red-headed chit who was only willing to promise to "love, honor, and *cherish*." But, to *obey* him? NEVER! The vicar of the little village church, St. Mary's in-the-Field, was equally obdurate.

"Marriage is a sacrament, my dear child," the elderly white-haired priest who had both christened and confirmed her protested. "You cannot rewrite the marriage service to please yourself. Nor can I alter it," he said sternly.

Alexa was unconvinced.

Rowan hastily intervened, hustling her out of the vicar's study, for he could see, as Alexa evidently could not, that further wrangling would get her nowhere. He himself did not greatly care about the wording of the service. The notion of a tamely obedient Alexa, while sometimes appealing, was too ludicrous to contemplate in any case. Their life together would never be easy but, of a certainty, it would never be dull, he reflected.

When they were out of the drafty Victorian vicarage and into the bright June sunshine, he ventured to remonstrate with her.

"*Must* you pit yourself against the authority and tradition of the Church, Alexa? It is only a word, after all. Does it really mean that much to you?"

"Yes!" she said stormily. "It does. I am not going to make any promises that I have no intention of keeping, Rowan!" Her lips trembled. "My marriage vows mean more to me than that." She flung up her head to dash the welling tears out of her eyes. "Whatever they may mean to you!"

"Now what the devil is that supposed to mean?" Rowan exclaimed with masculine obtuseness.

Alexa bit her lip and remained mute. The best wishes and wedding presents had started to trickle in and among them was an exquisite counterpane of cobwebby Belgian lace—the gift of Lady Frances Wyndham. Mama had exclaimed over its beauty and fragility and suggested innocently that it was the very thing for the bridal bed. Alexa hastily vetoed this suggestion. Longing to burn it but not quite daring to do so, she decided to relegate it to a guest room, for she wanted no reminders of Rowan's mistress to intrude on their wedding night.

"I didn't mean anything by it," she said sulkily.

Rowan looked at her sharply, wondering if

by chance the details of his last unpleasant interview with Frances had drifted to her ears. It didn't seem possible, for Chalmers had not driven him up to London on that delicate mission and none of the other servants would have had an opportunity of overhearing and thus gossiping about his affair with that lady. It must be the wedding present, he decided. He could cheerfully have wrung Frances's neck, for he knew that it was specifically chosen to embarrass him and irritate Alexa. Her "gift" had achieved precisely the effect she had intended, but, by God, he wasn't going to let it drive a wedge between him and Alexa. Devoutly hoping that it would be Frances's parting shot, for he had heard that she had gone abroad, he strove to divert Alexa's mind.

He had gone up to London on the morning train and motored back down in the afternoon in a smart little runabout that he had presented to Alexa as an engagement gift. She had been delighted with it and now, to put her in a more cheerful frame of mind, he suggested that she demonstrate the new skill that Chalmers had been teaching her.

Alexa fell in with the suggestion eagerly. She was thrilled with Rowan's choice of a gift and was proud of her newly acquired accomplishment. "Very well," she agreed. "It's a glorious day . . . and at least *I* won't put us into the ditch," she teased.

"Pride goeth before a fall . . . or, in this case, a skid," he warned her darkly.

Alexa laughed, then her face clouded over. "But Rowan, whatever will we do about the ceremony?" she fretted. "Time is running out."

"Leave that to me," he said authoritatively. "Since it means so much to you, I'll think of something." He squeezed her hand in a grip that made the bones ache. "Trust me, Alexa. I mean to make you a good husband. I mean to make you happy!"

His vehemence surprised her and, rather than reassuring her as it was meant to do, gave her a vague feeling of unease that almost amounted to a presentiment of disaster.

The "obey versus cherish" controversy was finally solved when the elderly vicar's young curate stepped forward with an offer to perform the ceremony as Alexa wished. *He* had no old-fashioned notions about the precise wording of the wedding ceremony— only some very practical ones regarding the advisability of accommodating the eccentric demands of a wealthy and influential parishioner.

Alexa was convinced that Rowan had won him over by sheer force of personality and when, later in the month, Prime Minister Asquith consented to receive a delegation of East End suffragettes, headed by Sylvia Pankhurst, she was persuaded that there was nothing Rowan could not do. In vain, he modestly disclaimed any credit for this volté-face on the part of the prime minister, pointing out that others more influential than himself had brought pressure to bear. "It's my belief that the prime minister sees the handwriting on the wall," he said thoughtfully. "He's beginning to realize that the issue of women suffrage is moving into the realm of practical politics."

"And not before time!" said Alexa with a sniff, remembering that gentleman's former intransigence.

But as her wedding day drew near, Alexa found that obtaining the vote and giving herself over to good works, as she had once planned to do, was beginning to seem less vital to her. She even found herself wondering if she hadn't at times been a rather silly young woman who hadn't really known what she wanted from life. There had been a time, she mused, and not so very long ago, when she would have said that she would willingly give up her life for the Cause. But that . . . that was before Rowan had come into her life. Before, life had offered her such bright and glittering prospects for a happy future—marriage to the man she loved, a honeymoon in Paris, a new wardrobe in all the dashing new styles. She feared she might be becoming distressingly light-minded. Yet even Mrs. Pankhurst, she reminded herself, rejoiced in pretty and stylish clothing and must surely be quite the most unfrumpish reformer ever known. Mrs. Pankhurst had even managed to combine a career of sorts with marriage and motherhood. What might not she and Rowan achieve together, thought Alexa, a trifle wistfully, if only . . . if only he loved her!

And if only she could banish this forboding feeling of impending disaster which sometimes descended upon her thick and heavy as a mist on the moors and just as intangible.

Chapter 14

The wedding day, that fateful 28th of June, dawned bright and clear, the brilliant sunshine making a mockery of Alexa's gloomy forebodings of disaster. And the ceremony went off without a hitch.

The church was sweetly scented with the blooms of summer flowers banked in profusion around the altar. There Rowan waited, his dress shirt white as snow, his elegantly cut coat and trousers displaying his width of shoulder and length of leg. He was the cynosure of all eyes, yet he stood calm and composed, as suavely imperturbable as ever.

The organ, a little off-key, surged and swelled throughout the old Norman church, and his best man, Owen Forbes-Hamilton, nudged him. He glanced back to see Alexa drift down the aisle in a beam of light which shimmered like an aureole round the bright hair covered with a gossamer veiling of Brussels lace.

She looked, he thought, angelically ethereal and fragile beyond belief, too delicate to make the long journey down the carpeted aisle without a man's strong arm to support her. But she did, seeming almost to float in an exquisite gown of creamy white that billowed and flared from a tight heart-shaped bodice.

His heart throbbed with a surge of passionate longing to initiate his willful yet innocent bride into the ways of love. Soon . . . soon . . . in a matter of minutes now, she would be his!

And then she was beside him and the curate began to intone the marriage service. Rowan, his voice a little husky with emotion, heard himself making the appropriate responses.

Alexa trembled but her voice was as clear and bell-like as ever, audible in the farthest pews as she made her vows. "I, Alexandra Mary, take thee, Rowan Roderick . . ."

It was over so soon, she thought, a little dazed. It took such a little bit of time to promise one's life away . . . to give it into the keeping of a man who might well trample on her affections, curb her spirit, and reduce her to the status of . . . of decorative household ornament and . . . and bedmate. She felt a moment's keen regret that she had ever succumbed to his blandishments—now

that it was too late! For already the
clergyman was intoning, "Whom God has
joined together, let no man put asunder . . ."

But Rowan, though hard and stern, would
always be kind, she reminded herself, at
least so long as she deferred to his opinions
as a good wife should . . . and so long as she
did not provoke him unduly.

Her heart jolted as she lifted her face for
the traditional bridal kiss, though she
expected his mouth to brush lightly across
hers. But he took her by surprise as his arms
enveloped her and the bold, heavy curve of
his firm lips fastened on hers in a kiss that
claimed her completely.

Although Rowan and Alexa were not
aware of it, they shared their wedding day
with another, much more illustrious couple
whose eighteenth wedding anniversary it
was. The Austrian Archduke Francis
Ferdinand and his morganatic wife, Sophie
Chotek, could have served them as a model
of domestic felicity, for theirs had been a
love match, entered into despite the disapproval of the Austrian emperor, for the
Archduke was his heir while Sophie was only
a poor and not particularly well-born lady in
waiting at the Hapsburg court. Sophie was
despised by the snobbish and sclerotic old
emperor, and the members of the court,
following his lead, held her in scorn and
contempt.

Nevertheless, the couple were devoted to

each other and to their three children, none
of whom were in line to succeed to their
father's imperial succession rights because
of their mother's humble birth.

The occasion of a state visit to Sarajevo, a
newly acquired part of the vast and ramshackle Hapsburg empire, coincided with
the date of their wedding anniversary. It
struck Francis Ferdinand as an excellent
opportunity for his Sophie to receive the
plaudits of the crowd, far from the stuffy
Viennese court where she had suffered so
many petty snubs and humiliations. It would
be an unusual honor for her, but, he decided,
no more than her due.

In Sarajevo, as in England, it was a day of
glorious summer weather. The streets were
lined with flags in honor of the royal visitors
and portraits of Francis Ferdinand decorated many shop windows. Large crowds
lined the streets to watch the cavalcade of
motorcars pass by. But there were few
cheers for the Austrian heir, resplendent in a
bemedaled full-dress uniform, or for his wife
who sat beside him, gowned in white and
wearing an enormous hat and veil. On the
seat facing them sat the Austrian military
governor who pointed out objects of interest
along the route.

They were proceeding towards the town
hall where a formal reception was planned
when a bomb came hurtling out of the air,
aimed at the Archduke. Francis Ferdinand,
who possessed extraordinary courage and

quick reflexes, caught it and hastily threw it into the road behind him. It detonated when it hit the ground, injuring several members of the escort party and a few innocent by-standers.

There was a scuffle, but the police quickly seized the bomb-throwing terrorist and marched him off for interrogation.

The Archduke ordered the cavalcade halted in order to learn what damage had been done and to insure that the wounded received prompt medical attention. When they had been dispatched to a hospital, he dismissed the incident with a cool, "The man must be insane. Come, gentlemen, let us proceed with the program," and the cavalcade resumed.

After the reception at the town hall, the Archduke and his wife insisted on paying a visit to the hospital to enquire after the injured. The military governor and the mayor of Sarajevo reluctantly agreed to the Archduke's request, for no one could believe that a second assassination attempt would be made that same day.

But they were wrong. There were no less than six terrorists mingling in the crowds—members of the notorious Black Hand society.

As the royal motorcar proceeded along the Appel Quay a shot rang out. The Archduke Francis Ferdinand slumped over, even as his devoted wife flung herself across him to shield his body with her own.

The assassin's gun spat fire a second time and Sophie Chotek collapsed in her husband's arms. "Sophie, Sophie," he groaned. "You must not die. You must live . . . live for our children."

But within a few minutes, both the Archduke and his wife were dead. And with them died an era.

At that moment, Rowan and Alexa were oblivious to the events taking place on the European stage. It was, after all, their wedding day.

They planned to honeymoon in Paris, but since the curate had come forward at the last minute with his offer to perform the ceremony, the church had been booked up until late afternoon. Rowan had no desire to spend his wedding night traveling, especially since Alexa had confessed that she was a poor sailor and likely to be afflicted with seasickness. So they decided to spend the first few days of their honeymoon in seclusion at the dower house, a small but comfortable building on the estate. It had been recently renovated and refurbished for Lady Mary, who, perhaps in anticipation of a stormy adjustment period, had averred that she had no desire to intrude on the privacy of a newly married couple. So it was arranged that she would move in later while they were in Paris, and in the meantime Rowan and Alexa took possession of it with a skeleton staff, which included Rowan's valet Parsons, and Hetty, who had been promoted to Alexa's lady's maid.

Hetty helped her mistress undress and brushed out her hair. "They do say as all brides are beautiful, miss—I mean, madame," the girl corrected herself hastily, "but you've got to be the most beautiful of them all."

Alexa smiled faintly. She was very nervous. "Thank you, Hetty." She studied her reflection in the dressing-table mirror, hoping that Rowan would find her so. She was very pale and her eyes were shadowed, conveying none of their usual vibrancy.

As if her thoughts of him had conjured him up out of thin air, Rowan stepped out of the dressing room, clad in a resplendent dressing gown. Hetty put down the hairbrush and murmured, "Will that be all, madame?"

"Yes, thank you, Hetty."

The maid bobbed a curtsy and withdrew.

It was an awkward moment.

Alexa swallowed hard. "What a . . . a handsome dressing gown, Rowan!" she exclaimed brightly. Even to her own ears, her brightness sounded faked . . . forced . . . but he appeared not to notice.

"Gaudy is the word, I believe," he said jocularly. "It was a gift from Lucinda," he went on to explain.

"Oh . . ." Alexa seized on Lucinda as on a lifeline. "Didn't Lucy look lovely today!" she enthused. "Rose pink is certainly her color. And the hat that Mademoiselle Madeleine designed for her is certainly the last word in hats." Unconsciously, her nervous fingers picked at the embroidery stitched to her peignoir. "I think Lucy and Dabney Cathcart will make a match of it, don't you? He is certainly smitten with her!" she exclaimed. "And they do make such a handsome couple. Why, at the reception . . ." she rattled on without pausing for breath.

Alexa next seized on her mother for a fresh topic of conversation. "Dear Mama, she always looks so well in powder blue. Did you notice how General Sir Henry Forbes-Hamilton was admiring her? He used to be a beau of hers many years ago. If . . . if only she hadn't quite spoilt her eyes by crying throughout the ceremony and . . ."

Alexa knew she was babbling but she couldn't seem to get control of her runaway tongue.

"Alexa . . ." Rowan sighed. And then he stilled it for her by the simple expedient of drawing her into his arms and applying his mouth to hers.

The kiss was tender yet fiercely possessive and far more persuasive than she cared to admit. Alexa found her fears melting away under Rowan's gentle ravishment, found her slender body instinctively swaying into his arms. As she pressed ever closer to his tall, powerful frame, her arms crept round his neck and her fingers laced through the thick, dark hair growing low at his nape.

He eased his mouth from hers and drew a deep, unsteady breath. "You mustn't be frightened, Alexa," he said thickly. "I'll be as gentle as I can, my dear."

"I . . . I'm not frightened!" Swiftly she denied it, but her wide, slightly apprehensive eyes told him that a small modicum of fear yet lingered.

She was being very silly, Alexa told herself severely. For . . . for what seemed like ages she had been longing for this very moment—for the time when the two of them would no longer be kept apart by the force of convention and circumstance . . . when . . . when he would have the opportunity to make her his own . . . but . . . but now that the time had come . . . the moment was near at hand . . .

At the base of her throat a pulse beat and swelled as though her heart had leaped up into it to flutter wildly out of place. Rowan, touched by her vulnerability, bent his dark head to caress the throbbing spot with sweetly exploring lips, sending little shivers of sensual delight skittering through her.

She whimpered as his lips traveled from the base of her throat to her slender neck, nuzzled it affectionately, and then moved along the corded path to her tiny shell-like ears. He made lightly flicking circles behind her ears with his tongue and then darted its point into the ear with a highly erotic in-and-out movement that sent tiny darts of

pleasure flickering through her. When his
lips closed over an earlobe, gently tugging
and sucking, she felt as if her bones were
melting.

Urgently she clung to his strength, having
none left of her own, and he, sensing that the
moment of her surrender had come, effort-
lessly swung her into his arms and carried
her to the bed, depositing her gently upon it.

She clung to him instinctively, drawing
him down beside her as an exquisite sense of
anticipation began building within her. It
felt, she thought wonderingly, like little
flames beginning to ignite and burn with a
kind of liquid fire, hot and molten to the
core, dissolving her form and substance.

A little shocked by her own eager reaction
to his caresses, she yet obeyed instincts as
old as time, opening her lips to his probing,
thrusting tongue, shyly yet eagerly returning
his kisses in full measure, slipping her hands
inside his dressing gown to run them over
the corded muscles of his back and
shoulders and then around to caress his
hair-roughened chest that so thrilled her
with its masculine hardness.

Yet when his big hands began tugging at
the narrow ribbons that fastened her filmy
silver-colored peignoir, a last faint tremor of
apprehension shivered through her. Noting
her quiver of alarm as he slid the gown off
her shoulders and down her arms to expose
her pink-tipped breasts, he murmured
huskily, "Trust me, Alexa."

Confidently and unhurriedly he led her through an exquisitely slow and gradual awakening and into an awareness of her own deeply sensual nature, and she, on her part, gave herself up utterly and completely to his masterful seduction.

As his kisses and caresses worked their magic spell upon Alexa, it occurred to Rowan that this was almost as new and fresh an experience for him as it was for her, for he had never before encountered innocence. The son of wealth and privilege, a consummate man of the world, he had had many mistresses, all of whom had been worldly-wise women experienced in the arts of love. His bride's very innocence and youthful ardor touched him profoundly, giving him the illusion that this was his own first taste of passion. It was as if he were experiencing the wonder of it all afresh, sharing her naive delight and wonder in the power of physical passion.

His eyes feasted on loveliness only half-veiled by gossamer folds, and she bravely allowed him to do so, wanting him to find her desirable, whimpering with yet unfulfilled yearnings as his hands stroked her back, her waist, her hips, glorying in the petal-like smoothness of her skin and the tender young breasts budded with pink tips.

When his warm, moist mouth fastened around those deep pink rosettes, it sent little shock waves and shivers up her spine. Willingly she surrendered to his touch and

answered it with a shy, yet bravely honest
passion of her own, indulging her curiosity
about the body so different from her own
with a frankness that both amazed and
delighted him. So that his robe might not
hinder her timid explorations, he doffed it,
smiling tenderly at her blushing confusion
as he took her hand and guided it to himself,
the clasp of her slender fingers arousing him
to new heights of passion.

When she had satisfied her curiosity con-
cerning the male physiognomy, he returned
to a leisurely exploration of her body until it
began to vibrate from his slow, warm, even
caresses, and the flickering flames that
glowed within her burst into a sweet conflagration engulfing her in sweet flaming
fountains of delight.

He cradled that most secret part of her
with his hand until the exquisitely delicious
spasms died away, finding his pleasure in
her release.

"Oh . . . Rowan . . . I . . . I . . . I didn't know
anything could be like this," she whispered
against his chest.

"It will be even better when you are fully
my wife," he promised her, aching to achieve
his own relief, yet reluctant to bring her even
a moment's pain or even discomfort.

But to his surprise, Alexa took the
initiative, pulling him down on top of her
and spreading herself to accommodate him.
"I *want* to be your wife in every way
possible," she said quite fiercely, arching

herself up to meet him as he, uanble to
ignore this blatant invitation, thrust deep
within her.

With his entry, a sudden sharp pain
pierced Alexa, causing her to gasp aloud. She
buried her face in the corded muscles of his
shoulder, digging her nails into his arms.
And then, within moments, she felt a
wonderful warm pulsing deep inside her, an
almost aching throb, and as he uttered a
groan of passion spent, she felt wonderfully
filled with him, wonderfully complete.

Cradling her in his arms, he held her close,
breathing feather-like kisses onto her face,
neck and throat and over her closed eyelids.

"Now I am truly your wife," Alexa said
wonderingly.

"Now you are truly my wife," he agreed.
"Now and for all time." Raising himself on
an elbow, he bent his head and kissed her
lips one last time, then lay back, pulling her
into the circle of his arms. And so they lay,
glorying in each other's joy until they fell
into the deep sleep of satisfied lovers.

It was Alexa, usually so sluggish in the
mornings, who was the first to awaken.
Rowan's arm was flung heavily across her
and she carefully inched herself out from
under it and, throwing a filmy bed jacket
about her bare shoulders, propped herself
up on pillows to ponder over her new status
as married (very-much-married) woman.

Had that passionate creature of last night

really been herself? she wondered. As she
thought of it in retrospect, color flared into
her cheeks, a flush that spread over her
whole body right down to her toes. Why, her
body had hardly seemed like her own last
night! It was as if a stranger had crept into
her skin and taken possession of her—someone she didn't know at all—someone she was
going to have to get to know.

What had happened to all those precious
ideals she had been forever spouting? she
asked herself. They seemed now like the
playthings of a child which must be set aside
now that she was a woman. A woman, she
thought with another blush, who had discovered that she was possessed of a very
passionate nature. Rowan's lovemaking had
tapped a vein of passion that she hadn't
dreamed existed, and everything else must
be reassessed in the light of her new self-
knowledge.

She simply hadn't known that love—the
physical expression of it—could be so sweet.
Only, of course, in Rowan's case, it wasn't
love, she reminded herself hastily. In no way
could she delude herself on that score! She
wasn't so naive or unsophisticated as not to
know that a man could desire a woman
without any deep emotional involvement
with her—without any tender feelings at all.
Not that Rowan hadn't been exceedingly
tender with her last night, she mused. He
had exhibited the utmost gentleness and, she
suspected, exercised considerable restraint

as he introduced his virgin bride to the ways
of love.

But of love itself he had breathed not one
word. She had not expected it but she had
half-hoped . . .

Hoped *what*? she jeered at herself. That he
would profess undying love for her? The
kind of love the poet's sang about? How
childish could she be! He was hardly likely
to do any such thing when he had only
married her to protect her good name and,
perhaps, to more effectively separate her
from the militant movement.

And so, of course, she had bitten back the
professions of love that had risen so
naturally to her lips, restraining her own
almost ungovernable impulse to tell him that
she loved him. It was one thing to bare one's
body to one's husband but quite another to
bare one's heart and soul. It would be un-
forgivably gauche, especially when she was
quite sure that such a confession would not
be welcome. Unutterably embarrassing to
him and to herself as well!

Her gaze wandered to his face and she
studied him wistfully. His midnight-black
hair and swarthy skin were in startling
contrast to the stark white bed linen. In
repose, the sometimes harsh and forbidding
contours of his face were muted, blurred by
sleep. She longed to reach out and tenderly
stroke his face, to run her fingers through
that thick thatch of black hair. But even as
she watched, his eyes, thickly fringed by

curling lashes that a woman might envy,
popped open and he was gazing at her, an inscrutable expression on that dark face.

Alexa quickly rearranged her own
features, perturbed at being caught eyeing
him like a lovesick schoolgirl.

"Er . . . good morning," she said brightly.

His heavy, full lips curved into a smile.
"Good morning, Mrs. Traherne." And then
his arms reached out to draw her down
beside him. It was, he thought, as though he
had an unquenchable thirst for her, a thirst
that grew greater the more often it was
quenched.

A discreet knock sounded on the heavy
oaken door.

"Damn!" Rowan exclaimed. "Did you ring
for tea?"

Alexa shook her head, adjusting the frilly
bed jacket he had disarranged.

Rowan sighed. "Yes, what is it?" he
growled.

"Sorry sir," the voice of his valet, Parsons,
was only faintly muffled by the door. "It's
Sir Edward, sir, ringing up from the Foreign
Office. He says he must speak with you, sir.
The matter is urgent."

To disturb a man on his honeymoon, the
matter must be grave indeed, Rowan
reflected, as he threw on his dressing gown
and thrust his feet into carpet slippers. No
matter what sort of flap was on at the
Foreign Office, the elegant and urbane Sir
Edward Grey was not one to overreact. A

crisis of some sort must be impending.

Rowan bent to brush a quick kiss on Alexa's lips. "I shouldn't worry, my dear. It's probably nothing of importance. Possibly one of the secretaries has misplaced a vital document," he suggested, without any real hope that such was the case. "I'll send Hetty to you with a tray, shall I?"

He was gone only a few minutes, but in that time Hetty had readied a tray for her mistress and drawn open the curtains so that bright June sunshine flooded into the room.

It was going to be another glorious day, Alexa thought contentedly, tapping the shell of a boiled egg, for Hetty had brought not only tea but a substantial breakfast for them as well.

She wondered how she and Rowan would spend their day. Perhaps go for a brisk gallop on the downs before the sun grew too hot, she mused. And then, in the afternoon, they might go punting on the river. She would suggest it to him.

"Well, is the country at war?" she said lightly when he came into the room, meaning it as a jest.

But Rowan's face was grave. "Not quite," he said grimly.

Alexa dropped her spoon in mid-tap. It clattered against the delicate china and went rolling off onto the carpet unheeded.

"This . . . this is serious then?" she said anxiously.

"Extremely serious. The Archduke Francis Ferdinand and his wife have been assassinated at Sarajevo." He began laying out clothes for his valet to pack. "I must go up to London straightaway."

"Oh, Rowan, no!" Alexa wailed.

"Oh, yes. I'm sorry, my dear," he said rather perfunctorily, or so Alexa thought.

"But somebody or other is always getting assassinated in the Balkans!" she protested.

"This isn't just anybody, Alexa," he said patiently. "It's the heir to the empire of Austria. The international repercussions . . ." his voice trailed off.

"Very well then, I'll come with you," she said impetuously.

But Rowan promptly vetoed this suggestion. "I think not, Alexa," he said regretfully. "I don't expect to be in London long. Sir Edward said something about a diplomatic mission. I may be sent abroad."

"And you don't trust me in London on my own—is that it?" she said resentfully.

"Let's put it this way. I don't want to come back to find you in Holloway!" His voice was stern, and, seeing her sulky face, he sat down on the edge of the bed and took her hand. "I want you to stay out of trouble while I'm away. No suffragette marches and demonstrations for you. Promise me that you'll keep clear of the militant movement while I'm gone, Alexa!" His grip on her hand tightened.

Alexa pouted. "Oh, very well," she said sulkily.

"Good girl!" He ruffled her hair teasingly. "I know you're disappointed that our honeymoon trip will have to be postponed, but so am I," he reminded her. "And I'd prefer to think of you waiting for me here. Just as you are, in fact." He eyed her dishabille with an approving grin, then sighed and stood up. "And now I suggest you finish your breakfast while I'm in the dressing room . . . later you can get dressed yourself to come downstairs to see me off."

But Alexa pushed the tray away, finding that she had completely lost her appetite.

Chapter
15

What does a bride do with herself, Alexa wondered disconsolately, when deprived of her new husband on the very first day of their honeymoon?

At first she had meekly done all that was expected of her. She had gotten up and dressed herself becomingly and gone downstairs to see him off. She had, she thought, behaved in an exemplary fashion. She had not shed a tear nor created a scene. It was, she told herself for the umpteenth time, a singular honor that Sir Edward Grey had chosen Rowan for this diplomatic mission and she was proud of him. With a stiff upper lip, in a proper "dutiful wife" fashion, she told him so.

He kissed her goodbye rather absent-mindedly, as if his mind were already half a world away. And then she stood on the steps and waved a lace-trimmed hanky until the motorcar was out of sight. Rather as if she were a medieval bride seeing her man off to the Crusades, she grumbled to herself.

Oh, it wasn't fair! she thought resentfully. Men got to do all the really important things in life while women were expected to bide at home and twiddle their thumbs and take up tatting. Was this what *her* life was going to be from now on? she wondered. Seeing Rowan off on one mission after another while she was left behind to occupy herself as best she could. And to keep out of mischief! For Rowan had found it necessary to hedge her about with restrictions and prohibitions before he left, extracting from her yet another promise to stay away from the militants and admonishing her one last time to "stay out of trouble!" Exactly as if she were an unruly child, thought Alexa, simmering with repressed resentment.

Yet for the first few days, she did. She took morning rides and long solitary walks and explored country lanes in her new little runabout, perfecting her driving skills so that she would be able to cope with city traffic when the time came.

And, of course, she scoured the papers for news. At first they were full of "The Royal Tragedy" as front-page headlines bannered: HEIR TO AUSTRIAN THRONE SLAIN! SCHOOLBOY PATRIOT GAVRILO PRINCIP AVENGES AUSTRIAN SEIZURE OF HIS COUNTRY! FRANCIS FERDINAND AND

CONSORT SLAIN IN STATE VISIT! AGED EMPEROR FRANCIS JOSEPH STRICKEN WITH GRIEF!

But as June passed into July, the news became sparser and was relegated to the back pages.

Alexa frowned, pouring over the papers with ink-smudged fingers. The *London Times* averred that there was absolutely no cause for alarm; tragic though it was, the assassination would make no difference to the political stability of Europe.

That being the case, she didn't see why Rowan did not come home. She knew he had been sent to Vienna. He had rung her up, leaving a message to that effect, for she had been out when the call came through. She had been disappointed that she had been unavailable to take the call herself. To speak to him—to ask him how long he expected to be away—and . . . and just to hear his voice.

But perhaps it was just as well that she had not had the opportunity to talk to him, she reflected. Because something in her voice might have betrayed her—might have revealed to him just how terribly she missed him. And that would never do. She didn't want him to think she was languishing because of his neglect. Oh, my, no!

He needn't think that she was going to sit by the telephone waiting for him to ring up, she thought with a toss of her red head. Indeed not! She wasn't going to mope and droop around or sit home alone any longer.

She would, she decided, invite a few people down for the weekend. Lucinda, for one, with Mama as her chaperone instead of that detestable Lady Salter. And Lucy's most persistent suitor, Dabney Cathcart, for another.

She debated with herself the advisability of inviting her own rejected suitor, Derek Cathcart, and decided that there would be no impropriety in issuing him an invitation. He was still Rowan's good friend and her own.

She also invited a sprinkling of neighbors and Rowan's young subordinate at the Foreign Office, Jeremy Fortescue, and Lucinda's shy friend, Lady Helen Hope-Stanton, to whom Jeremy had recently become engaged.

Alexa felt her spirits rise at the prospect of a party. It would necessarily be a small, informal gathering as there would be no host. But there was no reason, these days, for a wife to go into purdah in the absence of a husband. Besides, the guests were all close friends.

It was a pity that Rowan could not be present on this, the first occasion that she would entertain guests in their home. But this was not the first time he had been sent abroad on an urgent diplomatic mission, nor, probably, would it be the last. Very likely this was a sample of what their married life would be like and she might as well get used to it, she thought with resignation.

Dinner was a gourmet's delight, cook
having done herself proud, and Alexa glowed
over the many compliments she received.
The table was resplendent with wedding-gift
china and silver and an elaborately arranged
centerpiece of her own design, while she
knew that she herself looked especially
attractive in the new "harem trousers" that
were all the rage in London. Mama had
raised her brows over them but forbore to
comment now that Alexa was a married
woman and beyond her control.

The gentlemen lingered long at table, and
when the ladies grew restive in the drawing
room, Alexa excused herself and went off to
lure them away from their port and cigars. A
bridge table had already been set up in the
drawing room and the elder ladies were
impatient to have a rubber or two before
bedtime while the younger ladies' toes were
tapping to the tunes of ragtime music from
Lucinda's victrola, which she and Lady
Helen had brought out in the expectation of
being partnered by their dilatory swains.

As Alexa crossed the hall to the dining
room, she heard voices raised in a lively
debate on the political situation.

She sighed. She might have known that the
men would get onto politics as soon as the
ladies had withdrawn, it not being considered a fit subject for feminine ears. In
truth, she herself would greatly have preferred it to the ladies' gossip and aimless
chit-chat, especially as Rowan was so closely

involved with whatever decisions were being made behind the closed doors of European chancelleries. She had cornered Jeremy Fortescue before dinner and had tried to pump him for information, but, being young and full of self-importance, he had been extraordinarily close-mouthed, looking mysterious and protesting that he was "not at liberty to divulge any information."

Apparently Rowan's best vintage port had loosened his tongue, for Jeremy now held forth at some length on the possibility of Austria demanding reprisals, with Germany backing her up and Russia threatening to mobilize. Alexa paused and perked up her ears, listening intently and trying to make sense of it all.

"And if Russia mobilizes, France will surely do the same," said a voice that Alexa did not recognize. "France is champing at the bit to get revenge on Germany for losing Alsace-Lorraine—to the Germans in the Franco-Prussian War. The policy of 'Revanche,' that's what it's called," said the voice authoritatively.

"Bah! It'll all blow over. Just as the Moroccan crisis did in 1905 and the Agadir crisis in 1911." The opinion was expressed by a neighborhood gentleman who had been invited to keep the numbers even.

"What do you hear from Rowan?" asked Derek Cathcart of Jeremy. "As he's in Vienna, he's in a good position to know the score."

"Er, yes, that is to say, he's not in Vienna, he's at Bad Ischl but—"

"Bad Ischl?" Derek broke in, startled.

"That's a coincidence. I heard that Frances Wyndham is spending the summer at Bad Ischl," another unidentified voice remarked significantly.

A kind of dirty chuckle ran round the table. "There's one for the books—to spend your honeymoon with your mistress instead of your bride!" someone exclaimed.

Alexa's heart stopped—and then started beating again with a painful thud that left her weak at the knees. She could feel herself turning first hot and then cold—icy cold. She stood riveted to the spot, her hand clenched to the doorknob.

From what seemed an enormous distance away, she heard Derek respond to the insinuation in an angry tone, and heard Jeremy mumble something, but she couldn't take anything in. Her thoughts were tumbling round and round in her head to the exclusion of anything else.

Why wasn't Rowan at the chancellery in Vienna as he was supposed to be? Could Jeremy be mistaken about that? But, no, he was Rowan's English liaison—he would know if anyone did.

And if Rowan *was* at Bad Ischl it could mean only one thing, she decided swiftly. That he had brought his diplomatic mission to a conclusion and chose to dally at the European spa with his mistress! And that

was why Jeremy had refused to give her any
details about Rowan's mission. Why he had
not told her of Rowan's present whereabouts!

She never knew how she got through the
rest of the evening. Chiefly, she supposed, by
sheer dogged determination not to give way
to her feelings.

Hurt, shame, anger and outrage jostled for
pride of place, first one and then another
floating uppermost in the sea of despair in
which she was engulfed.

She was sure that the male members of the
house party were looking at her with all the
smug superiority of those who think they
know something that you don't. And by
tomorrow, all the ladies (with the exception
of Mama and Lucinda, probably) would
know too.

She would have to endure pitying smiles
and sidelong glances and the hush that
would come over the room when she entered
it. Oh, she knew all about it. Hadn't she seen
Mama endure the very same treatment when
Papa's philandering was bruited about?

Yes, she knew how to play the role of
wronged wife to perfection. One kept one's
chin high and one's smile bright and ignored
the whispers. And, above all, one did not let
on that one's heart was breaking in one's
breast.

Oh, how she wished now that she had
never married him! She should have known
better than to marry a man who was not in

love with her. She should have denied her
heart's desire.

But she had thought that she could somehow win his love—that, given time, he would
come to love her a little.

How faint and foolish a hope that now
seemed. They had been given no time at
all—or hardly any. Fate had snatched him
away from her after only one night together.

And perhaps he had welcomed their
separation. He had seemed cold and distant
at parting, expressing few regrets at leaving
his young bride, and being chiefly concerned
that she should comport herself with dignity
and propriety while he was away—or so it
now seemed to her. His insistence that she
not involve herself with the suffragettes
while he was gone no longer seemed
expressive of any deep concern for her well-
being. Rather, it was an arrogant
assumption of authority over her, based on
his determination that she should not sully
the family name by getting herself thrown
into prison.

As if *he* were not sullying their good name
by dallying with his mistress at Bad Ischl!
she thought.

It was, in the end, the combined forced of
pride and indignation that helped her to hold
her head high and get through the interminable evening.

But that night, in her lonely bridal bed,
pride and indignation no longer sustained
her and she wept, heartbroken, into her

pillows, using them to muffle her sobs.

Was *she* at fault? she wondered miserably. Had she somehow been inadequate as a wife? Was it because she was too inexperienced to hold him? She writhed at the thought, wondering if he was, even now, with Lady Wyndham. If he was comparing her to his voluptuous mistress—and finding her wanting as a woman!

Then an even more appalling thought struck her. Had he perhaps requested this assignment? Had he *asked* to be sent on a mission that would take him away from his too naive and sexually inexperienced bride and bring him into the proximity of his mistress? The notion tormented her all that long sleepless night.

The grey light of dawn had begun to filter through the curtains before she finally gave way to exhaustion and fell into an uneasy and fitful doze.

She was heavy-lidded and heavy-hearted the next morning, wanting nothing so much as to hang onto blissful sleep as long as possible. But with a houseful of guests, she could not linger long abed to nurse her wounded feelings.

Rowan, who thought her lacking in self-discipline, would have been amazed at the composure and self-possession she displayed as she went downstairs to face the day and the assembled company.

But by the conclusion of that long, terrible weekend, she realized that no matter how

successfully Mama had contrived to conceal
her heartbreak over Papa's defection, she,
Alexa, was not cut out to follow in her footsteps. She felt utterly demoralized by the
effort entailed in keeping up the pretense
that all was well. Her bright false smile felt
permanently glued to her face, and, hard as
she tried, she knew that her air of cheerful
unconcern must appear forced and artificial.
More than once, her composure had nearly
cracked under the strain, especially when
she surprised glances of curiosity or
commiseration on the faces of her friends.

No, she couldn't keep up appearances as
Mama had done for long. It just wasn't in her
nature. Nor was she willing to go into
seclusion, to live quietly in retirement on the
estate, an object of pity among her social set.
She was not going to play second fiddle to
another woman and she was not going to
follow in Mama's footsteps either!

By the time she had thankfully sped the
last departing guest on his way, she had
made her mind up. She knew what she would
do. She would carve out a new life for herself. A life that did not include Rowan!

That the last guest happened to be Derek
Cathcart strenghtened her resolve. It had
been a mistake to invite him down for the
weekend and she wished now that she had
not done so. She simply could not bear the
look of pity and compassion in his gentle
brown eyes.

She had tried, successfully, to avoid a tête-à-tête with him all weekend, but politeness dictated that she walk him out to the courtyard where Chalmers, already behind the wheel of the Rolls, was waiting to drive him to the station.

They strolled along in an uncomfortable silence until Derek suddenly halted and reached for her hand, clasping it between his own. "If . . . if there is every anything I can do for you, Alexa," he said awkwardly.

"Thank you, Derek, but I'm quite sure there won't be." She spoke briskly, for she wanted no tender scenes—no sympathy.

He looked at her searchingly, and she knew he could sense the unhappiness she was trying so hard to hide. "It must be very lonely for you down here with Rowan—er, with everyone gone." The pressure of his hands tightened and he spoke with sudden energy. "It's unconscionable of him to leave you alone while he's—"

"Away on his mission," Alexa interrupted swiftly lest Derek say too much. If he once put her fears and suspicions into words, confirmed what she had overheard, she knew she would break down.

"Thank you, Derek," she said again. "But, in any case, I won't be here much longer." Disengaging her hands from his, she said decisively, "You see, I'm going up to town, to take a nurse's training course at Guy's Hospital." There—it was concrete—all of a sudden she had made up her mind. She would burn her bridges behind her and go.

Derek looked stunned. "You are?" he ejaculated. "And Rowan? Does he know about this? And approve?" he asked incredulously.

"Of course. We—er, ah—we discussed it before he left." Long before, Alexa recalled. About a month before, to be precise—on that fateful night they had spent together which had precipitated their ill-fated marriage. And he had not agreed to it then, she remembered. But now he had forfeited his right to object to her plans. Unconsciously she lifted her chin defiantly. She would not be subservient to any man, least of all one who had left her for another woman!

"You'll miss your train if you don't get off," she said pointedly.

Derek, still bemused, picked up the case he had set down at his feet and said awkwardly, "Well, then, perhaps we'll run into each other now and then up in London."

"Perhaps," said Alexa without enthusiasm. "I expect to be very busy." She wanted no faithful Dobbins hanging about and she had no intention of drifting into an affair with Derek—if that was what he was angling for.

She watched his departure without a twinge of regret. Well, perhaps only one—that she had had the misfortune to fall in love with Rowan instead of Derek.

Do we always want what we can't have? she wondered as she trailed back to the house. Is it part of the human condition to cry after the moon? To yearn for the unattainable. For Derek still had a tendresse for her, she knew, while she, despite his betrayal of her, still loved Rowan and she knew she always would.

But that didn't mean she was willing to be his doormat. No, indeed! She would not be subservient to any man, whoever he might be! She was not going to turn a blind eye to his amours—to wait around with puppydoglike devotion for such scraps of his attention as he chose to dole out to her. She was no meek little mouse to settle for second-best in his life and his heart. Unlike Mama, she wouldn't be satisfied to share her husband with another woman. Not she!

Reminded of Mama, she squared her shoulders for the fray and went off in search of her. Now that she had made up her mind what to do, she was not going to let any grass grow under her feet.

Nor would she slip away inconspicuously, surreptitiously, as she had the last time. She was not, she reasoned, running away; she was going to London to take charge of her own life at long last, and Mama must be made to understand and accept her decision.

"You're going to...*what!*" Mama shrilled. She could not, at first, believe her ears and said so, more than once and in several different ways. Her incredulity surpassed Derek's and was expressed in a tone several octaves higher.

Alexa had thoughtfully provided herself
with a vinaigrette and an ample supply of
hartshorn and water. Now she thrust the
former under Mama's nose and reiterated
her intentions in what she hoped was a calm
and reasoned manner.

"But . . . but it just isn't *done,* Alexa!"
Lady Mary protested. "You will be exposed
to . . ." she shuddered, "sights that no really
nice young woman should be exposed to.
You . . . you may be required to . . . to care
for members of the opposite sex. To . . . to
bathe them and, er, perform other intimate
services for them."

"I *am* a married woman, Mama," her
daughter reminded her.

Mama blushed but stood her ground.
"Exactly!" she said triumphantly, for she
had a second string to her bow. "You *are* a
married woman, now, Alexa, and your place
is at your husband's side."

"But Rowan is not here, Mama," Alexa
pointed out with sweet reasonableness. "So
how can I be at his side?"

"In such a case it is your duty to bide
quietly here at home until his return, like a
good and loving and faithful wife," Mama
said stubbornly.

"And how faithful is Rowan, Mama?"
Alexa retorted, her patience giving way at
last. She had not meant to bring up the
subject, but Mama's strictures had irritated
her unbearably.

"Oh, my dear," Mama sighed. "You have

heard the . . . the rumors then. I . . . I had hoped . . ." her voice trailed off. "But it may be only gossip," she said hopefully. "You should have faith in Rowan and—"

"As you did in Papa?" Alexa's mobile lips twisted in a grimace of pain.

Mama sighed heavily. "Oh, darling, you're so very young. You . . . you don't realize what men can be. Gentlemen . . ." she faltered, "Gentlemen have their little peccadilloes and a wife must sometimes learn to close her eyes to them."

"Maybe that was true once, Mama, but it isn't true any more. The modern woman . . ." About to embark on a long diatribe about women's rights, Alexa felt her hard-won composure suddenly slip away. Her face crumpling, she wailed, "Oh, Mama, I love him too much to endure his lack of love for me. I . . . I have to go away, to make a new life for myself so that he won't feel responsible for me any more. He only married me to protect my good name. He doesn't love me at all, you see." She fished out a hanky and mopped her streaming eyes. "I . . . I thought he would come to love me a little. I thought I could make it work, but it seems I can't. I'm only a . . . a complication in his life.

"I . . . I *must* go away, to work out my own destiny," she sobbed, blowing her nose into the tear-wet hanky. "Don't you see that this is something I must do?"

"Oh, my dear child," Lady Mary sighed,

her own eyes wet. "I hope you're not making a mistake."

"So do I, Mama. So do I."

Chapter
16

Alexa felt more like a nun on the verge of renouncing the world than a nurse-probationer when the gates of Guy's Hospital closed behind her. She had removed her wedding band and, in her preliminary interview, with the Matron, had given her name only as Alexandra Traherne, daughter of the late Sir Reginald and Lady Mary Traherne of Nun's Farthing. To have explained that she was an abandoned? neglected? forsaken? wife would have negated her chances to be accepted as a probationer, she felt sure.

She took a deep breath and rang the bell. After a few moments, the door was opened by an old housekeeper who was dressed all in black except for a stiffly starched white hospital cap.

When Alexa introduced herself, the old

woman led her upstairs to a spartan bedchamber overlooking the courtyard. The one
modest little trunk Alexa had allowed herself had already been delivered and she
unpacked it in silence and then dressed
herself in her new uniform, a colorless
mauve and white pin-striped garment with
an apron cut to hide the figure. The apron
and the collar, cuffs and belt of the uniform
were so stiffly starched as to be able to stand
alone. She was also provided with an
absurd little cap which was supposed to be
attached to the very tip-top of the head by
means of what Alexa suspected was going to
be a highly unreliable pin. Thick black
stockings and flat black shoes completed her
new ensemble and made her feel more nun-
like than ever.

She had been told to report to the
children's ward upon arrival and so she did.
It was an L-shaped room with deep
embrasured windows on both sides, holding
somewhere between twenty and thirty beds.
The room had a warm, cheerful atmosphere
which Alexa approved of immediately.

Baths were in progress when she stepped
hesitantly into the room, and the ward sister,
who was dressed in a well-fitting blue
uniform to distinguish her from the lowly
probationers, Alexa presumed, gave her a
sharp assessing glance and assigned to her a
naked squirming two-year-old.

"For me?" squeaked Alexa who had
supposed she would only be expected to look

on and learn that first day.

"Of course, you," said the sister briskly, her heels tapping as she clattered away to another and more demanding patient.

Alexa looked dubious. She had never bathed a child in her life. She had no idea how to begin, and she felt as if she had never, in all her twenty-one, almost twenty-two, years, done anything so practical.

She held the squirming baby gingerly and dabbed at it with a dampened cloth, getting more water on herself and on the floor than she did on the infant. Nevertheless, the child squalled as if Alexa were torturing him.

"Oh, hush!" she murmured desperately, sure that the child's screams would bring authority on the run. But nobody came to the little boy's rescue, nor to hers, and gradually it penetrated her consciousness that hers was not the only small patient vociferously voicing a protest. Evidently bath-time was not popular, and, emboldened by her success (at least she hadn't dropped him), she went on to the patient in the next bed.

Supper went better, though by the time she had popped spoonsful of porridge into numerous fledgling mouths and had gone off duty to her own meal, she was too tired to eat. Dragging herself wearily off to bed, she had serious doubts that she would be able to stay the course.

It seemed as if she had no more than closed her eyes when, promptly at six a.m., her alarm went off. She lay for a moment,

bewildered, the center ceiling light glaring
into her eyes, wanting nothing so much as to
roll over and go back to sleep. Then, remembering where she was and that it was the
first full day of her new life, she scrambled
out of bed and hastily washed and dressed.

Morning prayers began the day for everyone who was not already on duty, and, in
chapel, Alexa sent up a petition that she be
given strength and patience to cope with the
small patients entrusted to her care and,
please God, that she would not make any
mistakes—at least, not any serious ones.

Breakfast was presided over by an eagle-
eyed sister who kept track of late arrivals
and improperly dressed nurses, of which
Alexa, to her mortification, was one. She had
been used to doing for herself when she and
Mama had lived alone in London, she recol-
lected, as with a red face she corrected her
errors in dress, but ever since Rowan had
come into her life there had always been a
maid, either Violet or Hetty, to see that she
was tidy. Well, she would learn to do without
a maid to dress her, even at the ungodly
hour of six a.m., and soon, she thought,
resolving to do better tomorrow, lest she
earn another reprimand. And it was some
consolation that one or two of the other
nurses had also run foul of sister's sharp
tongue.

After breakfast it was off to the wards to
take over from the night people. Guy's
Hospital, she soon learned, was run along

military lines. You didn't speak to a superior
unless spoken to, and since, as the newest
probationer, she was low man on the totem
pole, nearly everybody was her superior.

A sharp reproof from Matron, an elderly
lady dressed all in black with a white frilled
cap, taught her that you also did not sit down
while on duty. So for the first few days of
eight-hour shifts, the pain in her feet and
legs equaled and even surpassed the pain in
her heart, and since it had the effect of
numbing her mind, she almost welcomed it.

Gradually she toughened up and the
hospital routine no longer seemed so harsh.
Life became a round of simple dressings,
fomentations, bedpans, and the filling in of
charts, recording temperatures, pulse rates
and respiration. On the whole, she was sure
that it was better to be busy than not. At
least you had no time to worry about your
own problems, or the world's problems
either.

Only occasionally did she find time to per-
use a newspaper. It was indicative of her
state of mind that when she did she skipped
over the national news (in which Emmeline
Pankhurst and the suffragettes still figured
prominently) in order to turn to the foreign-
affairs section. But she found little information that would explain Rowan's protracted absence. It did not occur to her that
the very lack of news from Vienna might, in
itself, be an ominous portent.

More ominous was the trip the French

president, Poincare, was making to Russia.
But, since it appeared to be a long-planned
state visit, she did not think it was of any
significance.

Her perusal of the newspapers only served
to convince her that nothing of any importance whatsoever was taking place in the
chancelleries of Europe. Surely, if war was
as imminent as Rowan had hinted nearly a
month ago, something would have happened
by now and the newspapers would be full of
it.

Unaware that behind the scenes diplomats
were working to prevent a general European
conflagration, her lips tightened. She might
as well face the fact that Rowan had seized
on the royal assassination as a gilt-edged
excuse to abandon his too-trusting bride for
the fleshpots of a fashionable European
watering place and the company of his
voluptuous mistress.

If Alexa had turned to the financial
section, she would have learned that something was indeed going on. From July 12 on-
ward, a selling wave had hit the Vienna
Bourse and the Paris Bourse was electrified
by a famous Viennese stockbroker who was
in the know. But Alexa knew nothing of international finance, and even if she had glanced
at the financial section of the paper she
would not have known how to interpret it.

Listlessly she flipped through a couple of
pages. The Irish were agitating for home
rule. There was trouble in Ulster. But when

had there not been trouble in Ireland? she wondered disinterestedly, not bothering to read down the column.

An article on the outrages perpetrated by the suffragettes caught her eye—"the shrieking sisterhood," a hostile editor termed them. She sighed, knowing that despite Asquith's meeting with Sylvia Pankhurst, the battle for the vote was not yet won. She dearly wished that she could be a part of it again, but her promise to Rowan barred her from active participation in the Cause and she would keep *her* promises, she vowed, even though *he* had so little respect for promises made at the altar.

Tears pricked her eyes and the newsprint wavered and swam. Blinking back the tears, she jumped up, crumpled the paper and tossed it into the dustbin. She wouldn't think about him any more—she just would not!

She got up, blew her nose, washed her face, and began to dress in one of her prettiest frocks. It was her half-day and Derek had rung up and asked her to luncheon at the Savoy. She didn't particularly want to go out with him but he had been very persistent, trotting out that old saw about "all work and no play," and she had reluctantly given in. It would be better than sitting around and moping, she realized, and it would be good to get away from the hospital precincts for a while.

"So—how goes the nursing?" asked Derek when the waiter had brought their entrees.

"Splendidly!" Alexa's eyes, which had been roaming around the luxurious room, taking in the elegantly dressed ladies and gentlemen, glowed. "Next week I'm going to learn how to do injections—intravenous and saline. I can already do the prep for operations and cut abscesses," she boasted. Then her eyes drifted from her own grilled chop to Derek's rare roast beef which was oozing pinkish juices all over his plate. "Oh, dear, I'm afraid it doesn't make for very good luncheon-table conversation," she said apologetically.

Derek looked amused. "I'm a soldier, my dear, and therefore not likely to be squeamish," he reminded her. "At least I hope not," he added ruefully. "The way things are going, it's not unlikely that I may see action before too much longer."

Alexa was startled. "Action!" she repeated. "Why, whatever do you mean?"

"Haven't you heard? The Austrians have issued an ultimatum to Serbia. They say the terms are so harsh that no sovereign state could accept them."

Alexa was stunned. "But . . . but it wasn't in the papers!" she protested.

"I heard about it at my club. It'll probably be in the late editions." He looked at her curiously. "I thought you might have heard about it from Rowan."

She looked down at her plate. "I haven't heard from him."

"Oh, well, you know how it is." Derek

looked uncomfortable, and wished he had not brought the subject up. "He's probably tied up in conferences or something of the sort. And you know Rowan—he has that quality of, er, total absorption in the problem at hand."

"Yes—yes, of course," she mumbled. She felt a momentary spasm of gratitude to Derek for his attempt to save her face.

"But even if Serbia rejects Austria's ultimatum—even if those two countries go to war—we won't be directly involved, will we?" she asked, bringing the subject quickly back to politics.

Derek shrugged. "Who's to say? Rowan's been saying for years that Europe is sitting on a powder keg, needing only one little spark to set it off."

The little spark that had been spluttering and fizzling for weeks burst into flames at the end of the month when Austria broke off diplomatic relations with Serbia (which had agreed to all but one of the Austrian demands) and almost immediately began to bombard the Serbian capital, Belgrade.

"AUSTRIA DECLARES WAR ON SERBIA!" headlines bannered. "PEACE OF EUROPE IN KAISER'S HANDS!"

Alexa scoured the paper for news, wondering what would happen next and when Rowan would come home. She longed for his return, and yet, paradoxically, she dreaded it. What his attitude towards her new occupation would be she couldn't imagine. She felt sure of only one thing—that she loved her work and she was good at it and she wouldn't give it up for anyone—not even Rowan!

And why should she? she asked herself. She didn't intend to spend her life rusticating down in the country as Mama had done. She would not be content with scraps of her husband's attention whenever he wasn't busy squiring his mistress around London. For now that Austria was at war, Lady Wyndham would surely come home—if she wasn't back already.

It did occur to Alexa to wonder if perhaps she had not leapt to conclusions. After all, it was obvious now that at least some of the time he had been abroad Rowan had been engaged on government business.

No doubt solaced in his spare time by Lady Wyndham! she reminded herself bitterly. For he had been at Bad Ischl—Jeremy had said so. What business could he have had at that exclusive resort? she asked herself. None that she could think of—except to conduct an illicit intrigue with his mistress!

She followed the news with feverish intensity. Russia had mobilized in defense of besieged Serbia. Germany, ally of Austria, declared war against Russia, then mobilized against France, Russia's ally. One by one, the great powers of Europe fell into line like so many ninepins with a grim inevitbility that was almost guaranteed by their system of interconnecting alliances.

England was the last.

July had turned into August and still Rowan had not come home. It was Bank Holiday Weekend, and Matron, who was more far-seeing than most, granted an unprecedented amount of leave to her staff.

Alexa, who had nowhere to go and no one she especially wanted to be with, volunteered for extra duty. She watched a group of giggling probationers go off duty with a wistful sigh. Some were going to the seaside for the weekend; others home to their families. One girl, Molly, who had become her special friend, had invited her home to meet her brother.

"Come on, Alexa," Molly urged. "You've had hardly any time off since you've been here. My mum and dad would love to meet you. You'd get to meet my Bert—goodness knows, I've told you enough about him!" Molly giggled. "And my brother, Fred. He's a good-looker, is Fred. And he likes redheads," she went on coaxingly. "We could make up a foursome and go dancing. Mum's not so strict when there's another couple along."

Plump Molly cocked her head and eyed Alexa's slender frame critically. "And you could do with a bit of feeding up. Get away from this horrible hospital fare. You haven't lived till you've tasted my mum's steak and kidney pie. And her scones and jam tarts fairly melt in your mouth," she boasted.

But Alexa was resolute in declining the

invitation. She might have been tempted, she reflected, if she hadn't been so sure that Molly was intent on matchmaking. Not for the first time, she keenly felt the anomaly of her position. Pretending to be single and un-attached when in truth she was a married woman had its pitfalls, she reflected. Simply because of the irregularity of her position, she had met the other girls' overtures of friendship with a rebuff, but pretty Molly was as friendly and exuberant as a puppy and had penetrated the wall of reserve that Alexa had built around herself.

"Maybe next time," Alexa parried, knowing she didn't mean it but not wanting to hurt Molly's feelings. She had no wish to meet the good-looking Fred and complicate her already complicated life any further. "I've already informed Matron I'll be available for extra duty this weekend," she reminded her friend. "I can't let her down now. Besides, if Bert has you all to himself this weekend, he'll be more likely to pop the all-important question."

"Don't I wish!" Molly sighed. "Though we couldn't get married for ages—Bert's saving up to buy his own greengrocer's shop, you know." She patted her hair, examined her face in the little mirror over Alexa's dresser, and pinned her hat more firmly. "Well, ta-ta," she said, turning towards the door. "See you on Tuesday then."

By Monday, August 4, Alexa was dead on

her feet. Because the hospital was short-staffed, she had been shifted about from ward to ward to take up the slack as needed—chiefly on Casualty where she had been confronted, at various times, with a baby brought in with convulsions, a toddler who had swallowed a pin, several assorted brawlers who had been celebrating the holiday weekend rather too exuberantly, and the victims of a collision between a motorcar and a hansom cab. And then, when Casualty had quieted down, she had been transferred to the Surgical Ward to prep and scrub and assist at a number of unscheduled emergency operations.

But it was all worthwhile, despite her aching feet, she thought with a glow of pride. Casualty Sister had praised her quick wits and steady nerves. The consulting surgeon, Mr. Hardcastle, had praised her deftness in handing him the correct instruments as called for, and stern Surgical Sister had suggested that she apply for the crash course in surgical nursing that Matron was planning to set up if war was declared.

The German war machine had crashed through tiny Luxembourg on August 2 and was marching on neutral Belgium, whose tiny army was ill-equipped to stem the grey-uniformed tide.

Alexa was just about to go off duty when she was summoned to Matron's office. She had not entered that august precinct since her initial interview and she had a sinking feeling that she was being called on the carpet. But, for what? Had she perpetrated some frightful gaffe? Made some quite unforgivable mistake? But no, as far as she could determine, everything had gone as it ought.

She reached for a clean cap and apron, but sister said with a warning frown, "Go as you are, nurse. Matron said you were to report to her office *immediately*."

Alexa bit her lip. "Yes, sister," she said meekly and went off to take her punishment.

She hesitated outside Matron's door. Then, taking a deep breath, she rapped softly. A frosty voice invited her in. Alexa squared her shoulders and stepped hesitantly into the room.

She was so intent on the elderly woman in the crisp uniform seated behind the desk that she did not notice that the room had another occupant—a tall figure lounging by the window.

Alexa shut the door behind her and advanced a few steps into the room. "You sent for me, Matron?"

"I did," that lady confirmed. "It seems you have a visitor, nurse. Or should I say, Mrs. Traherne?" She gestured towards the figure in the window embrasure and Alexa's puzzled eyes followed the movement. "A gentleman claiming to be—" Matron's tone was icy with distaste—"your husband!"

Chapter 17

Alexa felt her heart give a great thump of joy. It was Rowan. Home at last!

Her first instinct was to cast herself into his arms, but she had learned self-restraint. Besides, the look on his dark face was so forbidding that she quailed before it. So she stood, taut as a strung bow, her hands clenched at her sides, and whispered, "H-hello, Rowan."

He inclined his head coldly. "Alexa."

Matron looked from one to the other. "This gentleman has come to me with an incredible story, nurse. He claims that he is your husband, and in his absence, you ran away from home in a fit of pique. That you came to us for training without either his knowledge or consent." She riveted a pair of stern eyes on Alexa. "Is this true, nurse? Is this gentleman your husband?"

Tearing her fascinated gaze away from Rowan, Alexa mumbled an assent.

Matron expelled a long breath. "Well!" she said, evidently at a loss for words.

But Rowan was not. "I am gratified to hear that you remember you have a husband, Alexa," he grated.

"I wish I could say that it is equally gratifying that you finally remember you have a wife!" she flashed back, her temper roused by his sarcasm. All of a sudden, she didn't feel the least bit meek or placatory.

"Now what the hell is that supposed to mean?" Quick as lightning, an irate Rowan stepped forward and grasped her arm, using his other hand to tilt her chin up to face him.

"What do you think it means?" Alexa glared at him defiantly, even as she tried to squirm free.

They stared at each other, two adversaries locked in mutual hostility.

Matron's sharp voice interposed between them. "I should be gratified if you would take your marital squabbles elsewhere! Nurse, your dismissal from this hospital becomes effective immediately. I suggest you go and pack your belongings."

Alexa shook herself loose from Rowan's grasp and turned an imploring face up to her. "Oh, but Matron . . . !"

"This is a hospital, not a refuge for bored society ladies," said Matron grimly. Seeing Alexa's woebegone face, she added a little more gently, "Not that we won't be sorry to lose you, several of our sisters have spoken highly of your work, and Mr. Hardcastle himself has recommended you for a course in surgical nursing."

"Oh, please, Matron . . . I . . ."

"Nevertheless," that lady went on resolutely. "You came here under false pretenses, pretending to be something you were not. The deception . . . in addition to the distasteful scene enacted here today . . . is inexcusable."

"I apologize for the inconvenience you have been put to on my wife's account, Matron," said Rowan smoothly. "Come, Alexa. We have taken up quite enough of Matron's valuable time." He grasped her elbow firmly and propelled her to the door.

Alexa glared at him mutinously but she could see that there was nothing for it but to go along quietly and with as much dignity as she could muster.

But as soon as they were out of Matron's sight, she wrenched herself away from him. "Now see what you've done!" she hissed, on the verge of tears, as she rubbed the arm his fingers had bitten deeply into.

Rowan was all solicitude. "I'm sorry. Did I hurt you?"

She rolled up her sleeve and peered at the red marks his fingers had imprinted on her arm. "Not much. Anyway, I wasn't referring to that." She rolled her sleeve back down and buttoned it at the wrist. "What I meant was—your getting me dismissed from hospital."

"I had no intention to do any such thing. You must believe me, Alexa. I had no idea Matron would go to such an extreme measure." He grinned mirthlessly. "You should have seen her face when I announced myself as your husband. I had, of course, no idea that you were masquerading as a single woman."

Alexa ignored his apology. "How did you know where to find me?" she demanded.

"From your mama, of course," he said patiently. "As soon as I got back to England and had made my report to Sir Edward, I went down to Nun's Farthing. Your mother told me you were here." His face twisted into a wry grin. "I'd gone down to the country in the expectation of surprising you. Instead I got a none too pleasant surprise myself. I hadn't expected you to sneak off to London almost as soon as my back was turned."

Alexa's eyes snapped. "I did not *sneak off*, as you put it . . . I . . ."

"Perhaps my choice of words was unfortunate," he conceded. "In any case, there are better places to discuss it than a hospital corridor."

This was undeniably true. Nurses brushed past them; attendants pushing patients in wheeled chairs and the occasional ambulatory making his way down the corridor—all cast curious glances in their direction.

"I suggest you go and pack. Meanwhile I'll make arrangements with the porter to have your trunk sent on. If you're coming home with me, that is!" he said, eyeing her sardonically.

"I don't have much choice, do I!" She lifted her shoulders in a shrug. "I have nowhere else to go. You've seen to that."

She had forgotten how high-handed Rowan could be, she mused as she stripped off her stained uniform and refreshed herself with a hasty sponge bath from the bowl and pitcher at her washstand.

If only he had contacted her in the ordinary way instead of announcing himself to Matron in such an arbitrary fashion—for all the world as if he *owned* her, she fumed. As if she were a piece of lost luggage he had temporarily misplaced and was now reclaiming—as if she were a possession and not a person, an individual in her own right with needs and desires of her own.

That certainty he possessed—the certainty of his own superiority—was absolutely insufferable, she decided. It was that, more than anything else, that had put her back up. For a moment—a very brief moment—she had been glad to see him. Oh, so very glad! And then he . . .

She shook her head and went on dressing, in a blue knee-length tunic over a darker blue ankle-length skirt which had a smart little jacket to match. It wasn't chosen to impress him—of course not—it was to keep up her own morale, she told herself firmly as she tossed the rest of her clothing helter-

skelter into her case and sat on it to close the
latch.

Rowan had already summoned a cab to
convey them back to Cadogan Square. The
streets were thronged with holiday makers
and an air of festivity prevailed. Alexa stared
stonily out of the window as if she were fascinated by the throngs of pedestrians,
ignoring—or pretending to ignore—Rowan,
who in any case seemed lost in his own
thoughts.

It was the first time she had entered his
house as its mistress—no longer "Miss
Alexa" to the servants but "the Madame"
and she felt as if she were being catapulted
back into another and far different world.

Rowan's longtime housekeeper, Mrs.
Brownell, fluttered round and took Alexa upstairs to take off her hat and jacket.

"Where is Miss Lucinda?" asked Alexa
casually. The house seemed unusually quiet
and her heart sank. She'd hoped that Lucy's
effervescent presence might have helped to
ease the strain.

But she was doomed to disappointment.
"Miss Lucinda is at a house party in Oxford-
shire, Madame," the housekeeper informed
her. "Lady Salter is, of course, acting as her
chaperone."

Ah, well, if she were to be deprived of
Lucinda's sympathy and support, at least
she would not have Lady Salter to contend
with, reflected Alexa philosophically as,
accompanied by Mrs. Brownell, she made

her way up the broad, curving staircase and along a long, carpeted hall to the bedroom reserved for the mistress of the house.

And then—"Oh!" she exclaimed as Mrs. Brownell ushered her into the room which she remembered from a previous visit as impossibly dark and gloomy. With unconcealed astonishment she gaped at the transformation. Gone were the heavy plush draperies, the massive Victorian furniture, banished along with the miscellaneous clutter of knickknacks and family photographs, so beloved of Rowan's mama, whose room this had once been.

Devoid of its fussy ornaments, the room seemed much more spacious and infinitely lighter and brighter. The walls had been distempered in a pale cream color and hung with a few good pictures in the impressionist style, Alexa noted with pleasure. The carpet was thick-pile and pale gold and there was an assortment of light wicker furniture scattered around the room—a comfortable chair, a divan, and a wicker table which held a couple of her favorite books and a stack of magazines, the topmost being a suffragette periodical.

"I hope everything meets with your approval, madame," said the housekeeper, her tone expressing some doubt. "The master had it especially done up for you while he was away."

"It's lovely," Alexa breathed, her eyes roaming round the room, taking in the bright cushions piled on the divan, the dainty escritoire installed at a deeply set bay window, in place of the rather hideous potted aspidistra that she remembered. Slowly she unpinned her hat and sent it sailing across the room to the divan.

Mrs. Brownell helped her out of the tight-fitting jacket, saying, "The master informed me that you would be dining at home tonight. It's rather short notice, but I hope that Cook will be able to come up with something rather special. If you would like to consult with her about the menu—"

"No, no, I'm sure that whatever she has planned will do very well," said Alexa hastily, as the door of the connecting master bedroom swung open and Rowan appeared.

"Do you require anything further, madame?"

"No, thank you, Mrs. Brownell. That will be all." Alexa watched absently as the woman bobbed a curtsy and tactfully withdrew, then turned, with obvious reluctance to Rowan. She felt awkward and ill at ease with him, though why she should, she couldn't imagine. After all, he was the one at fault, wasn't he? Not she—she hadn't done anything wrong!

There was an awkward pause and Alexa rushed to fill it in. "Er—this room—it's lovely, Rowan," she said a trifle shyly.

His somber face broke into a smile. "You're pleased with the changes then? I thought you might be . . . I fancy I've learned your taste by now. Perhaps," he added slyly, "I know you better than you know yourself."

An indignant Alexa was searching for a tart remark to puncture his complacency when he reached into his waistcoat pocket and withdrew a small jeweled case. "I trust you will find this equally to your liking." He placed the box in her hand.

Alexa stared down at it, dumbfounded.

"Well, what are you waiting for?" he said. "Go ahead. Open it."

She fumbled with the catch with nervous fingers. It sprang open to her touch, revealing an exquisitely wrought gold ring. Delicate filigree work enshrined two entwined hearts, the one engraved with his initial, the other with hers.

Alexa gasped her pleasure. "Oh, Rowan, it's exquisite!" she exclaimed.

"Fabergé," he said carelessly. "A little thing I picked up in St. Petersburg." He took the box from her and, setting it on the table, removed the ring and, lifting her hand, slipped it on her finger. She watched wordlessly, expecting a sharp comment on the state of her hands which were rough and reddened from her hospital work, the nails broken and chipped. But he seemed not to notice or, if he did, he withheld any criticism.

"Petersburg? You've been in St. Petersburg?" she repeated in surprise.

"Among other places, yes. Tsarkoe Selo, actually, where I had an annoyingly incon-

clusive inteview with the tsar." His face
hardened. "The man's a positive weather-
vane," he said with sudden irritation.
"Agrees with the last person he sees. And the
tsarina . . . .!" Rowan's tone was eloquent of
distaste. "If ever a man was henpecked . . . .!"

Under normal circumstances, Alexa would
have been fascinated with this private
glimpse into the characters of the Russian
autocrats but tonight she had more important things on her mind.

"But . . . but I thought you were in
Vienna?" she said carefully.

"I was, but only briefly. I've been all over,"
he said easily. "Vienna . . . Berlin . . . Petersburg . . . Belgrade . . . then back to Berlin
and then a short abortive trip to Norway."

"Norway!" she exclaimed. "What on earth
were you doing in Norway, of all places?"

"Trying to arrange a meeting with Kaiser
Wilhelm," Rowan explained. "He was incom-
municado—cruising on his yacht among the
Norwegian fords."

"Oh, yes, I . . . I remember now. That is, I
believe it was mentioned in the papers,"
Alexa mumbled. She twisted the ring on her
finger. Rowan hadn't mentioned Bad Ischl.
Deliberately? she wondered. She took a deep
breath. She had to know. She just had to!

"And . . . and Bad Ischl? You were there?"

"For a short time, yes."

Alexa's heart sank. Out of his own
mouth . . . ! He admitted it. He had been in
Bad Ischl with Frances Wyndham!

She gazed unhappily down at the ring on her finger. The two hearts entwined were nothing more than a sample of the exquisite workmanship of Fabergé. It didn't have any significance for him. It meant absolutely nothing.

Alexa had heard of gentlemen who presented their wives with a jewel each time they were unfaithful to them. Probably Rowan's gift fell into that category, she thought stormily. Why, her own mama had had a string of pearls that Papa had added to at frequent intervals. Most likely every time he took a new mistress, she thought cynically.

A sudden rush of rage welled up inside her. She was tempted to tear the ring from her finger and throw it back in his face. Scream that *she* would not be treated in such a cavalier fashion.

She twisted it round and round her finger—pulled it over the knuckle—and then . . .

Then the dressing bell rang.

Ordinarily, Alexa was of the opinion that in Society one was forced to spend a disproportionate amount of time dressing and undressing—changing from a riding habit to a morning dress to a walking dress, from a tea gown to a dinner dress . . . but tonight she felt positively saved by the bell. It was with a sense of relief that she heard its summoning clangor.

Oh, they would have to have it out sooner

or later, she knew, but suddenly later
seemed infinitely preferable. It would give
her a chance to get control of herself, to
quell the tumultuous emotions that were
tumbling around inside her. Yes, a decent
interval would give her a chance to think the
thing through. To explain to him clearly and
lucidly that they could not resume their
marriage while he kept a mistress. She
would have no part of a ménage a trois! And
she must do it in a dignified and civilized
fashion. She would not rail at him like a fishwife—no—she must maintain control of
herself and the situation. She must not let
him see how much he had hurt her—there
must be no undignified row. She would be
calm, cool and collected when she broached
the matter to him.

Later.

He had stilled her restless hands with his
own and his touch seemed to burn her like
fire. "Alexa," he began, "I'm sorry that our
reunion got off on the wrong foot. I . . ."

"Er—that was the dressing bell," she
reminded him a trifle breathlessly. "We—we
should change for dinner. We mustn't be
late. I . . . I understand that Cook has something rather special planned."

He disengaged her hands from his own.
"Quite so," he said tonelessly. "And on no
account must we disappoint Cook, must
we?"

Over a lavish dinner served by soft-footed
maids, the conversation was kept discreetly

impersonal. Alexa, who had not caught even a glimpse of the newspapers all weekend, so busy had she been, asked him about the war brewing in Europe.

"We'll be in it at midnight tonight," Rowan predicted, his face grim.

"Oh, Rowan, *no*!" Alexa exclaimed in dismay. She hadn't really, in her heart of hearts, ever believed that England would be drawn into Europe's quarrels.

"Oh, yes, my dear; I'm afraid so. His Majesty's Government has issued an ultimatum demanding German withdrawal from Belgian territory, in accordance with our long-term treaty with Belgium guaranteeing her neutrality."

Alexa frowned thoughtfully. "I can't understand why Germany is invading France through Belgium," she confessed. "Surely there's another way round."

"Ah, but German military strategy, the so-called Schlieffen Plan, demands a vast offensive into France through Belgium so as to achieve the speedy envelopment of the main French armies and their destruction in a quick decisive battle. Speed is of the essence, Alexa," he went on to explain. "Germany wants to knock France out of the war quickly and then turn her military might against Russia before she gets bogged down to a two-front war."

"Hmm—I suppose it makes sense," Alexa said thoughtfully. She was pleased and flattered that Rowan was going to the

trouble of explaining it all to her. So many
men would have taken it for granted that a
mere woman could not possibly understand
military strategy. Most men of her ac-
quaintance would have patted her hand con-
descendingly and advised her "not to bother
her pretty little head" about such things, she
felt sure.

Wanting to prolong the discussion, she
wrinkled her nose and confessed, "I don't
really understand why Germany should rush
at France just because some hotheaded
young Serbian shot an Austrian archduke. It
doesn't seem to connect," she pondered.

"It's complicated," Rowan admitted. "The
more so as every country involved feels that
it's defending its own interests against
agressors."

"But how can that be?" Alexa protested.

Rowan shrugged. "Austria is defending
the integrity of its ramshackle empire.
Gavrilo Princip was a Serb and Serbia has
been a hotbed of intrigue for years, giving
shelter and protection to Austrian mal-
contents," he explained. "Russia is inter-
vening on Serbia's behalf in the interests of
Slav solidarity. Germany, Austria's ally,
fears encirclement and isolation if Austria is
defeated, so she invades France, Russia's
ally."

"Through Belgium, whose neutrality we
have sworn to protect," added Alexa.

"Exactly." Rowan pushed his chair away
from the table, at which they had lingered

long, and stood up. "And that reminds me. I have to go out for a while."

"Tonight?" Alexa was startled. He was going out—leaving her—on his first night home? What could there be that was so urgent?

And then the light dawned. Of course, she thought. Frances Wyndham would be back in England now, here in London, and Rowan was rushing off to her side.

Pain so severe that it almost made her gasp stabbed at her heart. She felt crushed, hurt and humiliated beyond belief, but pride came to her rescue.

"Of course, if you must go . . ." she said stiffly, her quivering chin held high. She rose from the table, blinking back tears. "The servants will be wanting to clear away. I . . . I think I shall go up to my room. Have an early night."

She started to brush past him, but Rowan's muscular body blocked her path to the door. "Wait. I have an idea. Why don't you come with me," he suggested.

"Come with you?" echoed Alexa in consternation.

"Yes, why not? I shouldn't be too long and Sir Edward won't mind."

"Sir Edward?" Alexa parroted blankly. What had Sir Edward to do with it?

As if he could read her mind, Rowan said shortly, "I have an appointment with him in half an hour." He frowned thoughtfully. "We'll have little enough time together as it is, so—"

"Little enough time?" Alexa faltered. "I don't understand. Whatever do you mean?"

"The war, my dear. As soon as it becomes official, I intend to tender my resignation to the Foreign Office and wangle a commission in my old regiment."

Alexa went quite white. "But you're a diplomat, not a soldier," she protested faintly.

"My dear, the time for diplomacy is past, I fear," he said gently. "You wouldn't want me to be a shirker, now would you?"

Obscurely Alexa felt that she would, if it would keep him safe from harm! She bit her lip. "I suppose not," she said reluctantly. Somehow she hadn't thought he would go, even if there was a war on. Surely a man of Rowan's capabilities would be wasted as—as cannon fodder! she thought rebelliously.

"You'll take up a staff position, I suppose," she said hopefully, grasping at a straw.

But Rowan shook his head. "No red tabs for me. I expect to go to the front. It is what I was trained for, Alexa," he reminded her.

Suddenly she knew, beyond any shadow of a doubt, that all of the hurt and humiliation she had experienced was as nothing compared to the terrible prospect of losing him in battle. That her jealousy of Lady Wyndham was a petty and trivial thing compared to this new and terrifying threat of war and destruction.

"You . . . you might be killed," she whispered through stiff white lips.

He caught her chin in his big hand and turned her white, pinched face up to his.

"Would you care so very much?" he said gently.

"Care?" she said unsteadily. "Of course I care. I—"

"Strange," Rowan mused, looking deeply into her eyes. "I could have sworn you cared only for your causes. For improving the lot of women. For your independence and this new career you embarked on in my absence."

"I . . . I love my work. Of course I do," Alexa said slowly. "I wouldn't have taken it up if I didn't feel deeply about it. I do it well and I find it . . ." she broke off and corrected herself—"that is, I *found* it a source of satisfaction and fulfillment."

"There are other kinds of fulfillment, Alexa," he observed.

"I . . . I know that, now." She flushed, making an inconclusive little gesture with her hands. "Let me finish, please." She took a deep breath. "You have your work and your commitments and I have—*had*," she corrected herself again, "had mine. I don't see any reason that I should be denied the work I want to do just because I'm a woman and . . . and your wife." For a moment her voice rang with defiance. Then she paused, bit her lip, and went on in a softer tone.

"But . . . but that doesn't mean that I don't care about you, Rowan, because . . . because I do."

"Only . . . care?" he persisted. "Care enough to give up your work and your causes because I ask it of you?"

She had wanted so deeply once to pit her strength against the world's enormous ills. She had craved her freedom as much, almost, as she had craved his love. But now she found herself wanting only to be his.

She tried to twist away—to evade the moment of truth—to evade his mesmeric eyes, but she felt hypnotized by them. They were deep, stormy pools in which she felt lost, drowned. She felt herself sinking into their measureless grey depths, like a fragile little barque going down in a storm-tossed sea. She had a notion that the keen brain behind those eyes could read her every thought. So what was the use of evasion?

"Yes, yes, I would," she whispered. "You see, I . . . I love you, Rowan."

There, it was said. She had cast discretion to the four winds, abandoned her pride. She felt herself trembling, her heart racing like a mad thing.

He let out the long breath he had been holding and then she felt his strong arms enfolding her, his heart thudding as he crushed her against him. "Oh, my dearest," he murmured huskily, "I was beginning to believe that I would never hear those words from your lips. All those weeks apart it was all I could do to keep my mind on the task at hand—I tried to write you but I couldn't find the words to tell you how much—how very much I missed you. The only thing that kept me going was picturing you at home waiting for me to come back to you." He drew a long, unsteady breath. "Then when I got back and found you gone I went half-crazy with worry. I thought sure you'd come up to London to join your suffragette friends in Holloway. And when your mother told me you were in hospital, at first I thought she meant as a patient. That you'd taken part in a demonstration or got caught up in a riot, despite your promise to me. By the time I found out differently, I was in a black rage. And it was in a rage that I confronted Matron.

"I love you, Alexa—so much that all I could think of was protecting you, keeping you safe from harm. I've wanted to bind you to me hand and foot, subdue that independent spirit of yours, master you, if you like."

He shook his head. "What a fool I've been. I should have known you would chafe at the restrictions I set upon you . . . resent being cooped up like a bird in a gilded cage . . . and break out at the first opportunity."

"It wasn't altogether that," Alexa admitted, her face muffled against his chest as he stroked her bright hair. "I . . . *did* come up to London in a fit of pique, Rowan. You were right about that. I'd heard about you and Lady Wyndham, you see, and I—"

"About me and Frances Wyndham?" he
ejaculated. "Surely you don't hold me to
account for that. We did have a relationship,
I don't deny that. But it was over long
ago—long before we were married."

"But . . . but you went to Bad Ischl to be
with her," Alexa protested. "You *were* at Bad
Ischl, Rowan. You told me so yourself."

"Of course I was there. There's no secret
about that," he said, a trifle irritably. "The
Austrian emperor, Francis Joseph, has a
summer residence at Bad Ischl. When I got
to Vienna, he'd already left Schoenbrunn
Palace for his summer villa. It was of the utmost urgency that I consult with him, so I
followed him there. It's as simple as that."

"And . . . and you didn't see Lady Wyndham at all?" Her troubled eyes looked
searchingly up into his face.

"I saw her, yes. But only briefly. She *and*
her husband, I might add. I could see, even
then, that the peace negotiations were
getting nowhere and, as an old friend, I
wanted to warn her to prepare for the worst.
Advise her to pack up and come home before
all hell broke loose on the continent. I felt
there was a danger that she and her ailing
husband might well be interned as enemy
aliens if they lingered too long. As far as I
know, they took my advice and left the next
day. I haven't seen her since."

"Oh," Alexa said, in a small voice. There
was the ring of truth in his tone, and
suddenly she felt supremely foolish. In her

usual impetuous fashion she had jumped to quite the wrong conclusion.

She bent her head, hiding her red face in his dinner jacket, but he tipped up her chin with a caressing finger, forcing her to face him, saying tenderly, "My dear, my very foolish dear, I've never felt about any other woman the way I do about you. I know they say that passion is all the same to a man and who the woman is doesn't really matter, but that simply isn't true. After having you, after loving you, I certainly don't want anyone else—only you."

"Really, Rowan?"

Her lips were quivering temptingly near his own. "Really, my dear," he murmured huskily before claiming them in a long, lingering kiss, a kiss that was sweeter than any they had shared before.

It seemed only a moment later that Rowan's very correct town-house butler, Flemings, opened the door and stepped soft-footedly into the room.

Alexa could barely restrain a giggle at the sight of his scandalized face as master and mistress hastily stepped apart.

"Excuse *me*, sir—and madame," Flemings exclaimed with ponderous dignity. "I had thought you had gone out, sir, and that madame was in the drawing room. It is well past the usual dinner hour, sir," he added, a touch reproachfully, his eyes going to the as-yet-uncleared dining table in a meaningful fashion.

"So it is," agreed Rowan. Such was his self-possession that he appeared quite unabashed at being caught in the act of kissing his wife in the dining room at "well past the usual dinner hour."

"Dinner was delicious, Flemings," Alexa added mendaciously, for she hadn't noticed what was on her plate and, if asked, could not have said what the menu consisted of. "Please convey my compliments to Cook."

"Very well, madame."

"You can have things cleared away now, Flemings. My wife and I are going out for the evening. I expect we'll be quite late so you need not wait up. I have my key."

"Very good, sir."

"I wish I needn't go out," Rowan said regretfully when Flemings had disappeared. "The thing is I made only the skimpiest report to Sir Edward before rushing off to Nun's Farthing. I promised him a detailed report this evening. Of course, it's probably academic now," he glanced at the clock, "but he is expecting me." He looked down at her tenderly. "But you needn't come unless you want to, Alexa. You do look a bit done in."

"Oh, but I do want to," Alexa said quickly. She tucked her hand under his arm. "I want us to share every minute of our time together, however brief it may be."

She waited quietly in an anteroom while Rowan was making his report to his superior. Though it was very late, lights were lit all over the Foreign Office and busy secretaries bustled to and fro.

Somewhere a clock chimed and Alexa shivered. She knew that the hour by which Germany must reply to England's ultimatum to withdraw her military forces from Belgium had come and gone.

A few minutes later, Rowan came to the door of the inner room and beckoned her inside. "Sir Edward would like a word with you, Alexa," he said quietly.

"With me?" She got up uncertainly and followed him into the other room.

Sir Edward Grey, the tall, suave Foreign Minister of England, was standing at his window looking down on the Horse Guards' Parade. He turned round with an urbane smile as she entered. "Come in, my dear," he said warmly, clasping the hand she held out to him as Rowan performed the introductions. "We owe you a debt of gratitude for lending us your husband at such a critical period. I need hardly say that his services have been invaluable."

"I only wish his mission had been a success, Sir Edward," Alexa ventured.

"As do we all, my dear, as do we all." The older man, his face furrowed with anxiety, sighed. "Nevertheless, he did what he could. And you did your part nobly. It could not have been easy for a new bride to see her husband off on a mission of such gravity, leaving her alone. I deeply regretted the necessity of recalling him from his honeymoon, but, as I'm sure you understand, it could not be remedied."

Alexa blushed, wishing now that she had been as noble as Sir Edward implied. She mumbled something quite inaudible and looked away, down onto the Horse Guards' Parade.

"I am given to understand that you employed the time quite profitably, too," Sir Edward went on. "Taking up training as a nurse. Very foresighted of you," he said with warm approval. "Our country will need not only every man to do his duty in the hard times ahead but every woman as well."

"Umm, thank you, Sir Edward," she mumbled, quite horribly embarrassed at this undeserved praise. She was thankful that he could not know that it was neither altruism nor patriotism that had motivated her, but jealousy!

"Oh, look, Sir Edward," she exclaimed. "The street lamps are going out in St. James's Park. Is it because we must expect German zeppelins to drop bombs on us?"

"Oh, my dear," said Sir Edward sadly. He gave a heavy sigh. "The lights are going out all over Europe. We shall not see them lit again . . ."

A few minutes later, Rowan and Alexa joined the crowds that had thronged in the streets, releasing their emotions in long bursts of frenzied cheers and shouts and patriotic songs. A band had struck up Elgar's "Land of Hope and Glory" and everyone was enthusiastically singing along.

Alexa tugged at Rowan's sleeve and he inclined his head so that she could shout into his ear. "Everybody seems so enthusiastic!" she said, puzzled.

"They're drunk on enthusiasm, Alexa," he explained. "It's a kind of a fever, I suppose." He frowned. "It's been sixty years or more since we were last involved in a European war. No one knows how long and how frightful it's going to be."

"I heard someone say it'll be over by Christmas," Alexa remarked.

"Christmastime three or four years from now, perhaps." Rowan shook his head.

There was a frantic rush of feet towards Buckingham Palace and they found themselves drifting along with the crowd. The palace was ablaze with light. On the balcony the king and queen appeared with some of the younger members of the royal family. The cheering crowd fell silent as the band played "God Save the King."

"Had enough?" Rowan asked when the last strains had died away.

"Yes, oh, yes," Alexa nodded, slipping her hand into his. "Let's go home, Rowan. Let's go home."

They made their way on foot back to Cadogan Square, wending their way through the still-exuberant crowds. The house, when they reached it, was in darkness. The servants must long since have gone to bed, Alexa thought, or slipped out to mingle in the throng.

With a tired sigh, she went upstairs to lay aside her wrap, leaving Rowan to lock up.

Tossing her wrap carelessly across the back of a chair, she eased off her shoes with a little moan of pain. The walk back to Cadogan Square had not been particularly wise, she reflected, rubbing her much-abused feet. But she wouldn't have missed it for the world. Indeed, in Rowan's charismatic presence, she had quite forgotten her physical misery, that she had been on duty in the wards for eight hours preceding his arrival, and that her feet were sore and aching.

She felt a pang of regret that her nursing career had been cut short just now when nurses would be so desperately needed. But surely it was enough for her to be Rowan's wife—to keep the home fires burning while he was in the army. She must learn to be content. "You can't have it all, Alexa," she told herself as she brushed out her hair. "A meaningful career and a husband as well."

Seeing the light switch on underneath the door connecting their two rooms, she felt her heart beat a little faster and she hastened to struggle out of her frock and into a soft flowing negligee. But the buttons on the frock defeated her. It required the help of a ladies' maid to undo the multitudes of tiny mother-of-pearl buttons down the back. Should she ring for one? But it was well past midnight and she hated to disturb the maids at this hour. She twisted and turned, trying

to reach around, her slim fingers fumbling
with the fastenings.

That there was an obvious solution to her
dilemma had occurred to her at once, but for
some reason she found herself reluctant to
resort to it. Rowan was right there in the adjoining room and he was her husband,
wasn't he? Of course he was . . . but . . .

She caught her underlip between her
teeth, worrying it thoughtfully. So much had
happened since their marriage. Their
wedding night, which now seemed so long
ago, had taken on all the aspects of a dream
and she felt suddenly quite absurdly shy of
him.

But how ridiculous! she told herself. It
was silly of her to be so maidenly and
missish! Resolutely, she marched up to the
connecting door and tapped on it softly.

"Come in. It's not locked," Rowan invited,
his voice slightly muffled behind the door.

Feeling rather like the fly stepping into the
spider's parlor, she advanced hesitantly into
the room. "It's these wretched buttons . . . I
can't reach them," she explained a trifle
breathlessly. "Could you . . . ?"

"Of course." Rowan, who was already in
his dressing gown, finished knotting the sash
and came round behind her. Then she felt his
big hands at her back, expertly coping with
the tiny little buttons, and a shiver ran down
her spine.

And then she felt his lips, so warm and
firm and moist, plant a lingering kiss at the

nape of her neck, a kiss that roused a
melting, well-remembered sweetness deep
within her.

She froze into startled immobility while
her heartbeat skyrocketed and those teasing,
toying lips played havoc with her senses.

His hands were at her shoulders now,
tugging the material of her gown away from
them, baring them to his questing lips, and
Alexa felt her blood stir to a heated
reawakening.

Having given her bared shoulders their
due attention, he tugged the gown down
around her waist, spanning its measure with
his two big hands while his mouth made an
erotic journey up and down her spine, pro-
ducing unbelievably voluptuous sensations
that made Alexa tremble and her legs grow
weak.

Just when, weak with longing as she was,
she felt she could stand such pleasurably
sweet torment no longer, he seemed to sense
it, for he raised his head and pulled her into
his arms, drawing her close to him and
giving her the support of his strong, virile
frame.

His arms, with their whorls of wiry black
hair, engulfing her waist from behind, his
hands reached up to cup her breasts, the
thumbs flicking at her nipples until they
tautened into erect twin peaks, signaling her
desire for him, just as his male arousal
pressing so sensuously against the backs of
her thighs signaled his for her. Slowly,

languorously, he moved against her, heightening her arousal.

"Ro . . . Rowan . . . !" Alexa managed to gasp out. "I . . . I can't . . . this is torture!"

He uttered a husky laugh deep in his throat. "It *is* torture, isn't it?" he agreed. "Sweet, sweet torment." He moved against her sensuously, erotically. "And don't you think, my lady, that you deserve some punishment for the worry you've caused me?" he growled with mock ferocity. "Well, this is your punishment, my dear. Love's sweet torment!" His hands moved slowly, lingeringly, down her body to her waist, playing with her navel before undoing the strings of her petticoat so that it fell with a rustle to her feet and she stood before him naked.

Grasping her by the hips, he rotated her slowly so that his eyes could feast on her loveliness. "God!" he groaned aloud, "how beautiful you are! As beautiful as my memory pictured you all those long lonely nights abroad." His eyes hungrily devoured her loveliness as she stood before him, proud that he found her desirable.

"Well, my lady, are you ready for more punishment?" he growled, still mockingly ferocious. His hand slid seductively down her silken flanks; he drew her to him and, crouching, caressed her belly with his tongue, laving it in moist swirls, the tongue occasionally darting into and out of her navel.

Oh, God, this was too much! "Rowan!" Alexa tugged at his thick thatch of black hair to get his attention properly. "Rowan!" Tug. "Rowan! I . . . I demand equality!"

"What!" Puzzled, he raised his head to see a spark of mischief dawning in his bride's eyes.

"Certainly," said Alexa promptly. "Equality of nakedness!" Stooping, she snatched at the sash of his robe so that it fell open, revealing his superb virility. Her eyes widened but the little imp of mischief that lived in her was already roused and she yanked his robe away, leaving him as splendidly naked as herself. Teasingly, she held the robe just out of his reach.

"Why, you little witch!" he growled, snatching at it but, crouched off balance as he was, missing. He straightened and made another grab, but Alexa danced away, luring him to the bed, leading him a merry chase until they collapsed upon it in a tangle of arms and legs and merry laughter.

"Strip me naked, will you?" Rowan growled playfully. "This time there will be no mercy!" And he commenced to tickle her.

"No! Rowan, no!" Alexa squirmed away from him, writhing, giggling and protesting until suddenly all laughter died away, to be replaced by a breathless, "Oh, Rowan . . . yes . . . oh, yes!" as he began to work his magic upon her.

Their lovemaking was fierce and passionate as if they could hold the world and its problems at bay in the haven of love they created. It was his desire to lose himself completely in her, and she, on her part, wanted to be so completely and utterly a part of him that they would never be separated again—in spirit at least, if not in flesh.

But lovemaking is only a very temporary haven, Alexa thought wistfully the next morning as she watched Rowan make ready to go to the War Department to offer his services to King and Country. She knew that he would come home in uniform and, most probably, be in France with the British Expeditionary Force within the week.

She spoke of it sadly.

"Oh, I expect you'll soon be back in uniform yourself," he said encouragingly.

"Me? In uniform?" She looked at him wonderingly. "Why, whatever do you mean?"

He shrugged. "Only that I expect you'll want to go back to nursing now that war has been declared."

Alexa's eyes suddenly took on the sheen and shimmer of jewels. "Oh, Rowan," she breathed. "Do you mean to say that you wouldn't object . . . you wouldn't stand in my way?" It was such a volte-face on his part that she could hardly believe it. It seemed too good to be true.

He smiled wryly. "I can scarcely object to your doing your part while I'm off doing my bit," he pointed out. "Oh, I suppose there's a part of me that will always want to keep you sheltered and protected and safe from harm," he admitted, sitting down on the edge of the bed and drawing her into his arms. "But I can see now that I have no right to keep you from doing all that you're capable of doing—being all that you're capable of being—simply because you're a woman and my wife and I love you."

Alexa felt tremendously touched by this moving declaration, but . . . "It's too late, Rowan. Matron will never have me back," she said sadly.

"Oh, I think she will," he predicted confidently. "Matron will change her mind when the casualties start pouring in. She'll need every pair of trained hands she can get. And even if she doesn't, there are other training hospitals," he reminded her. "You'll be able to find your niche in one or another of them."

Alexa nodded somberly. She could see the sense of that. But the mention of casualties sent a premonitory shiver down her spine.

"Do you really think it's going to be a long war, Rowan?" she asked him anxiously.

"I'm afraid so. And it'll bring sweeping changes in its wake. Some good; some bad." Seeing the shadow in her eyes, he added hearteningly, "Why, I wouldn't be at all surprised if women didn't get the vote when all this is over. It'll give them the opportunity to show the men what they can do."

Alexa smiled faintly. "I heard on the streets last night that Christabel is back from Paris and Mrs. Pankhurst has declared a truce to militancy for the duration."

"There, you see," said Rowan encouragingly, "the winds of change have already begun to blow. Nothing will ever be quite the same again."

Alexa shook her head slowly. "You're wrong, Rowan. Quite wrong. There *is* one thing that won't change." Reaching up, she wound her arms around his neck and drew his face down to hers. "Our love for each other. That won't change. Whatever else happens . . . whatever else changes . . . our love will endure."